Robert Davidson is a writer and editor based in Highland Scotland. He is the author, co-author, and editor of many books as well as a published poet, lyricist and librettist, and is the founder of Sandstone Press. Before altering his life s course he worked in civil engineering, mainly in or around the water industry. It is this experience which informs *Site Works*. Books written by Robert Davidson have been short listed for the Saltire Society, Scottish Arts Council, and Boardman Tasker Awards.

Also by Robert Davidson

Poetry
The Bird & The Monkey
Total Immersion
After The Watergaw (Editor)
Columba (Poetry Scotland)
Butterfly on a Chestnut Leaf

Song Cycle
Centring on a Woman's Voice

Libretto
Dunbeath Water – an oratorio

Non-fiction
Winning Through
(with Brian Irvine)

Shadow Behind the Sun
(with Remzije Sherifi)

Cairngorm John
(with John Allen)

Fiction
Hegarty and the Doleful Dancer
(writing as Leon Murphy)

SITE WORKS

The Ness and Struie Drainage Project

ROBERT DAVIDSON

SANDSTONEPRESS
HIGHLAND | SCOTLAND

First published in Great Britain by
Sandstone Press Ltd
PO Box 5725
One High Street
Dingwall
Ross-shire
IV15 9WJ
Scotland.

www.sandstonepress.com

Site Works is a work of fiction. Names, characters, places and incidents either
are imaginative, composites drawn from memory or both. Any resemblance to
actual people, living or dead, businesses, authorities of any kind, events or
locales is entirely coincidental. No inferences should be drawn.

The publisher acknowledges subsidy from Creative Scotland
towards publication of this volume.

ISBN: 978-1-905207-63-3
ISBN (e): 978-1-905207-70-1

Sandstone Press is committed to a sustainable future in publishing, marrying the
needs of the company and our readers with those of the wider environment. This
book is made from paper certified by the Forest Stewardship Council.

Cover design by River Design, Edinburgh.
Typeset by Iolaire Typesetting, Newtonmore.
Printed and bound in Poland.

For Moira

Contents

1

A working man

It was getting on for 6:30am and it was Friday. I had only six hours sleep behind me but there was no time for another long morning of coffee and regret. Past the curtains, through the window, the sky was black as pitch. The pane had an edge of rime that would melt when the sun hit it. I woke thinking about the pumping station. There were another two, maybe three days in it. Derek the steelfixer was desperate to get on but before he could put his bars down the joiner had to get the soffit shutter in. To do that the walls had to be up.

Big Swannie, the new Contracts Manager, had given the Agent a bollocking about the time I was taking. The Agent, Mac, is a survivor from the old company and a gentleman. I tell him about safety considerations and the Clerk of Works breathing down my neck and he understands. I tell him about rain, how it washes the mortar away quick as I can put it down and the weather being too cold to make the stuff anyway and he accepts. When he passes these things on to Swannie he gets bawled out. Swannie sent him across the site to tell me to bring my other squad in. I told him it would make no difference; they couldn't change the weather. I didn't say they're working on a factory extension where they are under cover and the steady money isn't something I am going to risk. I'm losing enough on this job as it is. When he asked me if he should bring someone else in, Healey's men for example, I gave him the hard look. I don't work with other builders. Healey's just a brickie anyway.

I got up feeling dried out and sick, picked my clothes off the floor and threw the switch on the electric fire. Through in the kitchen I washed my hands and face and made a long spit into the sink. Light was breaking over MacRae's shed. This place is too far out of town but it's cheap. It was good to see the lambs being born and all the work that goes into the harvest, but a farm in winter is a bleak place.

Some mornings the mucus hangs off the beasts' noses in thick icicles. They hate the cold. They suffer, same as us workers. My hands go raw in the cold air, handling the bricks. Safety gloves have no heat in them. Real gloves get worn to nothing in half a shift. All around the cofferdam the ground is churned up. Wet clay climbs your legs and drops into your wellies. Turn your socks down over the tops and they get clarted with mud. I have bald rings round my calves where it rubs. My feet are filthy all the time. Wellies with steel toecaps freeze your toes and the steel cuts in when you walk. The teachers and the office workers don't know.

I made coffee and toast and gave myself ten minutes. There was a steady, acute thump on the right side of my forehead and my stomach was turning over. The toast went dry in my mouth, the tea acid in my stomach. I managed to finish both and threw a panadol down. Back in the room I put on trainers and a leather bomber jacket; I like to look halfway decent going back and forth.

The cold air hit me as I was locking up, so icy it picked out the rim of the nostrils and the quick of the nails. Worse than that was where it dug right into the body's core and made me know that I am limited. There is only so much in there. Not everything can be borne. Worse than that was the blow to morale. This was what I had to look forward to all day, these conditions, losing myself in work, doing the best I could against boredom. All I want is to get on with it when I'm out there. Instead I spend half the day taking blows and waiting.

The light in the shed went on and MacRae's boy, Neil, came out of the house and across the track to feed the beasts. He seems to like what he does. Maybe it's the prospect of owning the place when the Old Man gives up, or maybe he pretends just enough to get by. The beasts get excited when they hear him, moving around in their stalls. He tells me they show affection. Because he brings them food they think he's their friend. He gave me a wave. We don't say much.

In winter I drive a lot in unlighted areas and on farm tracks. This is what it is to be a builder in the Highlands. For this reason I always buy a white van, it's more visible in the dark. The present van is four years old and going on for 85,000 miles done. It's becoming unreliable. Soon it will have to go. This means another bank loan. For the same reason it's streaked with mud half way up its sides, right up to the Master Builders sign. I keep up with membership. It separates me from the Healeys of the building world when it comes to fine work.

What I like best is handling good facing bricks, keeping them dead plumb, dead square, matching in the coloured pointing. Being in the Master Builders keeps me in good with the architects, the ones who do one-off, individual houses. I like to think of these houses standing a hundred years from now. There was a time I wanted to sign my walls like paintings so people would know who built them. I take the same attitude into this other, heavier, work. It doesn't matter that it's a chamber that's going to be buried and filled with sewage. Some day after I'm dead it might be emptied and someone will go in and see. Nobody alive cares but Harry the Clerk of Works and he claims he's responsible for everything that's done right and none of the rest. It's an ego trip for him now where it used to be a religion.

The engine started third turn but the windscreen and the air-blower were both icy. I had to sit freezing in the stale fug left over from Malky's cigarettes, gunning the engine until it warmed up. When a soft patch appeared in the middle I went outside with the cloth and made it just big enough to see through. Back inside the van my head felt like it was going to split as I leaned over the wheel and peered into the headlight beams. I turned round the farmhouse and onto the track and headed out.

Grass in the middle of the track was coated with frost; the van lurched from side to side in the ruts. Now and again the lights picked out sheep eyes in the field. There's something hellish about a split eyeball staring at you from a sea of darkness. Listening to Malky puts these ideas in my head. He reads horror comics, collects videos like Rosemary's Baby and The Wicker Man. You could think he believes in that stuff. At the end of the farm track I turned on to the single-track road and, at the bottom of that, the main road into town. I drove through with the wipers going, gradually clearing the screen, past the police station and away.

My head had to focus through the last night's drink, quick movements would set it spinning. Concentration is a struggle at the best of times. My head goes everywhere when I'm driving, the job I'm going to, the last job, the next job, the number two squad, measurements. The wife doesn't invade the way she used to now she gets her money straight from the Bank. I don't see her any more and, if I don't see her, she fades. This morning I felt so rough I had to force all of my mind on to the road, deeply aware of my hands on the wheel, of gripping too hard; the tyres on the asphalt, how any sudden movement could have the van weaving.

Malky was waiting outside the garage in the Muir, just across from the pub where I'd left him. It almost looked like he'd spent the night in there and staggered out in the morning. We were both far gone when I took him home. The difference was he would have stopped then. Sandra would have made sure he was fed and clean before she put him to bed. She'd turn him out to meet me in the morning, knowing I would be up for work no matter what. Against that I went home to more vodka. Whoever invented Thursday pay for the troops should be shot.

Malky climbed down into the passenger seat. Neither of us said anything. I took off and gave him the look that said, *safety belt* – on. He pulled it across and pushed the catch home. I got us out of town and put the foot down. Malky reached into his pocket, took out a packet of cigarettes and fumbled one out. I watched him from the corner of my eye. He put the packet away and fumbled in the other pocket for matches. When he'd lit up and was shaking the match out he looked at the ashtray. It was full. He rolled down the window and tossed the match out. Without thinking he took the ashtray out of its holder and emptied it out of the window also. The driver behind us made angry shapes with his mouth. I let him pass and turned off the main road, taking the country roads. It would put ten minutes driving on the journey but the other driver's mobile phone could mean the police. Then there were tyres, brakes, all these things. But the MOT was up to date.

Malky took out his comic and settled down. He's as much gorilla as man. In this respect, as well as reliability and hunger for work, he's good to have around. There are Agents who dispute the measure, knowing they can sit on their lies and stare you down if you want to work for them again. Him just standing there when I hand it over makes a difference. Nothing needs to be said.

There are other builders the agents know will do the job quicker than me if they can get the Clerk of Works to accept the rubbish they put down. These guys would intimidate me off the job if they could get away with it. Not while Malky's around. Even Healey's Brendan respects him and Brendan's a pig when he's battling. He's loyal to me; I think he loves me in a way. Sandra knows she can trust me. She knows he'll get his full money every week, and that I'll drop him close to home. I don't usually bring him back exhausted and caked in mud or pished. It's only when times are thin I take on the heavy stuff, the pipelines, the roadworks. Most of the time he comes home from a nice house-building job, reasonably clean. More and more though, it's the heavy stuff I get.

The site is on a hill above the Beauly Firth. It's a sewer main, nearly three miles long, with staged pumping stations to get the stuff back up through the town and over the top. This means pipelaying going at the same time as building. Ductile iron pipes six metres long, gravel bedding, trench supports, all have to be trafficked along the temporary road. At the same time there are tracked excavators moving back and forth, cranes and piledrivers at the chambers, bricks and cement mixers. The Contractor's wayleave across the fields, the work space, is too narrow. With the pipe track open, pipe bedding on one side, arisings on the other, there's no room for the excavator to travel along and back. Conn has had the fence down three times, and he's a magic driver.

This is just one way the job is going wrong but it was the Client who arranged the access. Big Swannie is claiming delay and disruption. At present he doesn't know if he'll get his money back. This means a lot of tension between Swannie, his Agent, and the Engineer's staff. It means he's tight with his payments to the subbies and the suppliers. On top of this there are other bad things happening. Fact is, the job has gone to hell. My contract is to build walls to the main chamber, a big deep one, below the village. Everything about the job is vile. All I want is to build the thing once and correct, I mean to my own standards, get out and never go back.

There is a rough car park outside the compound. We stopped there and got changed at the back of the van. The sun was up but the air was still cold. Clear sky, it was a high-pressure day, a good day for work if I could only get going. Three long huts sit inside the compound beside the fence; one for the agent and setting-out engineer, another for Harry. The third is for the troops. The troops' had an outside cludge with the pan full to the top with pish and floating turds. There are people you tell these things and they don't believe these conditions exist. Some poor mug was going to have to dig down outside, break open the pipe and take the contents up his arm. It wouldn't be Malky. They couldn't give me enough money to make him do it. Inside the hut is where the men hang their jackets and change. This is where they sit when they're

rained off. The Agent had let the filth rise in the place for fear
of spending Swannie's money. Malky and I were having none
of this. We changed into oversocks still wet with yesterday's
sweat, wellies, donkey jackets, and walked the mile or so to the
cofferdam. I carried my tools on my back. Malky carried the
flask and sandwiches Sandra had made for us.

It was still a quarter before eight. Only Derek the steelfixer was
on site. Derek is the hardest man I've ever met. He picks a
frozen bar up first thing, when it's coated white with frost, and
just holds it tight in his hands. I tried to do this once. It felt like
burning, like gripping a hot poker. I couldn't straighten my
hand for half an hour. He says he only has to go through this
first thing and after that there's no more pain. He was sorting
out 30mm bars with his boy. This looked like roof steel for the
Pumping Station, which meant he would be delivering the bars
sometime through the morning. One of them at each end, they
carted them across to the gate where the crane could pick them
up from outside. I like Derek, but I'm afraid of him too. I once
saw him go to town on a concrete ganger who was pushing him
on for bonus. The ganger spent the night in hospital. Pride
wouldn't let him say anything. The police were never brought
in. Derek doesn't drink any more, doesn't swear or gamble. I
keep in as best I can. Healey does the same.

The access road was all churned up by trucks, but still hard
after the overnight freeze. In the wheel ruts there were knee-
deep frozen ponds. Below us was the chamber compound and
the cofferdam, the fence, the tops of the cofferdam piles. The
ground was shiny with tiny ice pools where our boot prints had
filled and frozen over. We couldn't hear the pump going.
When we got down we found it had been turned off overnight.
This happened every so often. When the locals had been
without sleep for long enough one of them would come down
and shut it off.

The access width isn't the only thing wrong with the contract. On Day One the pipelayers had come across a thick

gravel band about a metre below the surface. When the trench was opened it spilled ground water and kept spilling. Big Swannie turned purple. The Engineer said he should have expected this; Swannie said there was no way he should have expected it. Instead of dragging a trench box along to hold up a dry excavation he had to close pile and try to control the flow with pumps. When that didn't work he had to well-point. This is costing a fortune. The pipelayers are champing for bonus. Brendan, building the shallow chambers, is held up. This is why he has his eye on my job. The Pumping Station is four metres deep so has to be close-piled anyway. Swannie, being Swannie, bought in piles that had been used a dozen times before. Here and there the clutches have opened and water pishes in but this isn't so bad as in the trenches. I got Malky to dig a sump in the corner and drop the pump rose in. We covered it with gravel and, okay, the pump now handles the flow when it's working. But some bastard turned it off.

The water level in the cofferdam had stabilised near the top of the wall. Last time this happened the wall wasn't so high and it spilled over and filled the chamber. This time it had only filled between the cofferdam piles and the bricks. Malky tried to turn the starting handle to get the pump going, but the works were frozen. He gathered a few rags together, soaked them with diesel and started a fire under the thing. I drew the hap off the previous day's work and folded it into a corner, went out over the gangway and dropped on to the top scaffold staging inside the chamber.

By this time there was enough light to see to the bottom. It was deep shadowed but I couldn't make out any water. I took out my torch and climbed down to the next level. The wall looked sound. There was no glisten on the pointing where the torchlight hit it, no white efflorescence growing on the face. When I ran my hand across it came back moist, but I put this down to condensation. The next level was the same. My heart was thumping. This was a natural test for the wall and it looked like it was going to be okay.

Down on the base, where the outside pressure was greatest, it was difficult to tell. I laid my donkey jacket on the slab, got down on my belly and shone the torch all around the bottom course. It was bone dry, as far as could be seen. All around me were bits of scaffolding, dog ends, lumps of mortar, broken bricks. Here the smell of dampness and cement was strongest, that cold talc smell. It came into my head as awareness of place. I was here again, at work, a sort of home. I would always return.

Looking up at the patch of sky past the scaffold opening I could see it was beginning to cloud over. It would rain before the end of the day; maybe there would be snow. Up above, the pump started, slowly at first then more steadily. The gravelly roar arrived over the top of the wall, followed by the coughing noise it made when it started throwing water out into the ditch.

I climbed back up and laid out my tools on the top staging. It looked good, the whole thing looked good. The time spent was worth it. If Healey had built it, the way he was building the small chambers, the courses would have been all over the place. Water would be coming through and it would never seal. Harry would have accepted none of it but the wall would be up – built. Eventually the Engineer would have settled for the best he could get, knowing it would never be seen except by some future workman with other things on his mind if he was down there at all.

I opened my bag at the corner of the staging where I couldn't trip over it. Between the piles and the walls the water level was steadily falling. Malky was filling the mixer with diesel. We had an alkathene pipe running overground beside the track from the mains connection. Naturally it was frozen. We'd have to wait for the sun to free it if we were going to use it to make mortar according to spec. He turned the tap to the on position and left it. The water would announce its own arrival. Meantime he shovelled sand and cement into the bucket and gave it a few turns.

I got him to hold one end of the steel tape at the two near

chamber corners and checked the diagonals. I knew I'd done this the previous night and that I would do it again last thing as well as several times through the day. The sizes can't change but I check them anyway. I'm obsessive about checking. When I've nothing positive to do I go check something. In the van I find myself wondering if I checked sizes before I finished, if I packed my tools right, if I locked up properly. I wake up thinking about these things. The following morning it always turns out I have. I mean it – always.

The Contractor's troops were starting to drift out of the hut and about the site. I had asked the Agent for a crane but it hadn't appeared. It was tied up with the pipelayers. As usual he was pressing me on time but not providing the plant when it was needed. It would have to track across half the site to get here. If Brendan was involved there was no telling when it would arrive. He would tie it up as long as he could. I climbed out of the Chamber again while Malky took a Stanley knife to the plastic on the first palette of bricks. He passed them to me in pairs and I tossed them on to the staging.

This was coarse but I couldn't wait. As usual there was big wastage. I would have to build the broken bricks in as best I could and drop the rest into the chamber. The troops would clear them out before the joiner came in. After a while we got a rhythm going and got the bricks across. I climbed back on to the staging, put the string lines up and tested them with the long bead.

It was nearly 9:00am and nothing was done. I had come in wanting to lay bricks from 8:00am right through until the light stopped us. Now we were ready to start but the water pipe was still blocked. I got Malky to lower a bucket down between the cofferdam and the wall. The ground water was pure as anything that comes out of the tap. So long as Harry wasn't around we could use it. I made a start scraping out between yesterday's courses, making ready for pointing, while Malky finished the mix. When it was ready he tipped it into the

barrow and pushed it across the gangway. I took the mortar
board from its lean against the wall and put it down on the
staging and Malky dropped the first mix on the board. Now I
was cooking.

I filled the trowel with mortar and dropped it on the wall
head and spread it. Malky makes good mortar. You can tell by
looking at the colour and feeling the way it slides off the blade.
It would pass any test Harry could dig out of his books.
Malky's been working with me for three years and the time
we spent mixing on the early jobs, just doing it over and over
until it was right, was well spent. He gets it right first time,
every time. Never mind the state of his head, that it's full of
drink or Sandra's been nipping it.

I positioned the first of the new bricks, the most important of
the day, in a stretcher across two headers. The trowel edge
showed it flush with them, both ends. The string showed a
dead level. This was the one to take care with. The rest would
be easier. I moved out of thought and into rhythm – spread the
mortar – pick up the next brick – mortar its leading edge – lay
the brick – check the string. Now again, faster this time. Scrape
the wall clean where the mortar runs down. Don't let the drips
and snotters take a set. Keep going. Merciless with the lash, as
Harry says.

This was the best of it, working steadily – no thought
required. It all happened between the hand and eye like they
spoke to each other. Malky lit a cigarette and sat on the palette
with his comic. I wouldn't have to tell him when to start the
next batch.

The pump revved up as it started sucking air. This meant
the water level in the cofferdam was down to sump level.
There was still water pishing through the clutches on to the
concrete base but the pump had beaten the flow. Malky hung
his donkey jacket over the fence gate, folded his comic into a
pocket. He picked up a shovel and climbed down the ladder we
had tied to the cofferdam walings. This was at the corner we
had part backfilled with a gravel and sand mix. With just about

his body's width to turn in I could hear him digging his small hole, leaning the shovel against the steel piles and fumbling at his belt. Sound travels between the hard surfaces like it was a tunnel. I picked up another brick, mortared one edge, and laid it. When he got back he went straight to shovelling sand and cement into the mixer. Without warning the hose started throwing out water. Just in time, as it happened.

Malky picked up our two safety helmets from the corner of the compound and smacked them together to catch my attention. When I looked up he tossed mine down for me to catch. I looked along the track to see Harry's white helmet bobbing up and down, then his duffel coat. When he arrived Malky was feeding water into the mixer from the hose and I was dipping from the knees, head up to keep the helmet steady, as I lifted the bricks. He made his cursory hello with Malky and crossed the gangway. I was ready to move the string line again. This time I hung the plumbs as well. Harry nodded approval and put his ruler between the strings and the bricks, nodding again and again. Keep going, he said. Merciless with the lash.

I respect Harry, and because I respect him I enjoy his approval. We have long conversations about building. He's worked on buildings all over Britain, big architectural projects, London docklands, big new houses, specialist work on ancient buildings. When he goes on about the time he was in West Africa I kid him about 'that big pyramids job in Egypt'. He knows all there is to know about building, all the mortar mixes, how to colour them. We talk and talk about these things. He knows all the bonds. No point arguing about what English bond really is, or garden bond, or the rest. He quotes chapter and verse. Better than that though, he's done it all. He also knows all the ways to cheat, so if you try he generally finds you out. Harry and Healey's men are in a permanent state of war. Harry would hunt them off the job if he could but, of course, Big Swannie likes speed. I know if Harry wasn't so precious about the quality of brickwork in this chamber I'd be off the job. That's not why I keep in with him though; we have an affinity. By God, he likes to talk. Some time in the pub we'll really get down to it.

After he checked the strings and the diagonals he walked all the way round the cofferdam, looking down on the wall head. Any one can lay English bond when the wall only goes to a one-brick width. Its when you step out another brick or, worse, half a brick, it gets difficult. This is when the likes of Healey's men get lost, building on that extra width as just another skin, not building it *in*. All the extra strength it has then comes from the brick's weight, not the build. It's just two walls leaning against each other. What I had built was the true English bond. Harry knew this. He went round and round the cofferdam admiring. When he had done all this we talked for a while about the site, what was going on, all that was going wrong.

Harry hates Healey more than I do. He has no time for Kelly, the General Foreman, either. To his face he tells him he leaves lousy work behind. The true bottom-acid of his bile though, is kept for Swannie. Harry despises the profit motive that is all James Swann lives for. On a slightly lesser ranking of hatred is his own boss, the Resident Engineer, who forever compromises on standards and pays out for bad workmanship over Harry's head. Meantime Malky made a roll-up and took out his comic. He knew Harry valued him as much as the turds he'd just buried on the base of the cofferdam. This meant they paid each other no attention. To Malky the Clerk of Works was just another delay. To Harry, Malky was a talking shovel and the less it talked the better.

After a while Harry moved off along the track to the pipelaying operation and we got back to work. As Malky tipped the next batch onto the board the general foreman appeared. Kelly looked nervous. He knew I didn't like to be interrupted and that I wasn't under his control like the other troops. The Agent wanted to see me in his office. I used up the batch, making no haste to do what I was told, making sure that every brick was laid just *so*, before rinsing my hands under the hose and walking up the track. Malky set to making himself useful while I was gone, hosing down the mixer and brushing the cement slurry into the cofferdam. If I was away long enough he would know to take his tea so we could start again when I got back.

The office and stores compound was buzzing. Troops were going in and out to pick up bags of cement, bits of pipe and fittings, all the rest of it. Derek was nowhere to be seen but the chamber steel lay stacked beside the fence, waiting to be lifted. I guessed the mobile crane that was bouncing down the hill was coming to do the job. One of the flat lorries wouldn't be far away. The Agent's Ford and Swannie's Beamer were parked outside the hut. The Agent would be in fear and trembling. What I felt I wouldn't show. I made a loud knock on the door and waited for the shout.

Swannie was at the filing cabinet when I went in. The Agent was standing beside his desk instead of sitting, looking like something spare. Swannie told him to make coffee and pushed the cabinet drawer shut with a bang. Everything he did was like this. Every gesture was an assertion of position. Every look was half assessment, half threat. The Agent put a mug of coffee on the desk for Swannie and gave me one too. He didn't make one for himself. He would know Swannie's way the way I knew the ways of all Swannie's kind. If he gave himself coffee he would receive the hard look. Then there would be something menial he would have to do in front of me. If he tried to find something to do for himself he would be told to do something else. If he so much as wanted to go for a shite he would be told to wait.

I stood quiet while Swannie sat and read from a file, sipped at his coffee, lit a cigarette. Humiliation was his favoured currency. I got the name right in my head, Mr Swann, and tried to look casual. Finally he got round to it.

He wanted the chamber roof cast on Tuesday; it would be an all-day pour. This meant the steelfixers in on Monday, the joiners before them on Sunday. Obviously he was going to defy the no-Sunday-work rule that was usual in this area. For the joiners to work on Sunday I had to be finished by Saturday night. I don't like to work Saturdays. I like football. As does Derek, but he wouldn't be required until Monday so long as his steel was beside the Chamber tonight.

There was no chance of me finishing in daylight, or even by the end of Saturday unless I worked on. This meant lights. He was having Brendan bring them to the chamber as we spoke. I put down my mug to go but Swannie wasn't having this. Before I could leave he had to harangue me about my inadequacies. I stood and took it. This is what you do if you want to work. Of course Pat Healey is his boy and his men are favoured. If it wasn't for Harry's perfectionism on this brick chamber in particular I'd be off the site. None of this needed said.

I made my second skin and let it all blow past me. I would work on under lights into Friday night. Next day, Saturday, I would come in and work to a finish. No matter what I did or didn't like. There would be nothing extra on the rate. This is how it would be. My increment of hate for Swannie was just one of many on a hoard he had been growing over the weeks. He didn't care. Right now though, what was uppermost in my mind was the chamber compound where Healey's men were erecting the lights. I was thinking about Malky. I was thinking about trouble.

Outside in the compound Derek had reappeared and was organising the steel lift on to a flat lorry. I stopped to tell him what was happening with the chamber. Of course he already knew. So would the joiner. I was last. I was weak enough to unload on him about Swannie, about the hate that was building up in me. Derek was impassive, as tough of mind as of body. He takes it all and gets on. He knows he works for money and hardening his mind against humiliation is as necessary as hardening his hands. A straight face dealing with Swannie, and for that matter Healey, is as necessary as a straight back for lifting steel bars. These are the necessaries – tough hands to do the work, and thick skin to endure the insult.

When I got back Malky was facing off three of Healey's men with the mixer's starting handle. Saying nothing he stood inside the gate with his legs flexed. They had the jeep and trailer. Bits of lighting equipment stuck out from the sides like a spider's legs. Brendan was laughing at him, sneering at him and calling him out. If they were to get in to the compound before the mortar had set on the last course they could do damage. They might do damage anyway. Healey would like us to be slowed down. The walls were up so far even Brendan could finish them. Swannie would like this too. Healey was his boy.

I never forgot this – Healey was his boy.

Malky's expression didn't change, never showed the doubt I knew he would feel, the anxiety when I wasn't there. He's a soldier. When they got out of the jeep and started unloading the equipment he moved nervously from side to side on the balls of his feet. Anything could happen. I hurried down. Walking from the other side I could see Harry. Finished at the small chambers he was heading back to the huts.

We got to the stand-off together, Harry's presence changing everything. Of course he had it all sussed. He took out his date-and-time camera and snapped the walls as they stood, gave me a few words of appreciation. He said he'd be back in the afternoon and moved on. Malky threw the starting handle beside the mixer and let Healey's men in. They weren't likely to try anything now.

I looked at my watch. It was coming on for 12:00pm. Better we were out of the way. I gave Malky the nod and packed my tools on to my back. It was worth an hour to keep out of these guys' way. At the van we ate the pieces Sandra had made and got out of our wellies. Instead of drinking the tea I drove us to the pub. If we were working late the tea would be good to have at about 4:00pm.

The corner before The Islander has an electricity sub-station I did work on years ago. There's every reason I might park the van there if anyone was wondering. We walked the rest of the way. Annie behind the bar knew us by this time, knew to pour a pint of lager for Malky as we came in, a big Whitbread for me. I got us a bridie each, to sit on top of Sandra's pieces, and we hid in a corner out of the way. The more I thought about James Swann the more I churned inside.

It wasn't that he wanted the work moved along, or that we were going to lose the best part of the weekend for nothing extra on the rate. All that's part of the game. It was the lack of respect for craftsmanship. It was for not recognising it in the price. It was for the victory it handed to the likes of Pat Healey, the triumph of crap over quality. The no-respect was handed on to me and through me to Malky; through Malky to Sandra and the boys. Come to that, through me to the ex, and the girl. No-respect was the message sent to the whole worthwhile world of doing and making and being.

Malky soon had his nose in his comic but his lips weren't moving. I've long since stopped asking what he gets out of these things, how he can go over the same pictures over and over again. As I looked at him, wondering how to start a conversation without spilling out all this bile or going over some old well-rutted ground yet again, he fumbled his cigarettes out of his pocket, lit up and dropped the spent match into the ashtray without looking. Malky knows the score. He takes just the one pint, usually doesn't even finish it. He was smoking away, drinking very slow, keeping his eye on the page and never looking at me all the while. Yes, Malky knows the score. I got another big Whitbread from the bar and watched the hands on the clock go round.

Harry put his head through the door and went away again. I would have liked to speak to him. He has his difficulties with

the Resident Engineer. Harry stands for quality in workmanship, standards. He takes a stand on all these things. I know,
I've watched. Time after time the RE makes his compromises
and pays out on crap. The job moves along, eventually it will
be built and it will work. It always does. The public will judge
on what it sees on the surface, a gardening job, a paint job,
whatever. The public couldn't care less about what it can't see.

Yes, I would have liked to talk with Harry over a few pints.
The times we've spoken on the scaffolding, the things he's said
about Healey, hinted at about the RE, tell me he's a craftsman
and a true believer in craft. We could get on all right, talking
about jobs we've been on – that big pyramid contract in Egypt.
I want to know how he handles the humiliation of working for
lesser men. Does the Engineer speak to him like he was dirt?
Does Swannie? Mac is okay. The two of them, Harry and the
agent, get on okay. They have cups of tea and jammy buns at
their Thursday meetings. I guess the both of them are prison-
ers just as much as Malky and me. They can say what they like,
agree what they want, it's Swannie and the Engineer, the guy
in Glasgow, the guy above the RE, doing the business.

Two pints is the usual limit, but it was Friday and we were
working on. I took another Whitbread. Malky didn't want any.
He hardly touched what he had. As I say, he knows the score.
Half way through this third I wanted more, but I was all bagged
up with gas. I left the bottle about a third full but, while Malky
was calling Sandra to say we'd be late, took a vodka at the bar,
trebled it with lemonade and threw it down. Outside, the cold
air was like a slap across the face. The clouds had closed up
and there was a bitter wind. We checked the road both ways, if
the worst came to the worst Malky could drive. No police. We
drew our jackets in tight and hurried to the van.

Swannie's beamer was away from the compound when we got
back. He would be off to another site to give another Agent a
late, surprise visit. This is his way, he turns up at odd times to
keep them on their toes. He walks his Agents and foremen at

breakneck speed around the sites, questioning everything, criticising every decision, listing everyone's inadequacies, pushing anger out all the time, turning on his heel, suddenly rearing up like he's about to do violence. As far as I know he's never landed a blow. Through the office window we could see the Agent tidying his desk. Friday afternoon, soon he would be away. Probably he would drop in on the Saturday to see what was doing. We would be here, along with maybe a few of Healey's men. Derek would be at the football. That was why he had the mobile crane down at the Pumping Station when we got back, unloading reinforcement to make a quick start on Monday morning.

The crane was covering most of the gateway with the flat lorry just in front. Derek was up on the flat, tying on the steel for the lift. His boy was in the compound, organising the landing and doing the untying. They were going to take at least a half hour. In that time all we could do was lay out the tools, break open another palette and throw more bricks down on to the staging. After that we were standing.

Half the day had disappeared this way and now the wind was cutting through us. Across the Firth there was cloud half way down the hill above Beauly and wisps of snow were drifting across the water and on to the site. Seeing how it was going the pipelayers wrapped up for the day. So did Healey's men, calling out to Malky as they walked past. Malky turned his back on them. Sooner or later there would be trouble. Probably it would not come on the site. Most likely it would burst out of nothing in a pub. Sooner or later, though, it would come.

Healey's men hadn't set out the lights as they should. They'd just dumped them. As soon as Derek's lorry was rolling along on the ruts in the access track, back to the compound, we put them up ourselves. Malky filled the genny with diesel and pushed the button. The lights flashed once and came on first time. Now we were ready to go. I took my frozen arms and legs on to the staging and set up the string lines again.

My fingers were stiff and clumsy but that would pass when the work started properly. Harry's presence had prevented Healey's men from doing any damage to the morning's work. It was only after Malky had shovelled sand and cement into the mixer we discovered what they had done. The starting handle was missing. They had taken it, or dropped it down a hole somewhere, or buried it, or whatever – but it was gone.

Already the natural light was fading. Snow was blowing in more steadily. I manhandled the mortar board on to its edge on the staging and leaned it over in Malky's direction. He got his hands out wide around the edge and lifted enough for me to get my hands round it down below. Together we managed to heave it over the gangway without dropping it into the cofferdam.

Malky mixed the mortar by hand, shovelling three of sand on to the board, then two of cement, forming it into a doughnut. Water he measured in from the bucket. It was all judgement anyway. He could both tell from the look and the feel of it as the light faded whether the mortar was good. By the time the first brick was down the natural light was almost gone. I struggled against the cold for rhythm and eventually it came and my mind went where it always went, to the nooky. I have a class number on hand, a teacher. I guess she has herself a bit of rough. She's married. Doesn't matter. It's sex she wants from me. The husband sits around all day, behind a desk, in a car. Things like playing squash, going for runs, don't harden a body like building does.

Sex is where my head wanders when the body works by itself. Malky clicked the safety helmets together. Harry was coming back. I looked up and shook my head. Harry isn't daft. There was no one else working, nothing but snow was going to fall. What could happen? No one could see us from the road. Better with the woolly hats on, it was warmer. I was into my rhythm by now, didn't want to stop – mortar the wall head, mortar the brick edge, lay the brick, check the string. Again. Again.

I could hear Harry talking to Malky, trying to get sense from him. He was asking what time we would work to, how we were measuring the mortar mix, if we had enough deisel for the genny. Malky sent him to me for answers. There's no telling what's in Malky's head when he's not actually shovelling. He has a great capacity for waiting. I waved up with the trowel and Harry came across the gangway and dropped on to the staging. By now the wind was whipping snowflakes across the top of the cofferdam. Harry was coated white down one side. I took a step back to make room for him and hit the kickboard.

I almost went over into the chamber. Harry grabbed my arm and started to speak. Half way through whatever he was saying he stopped and looked into my eyes. His own eyes closed and I could almost read his thoughts through his eyelids. Oh no, he was thinking. Oh no. He went back up and spoke to Malky, pointing in my direction and shaking his head. Then he went away. There was nothing more to be said.

Soon all the natural light was gone and it was black as tar except for our little theatre of light on the side of the hill. I checked my watch; it was past 5:00. We drank Sandra's tea; Malky as he stood in the snow, me between picking up bricks. Mortar the wall head and the brick edge, lay the brick, check the string; another brick laid. I checked my watch again. It was 6:00.

At 7:00pm I looked up for more mortar. Malky was thick covered with snow. I had some little shelter from the brickwork behind me and from the cofferdam wall. Also I was moving all the time. He was out in the open with no cover at all. As I watched he shivered again, hugely and violently. I called him over into the light. His hands and face were both blue. I got him to pull the hap over from the corner of the compound and we covered our work. There was still tomorrow. We filled the pump with diesel to keep it going through the night. I packed my tools onto my back and turned off the genny. The lights flickered and went out.

We locked the compound, left the padlock key under its stone at the corner and made our way back to the van by torchlight. When we got back to the office compound we could still hear the pump roaring in the sump, but not the ground water pishing through the pile clutches on to the cofferdam base. These had been the ground notes of our day from start to finish.

It was only when we were back at the van, out of our wellies and inside that I realised how deeply the chill had bitten into Malky. Under the window light his hands were still blue. They trembled so much when he tried to light a cigarette I had to strike the match for him. I was frozen but Malky was worse and he was soaked through as well. I drove us back down to the Islander and put a whisky and lemonade into him. I took nothing myself. Soon he'd stopped shivering and was running his hands up over his face and through his hair, shaking his head and grunting. We got back into the van and drove back to the Muir. It being Friday I stopped off at the pub. Malky took another whisky and I had a couple of vodkas.

There was never any doubt about him turning out the next day. I don't pay him so much he can go past the o/t. Sandra was on my side so long as I kept him in work. Whatever else, she didn't want him back in the slammer – and without a job it would only be a matter of time. It would be another story if she saw him frozen, or if she knew the sort of heights we some-times work at, or the state of some of the holes. The Pumping Station wasn't as bad as most, thanks to Harry.

Malky got involved in a futile discussion about the Rangers with one of the bartenders. These are things I don't talk about too deeply with him. He gets too excited. I like football but mostly what I care about is work and women. Transfers, results, league positions occupied Malky's mind when it wasn't full of horror comics. You'd think the work he did wasn't horror enough. Sandra still didn't know we were going out the next day. I got him to call home and tell her, this way she would be settled to the idea by the time I got him home. Of course I would be invited to eat. This was good. I bought him another and, weighing up the drive back to the farm carefully, had another myself.

The two boys met us at the door. Washed and pyjama'd they were ready for bed. It's always good to see Malky with his family. A different man, he's responsible, caring. When I'm over I always make a point of giving him his place, of not being the boss. He worships his wife, as well he might. She's the anchor on his life. Of course seeing them together always stirs up bad thoughts but these have to be lived with and can't be dwelt on. I accept. With women I am what I am, not capable of respect never mind worship.

Sandra came out of the kitchen to meet us in the living room. The smile fell from her face when she laid eyes on him, caked in mud. When he tried to speak I realised he was drunk and thought it better to say nothing. Although I can hold my drink better than Malky I wouldn't be far behind. Sandra sat us down and put the boys to bed. She went back into the kitchen and took the dinners out of the oven. The two of us ate in silence. Already Malky was falling asleep. He was eating on automatic pilot by the time we finished. Sandra had the bath running as I went to the door. I tried to kiss her but she was having none of it, and then I was back out in the cold again. Twenty minutes from home, I had two police stations to pass, one further along in the Muir, the other in Conon, before I got to Dingwall. Some day they'll get me.

How else can I live? Working the way I do, living on my own as I have to, drink is central to the whole thing. Sometimes it's like it's what I live for. Monday afternoon, when it was out of my system, I would phone round the architects. One way or another I would get some decent work. I don't want to spend the rest of my life freezing down holes in the ground.

As I drove I could feel the weight of a good facing brick in my hand. I was colouring the mortar in my head. This is the work I'm trained to do, the work I can talk about all day. Harry knows. Harry respects me the way I respect him. These are the things my mind plays on when it should be on the road. I gave myself a shake and checked the speed, not too fast, not too slow.

At night I drive with my heart in my mouth. Once a prowler fell in behind me, shadowed me from the Muir to Conon, then it put its light on, swept past and away. Some emergency, somewhere else, or I'd have been locked up. It could happen any night, most mornings. I got back to the farm, bounced up the track and climbed out. The beasts were sounding off but that was because the van had disturbed them. Soon they would settle. I wish I could say the same for me.

I took my jacket and trainers off, the only clean things about me, and hung my trousers behind the door. They could be brushed more or less clean on Sunday. There would be no job to go to on Monday. I would wash them then, spend the day on the phone. Inside I switched on the electric fire, threw my underwear into the basket and went directly into the shower.

This was when I discovered how tired I was. With the cement and the mud trickling down into the tray I put my head against the wall and shut my eyes. It felt like they might never open again. At home I wear tracksuit bottoms and an old pullover with elbow patches. I took a bottle of vodka and a bottle of lemonade out of the cabinet before falling onto the settee and jabbing on the TV remote.

This was it. This was it. This part of the day was for me alone. In two hours, maybe less, I'd be in bed. I poured a big one and doubled it with lemonade, flicked across the channels. It was all junk, so I left it where it lay – hospitals, one for the ladies. The vodka went down and I poured another. I had to hold back. There was no point rushing for oblivion, and I had to get out again next day.

I couldn't settle though. For all I was exhausted, my legs were stiff and my shoulders hurt, I had to get up and walk about. Who the fuck did Swannie think he was? He'd treated me like dirt. He had spoken and I had jumped. For all I had put on a straight face and said little, I had jumped. I knew it and he knew it. There was no hiding it. We both knew. I would be off the job on Monday, never wanting to come back, and I had taken it in silence. He had kept going until he was sure that I was buckled, and sure that I knew it.

Why take it? Because I know, in my heart of hearts, that this is where I am now. This is what I have to do to make any kind of living. There won't be many more big houses. This is where we were going from now on, Malky and me, down these holes. No more quality work, quality drawings, quality clients, this was another world we had landed in.

In this world the Pat Healeys write the rules. Get it done quick, defend your ground. Get in with the right Contract Managers. Which Contract Managers are the right ones? The animals. I remember something stupid, something about having to operate *now*, being said on TV while I was running my hands across my face. This was despair. I couldn't go it for long, not like this. I had to adjust somehow.

I thought about rolling a joint but I know my moods and this one wasn't right. What I really wanted was to call the girlfriend, to get her over here, but Friday night her husband would be in. There were the kids. What if one of them answered? No, I'd have to wait for Tuesday afternoon like we agreed. It wasn't sex I wanted. By this time I just wanted to rest my head between her breasts, put my hand between her legs and go to sleep. Just that.

So you'd think I'd sleep well, go out like a light – black velvet until the alarm goes. Not so. The vodka kept me awake. There were all the usual flash memories that won't give me peace, all with hurt in them – site agents, contracts managers, women, police – the most recent was Sandra crying in the kitchen after I took Malky home.

All night the Pumping Chamber kept coming back, how I'd kept those walls square and plumb from the base right up to these last courses below the roof slab and, damn, I hadn't checked the diagonals last thing. Through the night the determination grew in me to keep it right all the way to the top, not to compromise. If it took until Tuesday, so be it. If Swannie barred me from all of his sites, that was okay too. I would do it. Then I would never work with these bastards again. I'd get back into buildings, quality buildings, or I'd get out.

Some hope. There's rent to be paid, money to the wife – and I know from the past that I can't face the long empty hours being out of a job brings. I'm a worker. Malky and me are both workers. We do it because we do it. There's no more explanation. We're workers. So are Swannie and Healey, although they're animals as well. I'm a master builder. Rest, my God, I needed rest more than I needed money. It was in one of those in-and-out-of-sleep moments I had to face the truth. No, the architects don't want me any more. Too much drink.

Next day I felt worse, less because of the lack of sleep than because of the vodka. I got up, washed, fed myself. I put on those cold wet clothes again. Malky and I are so close now I can almost feel Sandra pushing him out of bed. He would be at the Muir garage, same as usual. He's reliable. Sandra and the boys make him that way. They're his purpose.

The cold hit me again as I was locking the door. It feels like it shrinks your face. The moon sent its white light across the patchy snow in MacRae's fields. In the corner of the door lintel a cobweb shone like silver. Like me the spider works through instinct. It just gets up and gets on with the job without thought. Every so often it turns out something perfect.

They say there's no labour without dignity. I don't see it. Better to be like the spider and not think in those terms. It's just life, an endless round of work, loneliness, humiliation and drink. The beasts with their frozen snotters have as much dignity. I have a past. I guess I have some kind of a future. The present is in finishing off this chamber with Malky. That's it. There's no more.

2

Extracts from the Water Authority's Report on Tenders for the Ness and Struie Drainage Project

This Project is the latest in a series to be undertaken in sequence along the Ross-shire, East Sutherland and Caithness coast and is programmed to follow on from the Black Isle (Beauly Firth) Project now approaching completion and preceding three more located further to the north, Lochdon, also in East Sutherland, and Dunpark and Fishertown in Caithness.

Although not geographically distant the communities of Ness and Struie are separated by a range of relatively low hills. They have a combined population of around 1000 people that is more than doubled in the middle third of the year by summer residents and tourists. Both are served by septic tanks which have been the subject of complaints from the local Community Councils over many years.

★ ★ ★

The septic tank for the coastal village of Ness has its outfall directly into the North Sea. Given that it is considerably undersized for the summer population, and its location renders access for the Authority's tankers virtually impossible, it is never emptied and there is frequent contamination of the shore by gross solids.

The septic tank for the inland village of Struie discharges its effluent into a slow moving stream that has its lowest flow in the months of highest usage. This leads to a very considerable odour nuisance with, it is claimed, an effect on tourism and the local economy. The Environment Agency has written to the Authority's Chief Executive threatening fines if these conditions are not addressed within the next financial year.

The Authority's Operations and Maintenance Department has stipulated a single Works rather than the Consultant's preferred option of two. Predictive calculations indicate that the additional costs involved will be justified over a forty year lifespan.

The Authority has retained the services of the Consultant Engineer used for the Black Isle (Beauly Firth) Project, The Russell Partnership of Glasgow, with Sir Graham Russell designated as the 'Engineer for the Works'.

★ ★ ★

The Russell Partnership's strategy for meeting these requirements entails the construction of a new sewage treatment plant on the coast approximately four hundred metres south of Ness, where any odour nuisance will effectively be removed from the village. The Works will consist of a collection chamber close to the A9, two circular concrete settlement tanks and an outfall to sea for treated effluent.

The flow from Ness will be taken by a new concrete pipeline to the collection chamber and the existing septic tank demolished.

The flow from the inland village of Struie will be pumped uphill in a 150mm diameter uPVC flexible pipe where, at the top, it will enter a new, reinforced concrete culvert which will be two metres in section, large enough for any future increase in flow should the Planning Department's plans for future housing development be realised. At the east side of the hill the flow will enter another new concrete pipeline to flow downhill and under the A9 to the new collection chamber where it will join with the flow from Ness and enter the new sewage treatment plant.

The culvert and pipelines will all be underground with top surfaces reinstated to the satisfaction of both the landowners and the Environment Agency.

★ ★ ★

Our Consultant proposes to supervise the Contract with a permanent Resident Engineer and Clerk Of Works. Costs for these necessary positions have already been built into the Overall Project Estimate.

The Allowable Contract Period will be six months beginning on 1st January. This should lead to least disruption of tourist activities as well as conform to the Authority's planned spending profile and work will run on from the Black Isle (Beauly Firth) Project.

★ ★ ★

The recommended tender has been placed by Strath Construction Ltd. However, the company has been purchased by Syme Atwood (Contractors) Leicester, and is now their wholly owned subsidiary. Strath Construction is well known to this Authority and has carried out many Contracts of this scale and approximate value.

In purchasing Strath Construction, then in the course of completing the Black Isle/Beauly Firth Project, Syme Atwood acquired the local base necessary to meet the Authority's stipulated requirements. It is likely that the acquisition will bring economies of scale that will ultimately be to the Authority's advantage.

★ ★ ★

The Contract duration will be eight months. The Contractor has committed to employ locally.

3

Commitment is the name of the game

Mac hung up as quietly as he could and checked the clock. 6:35am.

Five minutes on the phone had seemed like ten. So much, too much, was going on. So much happening at once, there was so much to keep a grip of at once, his hand had that slight tremor it began when his marriage was breaking up. It rested on the phone as he looked through the window into the street below, as though to prevent it leaping up against his ear to command his time and attention and fill his mind.

A fighting east wind hurled big raindrops against the hotel opposite his flat. The executioner's wind his General Foreman called it, the one that cuts through you. Water filled the drainage channels at the road's edge and swirled over the gratings before disappearing through the gully frames and away. It was black as pitch outside the cones of the streetlights.

Paul's mother had answered and called him to the phone. Mac had diverted him from the site on the Black Isle to the new job in Ness, East Sutherland. From the Williamson house in Dingwall it would take him just over an hour to get to the site. The new sub-agent, Trevor Sharp, was staying in the hotel there until he found digs. If the weather up north was as bad as here in Inverness, if it continued through the day, nothing much would be done on the ground but at least they would get to know each other. They could take refuge in one of the huts and go over the drawings. The sub-agent/engineer relationship, one of the most important on site, would begin to be

established. Paul wasn't required on the Black Isle job any
more, not really. So Mac made the decision at four in the
morning when he would have been better asleep.

Today he, Mac, would not be able to make a start before
8:30, desperately late at a time when he was vulnerable. He was
still quantifying materials for the buyer, which would have
been done, *done*, if Alan Syme had not paid off his site agent
after the Syme Atwood take-over. Now his workload was huge.
The job was so tightly priced even a few per cent saved on
materials here and there would make a difference. Syme's first
visit to the office three months before, its tone and force, had
shaken him. The new order wasn't properly established then,
but the old one was certainly destroyed.

Syme had spent six hours grilling him about Strath Construction's operational set-up. There had been no preliminary
conversation, no exploring of any social overlap. On the
second day Syme had laid down the law about the immediate
future, downgraded him from Contracts Manager to Site
Agent and introduced him to his new boss, James Swann.
Swann had told him he would be spending all his time out on
the sites, not to come in to the office unless he was told.
Angrily, wearily remembering, Mac shook his head. He had to
prove himself again.

'Dad!'

Alison was in the doorway, wide-awake, bare-foot, cleaning
her glasses on the hem of her pyjama top. She was fourteen.
When she stayed in his flat, those too few occasions, it always
surprised him how grown up she was, the big advance from
last time. Soon there would be boys. Oh yes, there would be
boys.

'Are you all right?'

'Sorry, Ali. Did I waken you?'

'I'm worried about you. There's something on your mind.'

'Just work, Sweetheart. Changes happening. Remember I
told you? It's not pleasant. I'll come through.'

'You wouldn't lie, would you? It's not about Mum and you?'

'No, I wouldn't lie to you, not after all we've been through. It's not about Mum and me.'

Her eyes behind her glasses were bright, alert to every nuance in his voice.

'You're not going back to sleep, are you – want some tea?'

'Okay,' she said. 'I'll make it. You sit down, Dad.'

Alison went through to the kitchen and made tea. When she came back she sat opposite him, on the floor with her back against the other chair.

'So what's happening?' she asked.

'The new owners aren't happy about the way things have been run. My old boss is gone. They've put a new man in his place. My Agent has been sacked as well.'

'Mr Matheson is gone? I liked him.'

'We all did. The new man isn't like him. He has to get results quickly. We've been losing money; that's how Syme and Atwood could buy us. He has to turn that round.'

'You must want that too.'

'That's right. It's in everybody's interest to turn it round.'

'Could he sack you too?'

'No, Sweetheart. I have a contract.'

He was half lying to her. More likely they would try to sicken him off. There would be compensations but they would not be so very great and he couldn't afford not to earn. Where he would go afterwards he didn't know, nowhere in the Highlands. There was war damage to be repaired in the Middle East where he had worked before, although that was in a time of peace. He had already put out feelers and some opportunity might come up, but the sand and the flies would mean being away from Alison, losing what little of her teenage years he was entitled to.

'But he could make it – difficult for you?'

Mac hesitated too long. Alison pushed herself across the floor and leaned half against his chair, half against his leg. She rested her head against him and he put his hand on her shoulder, looked down at her hair that was so like Patricia's hair.

'I'll survive. Commitment is the name of the game.'

'You'll be okay,' she said. 'You're strong.'

He squeezed her shoulder. 'You're encouraging me. Don't you know it's supposed to be the other way round? How are you getting on with Ronnie?'

She squeezed his leg in return. 'Mum asked me not to talk about that.'

'Okay.'

'He's all right. We don't have much in common. He's not remotely like you. He likes football.'

'Ugh! Listen, if you ever hear them up to anything at night I want you to bang on the wall and shout through that you're trying to sleep.'

'Dad, that's really embarrassing! What time are you leaving in the morning?'

'I'll take you into the Academy. Then go straight to Ness.'

'Will the new man be there, the one who got your real job?'

'Did Mum tell you that?'

'What's he like?'

'His name's James Swann. You can call him James.'

'I'd rather call him Mr Swann. I don't like him.'

'You haven't met him. He's a bit younger than me; thirty-eight or nine, sandy hair, gets angry easily. He's got a nervous tic that gets worse when he's excited. Wait till you see; the men will give him some nickname.'

'Blinky Jimmy!'

He put his hand on her head and shook. 'You'll get me into trouble, you. The partner flew back down to Leicester last night. Who knows what's in their minds down there? They're extending their Scottish operation. Actually they call it 'North,' meaning from the north of England up. They'll have longer term plans.'

'Will you be part of them?'

'Maybe, maybe not. If not, just another couple of years.'

'What happens then?'

'You'll be old enough to leave school. You can get a job, move in here and look after me.'

'You're terrible.'

'Don't monopolise the shower this morning,' he told her, but she did.

As usual she tried his patience in the morning. It was the headspace she took up when his mind wanted to range through site deliveries, human resource, plant locations and returns, storage of materials, programmes, progress, valuations, the overall consumption of Strath Construction by Syme Atwood, the future – what future? – the end of his career in the Highlands. They needed a Scottish base to bid for the string of coastal sewage treatment plants the Authority was obliged to build and already they had two. Their methods worked.

With Ewan Matheson gone he was the firm's oldest hand. At 44! Damnation, but he could see the future only too well. Big Swannie was the new Contracts Manager. Trevor Sharp was young, bright, an Honours Graduate, recently Chartered, uncontaminated by Strath Construction thinking. He would be the Agent who finished this job. It was written in the stars. Mac would be lucky to survive. Swann was a Contracts Manager looking for a Directorship. He would want Mac out and Trevor remade in his own image.

Alison was Mac's priority. He had to remember that and give her his full attention. Getting into the car he realised they had hardly spoken since that early morning cup of tea.

'We've hardly spoken,' he observed, driving off.

'It doesn't matter,' she told him. 'If we were together all the time we probably wouldn't speak at all.'

How did it happen, the development that occurred in the big leaps of time they were apart? The brassiere had appeared from nowhere. That was Mum's business anyway, but she could have given him some kind of warning, some kind of discussion, about the sudden alteration in shape. She knew about sex, sometimes he felt she knew more than him. They joked about it. Of course, the break up had primed her early. Soon she would be experimenting with boys, perhaps already was. Time apart from her went by in great soaring leaps with brief, longed for, touchdowns and painful pushoffs.

She kissed him on the cheek and stepped out into the rain.

Her ears were pierced! He noticed as she leaned out of the car. How could he have missed it? Why hadn't she said? No one told him these things. There was no preparation.

'When will you be home?' she asked. 'Must run.'

'8:00. No, 7:00. Make that 6:30pm.'

Driving out of town and across the Kessock Bridge the rain eased and by Tain he had driven out of it. His heart lightened. Paul and Trevor would be, at least should be, seting-out the wayleave fences over the hill. He broke the speed limit to get to site by 10:25, smashing his record, rounding the bend that revealed the new site establishment beside the A9 dual carriageway, the hill to his left between it and the works in Glen Struie. Eventually the pipeline would come down there and cross the road. What a hell of sliding mud it would turn into if it rained, he reflected.

He turned carefully off the road and into the new compound. The compound fence was complete, the first fence to be established. Looking beyond it, down past where the settlement tanks would go, and the outfall, the oil rigs seem surprisingly close to shore.

He parked where he could and entered his hut. The desk was in place, a seat, drawing board and empty filing cabinet but it was still icy cold. John Kelly hadn't turned the electric heater on. These plasterboard boxes didn't retain the heat. They needed a constant supply of energy. He went back to his car for his coat and, inside again, put it on and stood by the window.

The troops were working on the other compound huts and laying out materials. Beyond them were the shoreline and the North Sea. His own hut, which he would share with Trevor, was the first of four to be complete. Paul would share with the General Foreman, John Kelly. Beside that would be Stores and beside that again, the mess. The greater part of the area would be given over to larger items that wouldn't fit in to the Stores hut, reinforcement steel, shuttering frames, diesel tank, huge segmented chamber covers that would be cast onto the underground pumping stations. The concrete batcher was also up, but had no sand or aggregate in its bins yet.

The car park had been scraped down and roughly levelled by a JCB, arisings piled in a heap of frost-bound lumps at the far end of the compound. The same machine was standing by a pile of road stone, the driver waiting while a layer of geotextile was rolled out before starting to spread. There wasn't nearly enough space, but there never was. They would get by. Meantime he was chilled to the marrow. At the door he called to John Kelly and pointed to the generator.

Kelly checked the fuel level and mouthed the word 'okay'. He inserted the starting handle and took it in both hands, his shoulder muscles bunching under his shirt as he pressed metal against cold metal and the handle slowly, reluctantly, turned. The man was as strong as an ox. Another turn, another, and he threw the switch. The genny coughed and shuddered and shivered into life, the hut light went on and, in a minute, the metal front of the heater expanded and boomed outward.

John Kelly's dark face was weather beaten and seamed and ancient and looked like it had been carved from bogwood somewhere in ancient Ireland. His was the way of the shortcut and speedy finishing but they understood each other and, usually, made it work.

Mac used his mobile phone to call Paul. As expected, he and Trevor were on the other side of the hill. He was thinking about driving round, giving the hut time to properly warm when James Swann's car pulled up. Swann climbed out of the car with his briefcase under his arm, scowling at Kelly and the troops as he locked the car door. Something between anxiety and challenge went through Mac but he knew it would be better not to confront him. The man was always energised and restless, always on the cusp of anger. He could do violence; at least he gave that impression. If it came to blows Mac would probably come off best, or so he felt, although Swann was a couple of years younger and half a head shorter and broader in the shoulder. But, there would be no winning that one. One blow and he would be down the road.

If it was only that simple, he thought – but the name of the game was commitment, even when it was reduced to humiliation and endurance. There could be no resolution other than one that came through events and, for the present, he would have to absorb, simply absorb. Already, since the takeover, he had it down to a fine art. Swann inside dropped his briefcase on Mac's desk, eyes ranging, blinking, around the four bare walls.

'Where's Trevor?'

Mac decided not to give a 'good morning' either. 'Round at Struie, with Paul.'

Swann looked out of the window.

'Joiners. These are the eight we carry on the books?'

Mac joined him by the window. 'All steady types, reliable. Good men.'

As they watched, one of the joiners held out a hand to check for rain and looked at the sky. He said something to the others and pointed to the corner of the compound where the mess hut was to go.

'Not that good, or we couldn't have bought you.' Swann looked at him pointedly. 'Or maybe it's Ewan Matheson you blame. What do you say, Mac? Was it the workforce or the management lost all that money?'

Mac knew he couldn't defend the slackness that had crept into the company over the last three years.

'Maybe it was just luck.'

'Luck has to be managed out of the picture.'

'We took a hit on the Gairloch road when we under priced the rock items. There was ten times as much as the Document predicted. If we'd overpriced by just a few pence we would have made the hit.'

'You could have fought that.'

'We did. We lost.'

Satisfied, his point made, James Swann held a hand over the radiator to make sure it was working.

'Tea? Coffee?'

'Later. I want to see the two tanks. You drive.'

As Swann pulled round his safety belt Mac reversed carefully past the joiners and turned towards the road. He slipped into first gear and wobbled slowly across the uneven ground to the gate. Another lorry was approaching. He reversed while John Kelly waved it in, pulled forward again and made his right turn on to the dual carriageway.

A police car had drawn up on the verge, the two officers looking carefully at their traffic controls. One had a 60m tape in his hand. The other held a drawing. They were about to go over all the details. Mac put his mobile phone in its recharging holster on the dash and pressed 3. John Kelly answered.

'John,' he said. 'Police checking the controls. Who put the cones out this morning.'

'Me.'

The GF sounded as if he was speaking from inside a diesel barrel.

'Trevor and Paul set it out yesterday. The chalk marks on the kerbs were all clear enough. It should be okay.'

'Good.' Mac pressed the off-button.

'You weren't sure?'

'First time, it was worth checking. What I wanted to know was that Trevor and Paul did it together. If it was just Paul I would have worried.'

'Who have you got on 1 and 2?'

'My daughter. My wife.'

'I thought you were apart.'

'We are.'

Mac tried not to let his hands tighten on the wheel, tried not to show how this needless probe had got through his defences and, worse, called forth his answer. This one had taken him by surprise. He drove with his stomach churning, knowing he had just accepted another humiliation: accepted when he might have deflected. To make it worse it felt as if he had accepted on behalf of Alison.

Ness amounted to two hundred or so houses exposed to the elements just before the Point. Mac slowed down and turned into the hotel car park. When he had turned the engine off and taken his pair of lifting irons out of the boot they crossed the road to the septic tank. The wind from the North Sea whipped at their trouser legs, their coats, chilling them.

'The executioner's wind that cuts through you,' Mac said.

'And blows the smell back into the village. No wonder they complain.'

Mac pointed at the rubble that had been placed around the concrete tank to protect it and hold it in place.

'All these boulders were taken from the road widening about thirty years ago. The tank was built at the same time.'

He inserted one of the lifting irons into an opening on the first cover, turned it in its socket and gave a light tug upwards. It eased slightly in its frame.

'Good, it should lift,' he said. He put the other iron in its socket and looked at James Swann. 'I can't do it alone.'

They each took a wide, knees bent, stance and hauled the heavy frame upwards to swing it over and across. Peering through the triangular opening into the dark entry chamber their eyes slowly adjusted. Below them the inlet channel from the village ran into two pipes, each one entering a different side of the tank. As they watched, a large thick turd floated through and dropped into the settlement chamber.

James Swann looked along the line of the tank, past the built up ground on to the stony beach where the outfall pipe lay exposed on the surface. The pipe was rotted and broken and faecal matter was lying in lumps between the stones.

'Hasn't been emptied since it was built,' Mac said, taking

himself upstream of the entry chamber, making a large circle with his hands. 'This is where we build the interception chamber.' He turned to look along the shore towards the compound, John Kelly and the troops small in the distance.

'So we build a new chamber here and a pipeline to meet the new pipeline that will come over the hill from Struie to the compound area. When the new Works is in operation we'll empty this tank, knock its top in and backfill. Basically hide it. The estimators haven't put much in for landscaping but if we skimp it's this we'll be judged by.'

'We want paid for that,' Swann told him. 'I'll get Trevor to go over the document, see if he can find an opening.'

Mac didn't point out this was his job. Intended or not the message was all too plain.

'Now,' said Swann, 'round the hill to the other tank.'

As he drove towards the Point and the corner that would take them on to the Struie road Mac looked north, along where the coast doubled back on itself, at the Sutherland cliffs that eventually ran up to Caithness.

'Beautiful country,' he said, but James Swann didn't reply.

The Struie Burn broke over boulders, running almost transparent in the winter light, its bank lined with leafless alders and willows.

'This river could hardly be cleaner,' Swann said.

'I wouldn't drink it. You'll see why when we get to the village.'

Half way along the road they drove past where the fencers were laying out their materials to start on the way-leave and, shortly after, drew up beside a dilapidated mesh fence with a Water Authority sign placed inside. The septic tank was a concrete box cut into the bank, half the size of the Ness tank. The outfall pipe dropped directly into the river. They got out of the car and entered the compound, Swann waving his hand in front of his face.

'What do they eat around here? Road kill?'

'There's not the same wind to take it away. Look down there, where the pipe discharges into the stream.' Mac pointed through the water to a smooth layer of silt that covered the stones at discharge point. 'And look there.' Faecal lumps were lying along the water line further downstream.

'They'll stay there until a big rush comes down. As at Ness the sewage goes straight through. No effective treatment. So we replace the tank with a Pumping Station and lay a new pipe downstream to where you saw the fencers. There the pumping main turns uphill. Top of the hill we build a concrete culvert, then down the other side in a concrete sewer to meet the Ness flow.'

James Swann was hardly listening. 'This is where the Resident Engineer's hut goes?'

'Authority property, so we didn't have to negotiate.'

'And well out of the way of most of the works. Good.'

'Well out of the way.'

'Trevor and your boy are on the way-leave now? I mean right now. I didn't see them.'

'They would be up the hill.'

'On the other side is the wayleave back down to the compound? I might go back that way on foot?'

'It's not set out yet but – sure.'

'Let's go see what they're up to.'

Mac opened the boot and changed into his yellow dayglow jacket. He took out two safety helmets and gave one to James. The two men pulled on wellies and walked back down the road. Above them on the hill the two setting-out engineers were ranging around with tape measures. About a third of the way up a theodolite had been placed over a seting-out peg. The fencers were putting wooden stobs and rolls of wire mesh into a trailer behind a quad ready to carry up.

A second group had already begun at the bottom and were now driving in their third stob. Two holding it in place with stabilisers while a third hammered it into the ground with a 2kg mallet. Swann turned to Mac as they climbed.

'What century is this? There are machines that push these things into the ground in half the time. Don't you know we carry safety responsibility for these men?'

'There isn't one available this side of Inverness right now, and if there had been it couldn't have matched Sandy MacKenzie's price. Take it from me he'll finish on time if he has to work in the snow.'

Swann lengthened his stride, lifting the uphill pace without answering.

By God, Mac thought, the man could climb. He found himself labouring and breathless Up ahead Paul and Trevor were squaring off from the pipeline pegs, taping out fence offsets. Swann strode uphill and past them. Mac laboured up and called Paul and Trevor across.

'Did he speak? Did he say anything?'

'Didn't so much as smile,' said Trevor, respectfully. It appeared Trevor didn't know he was Mac's replacement yet.

'Watch him, boys. He could sack you without an extra blink.'

'I know it,' said Trevor.

'He said something to me,' said Paul. 'Accuracy. Just that one word – accuracy.'

Swann was waiting at the top of the slope. 'They're working steadily enough anyway.'

'I'd say they're committed.'

'Umh.'

Swann's eyes were on the animals that grazed the hill. Close to the road there were black cattle; from about half way up it was all sheep.

'Met the farmers' agent yet?'

'Not yet.'

'Well, get on with it. He'd not be the first to see a way-leave slightly out of position and let it go until we couldn't go back and then stop us and hurt us. Those fences have to be on the nail. Take a tape to a few of the pegs yourself, you and Kelly. Be sure; be absolutely sure. When MacKenzie is done get

these two to go over the whole thing again. Make sure everything they do is checked.'

'Of course'

'Don't "of course" me. You'll have my trust when you've
earned it, and you'll never have it all. I'll always be looking over
your shoulder, Mac. Never forget that. This job has a two per
cent. It can't afford mistakes. C'mon, we'll walk to the other
side.'

Mac looked back down the way-leave at Paul and Trevor,
down again to the fencers and the Struie road. The engineers
would have to pack up in the early afternoon. At this time of
year, this far north, the days were short and hard. The air was
colder. James Swann would not know to make allowances. But
he had already strode off. Mac turned and followed along the
line of pegs.

At the seaward side they looked down another steep slope to
the compound where Kelly was organising the work force, not
doing it well. A flat lorry was waiting at the gate, preventing
another lorry from entering. There was a bank of traffic held
up on the dual carriageway. One of the joiners took out a tin
and began the casual rolling of a cigarette.

'Behind us,' said Mac, 'the route we've just walked, is the
culvert. I want to do that before the pipelines. Otherwise the
ground will turn to slush and we'll struggle to get concrete up.
This is where our joiners will be going as soon as they finish the
compound.'

'No they won't. I'm bringing up a grip squad from Glasgow.
They'll do this in half the time.'

Mac's heart sank. A self-employed squad would look to
Swann's authority. They would look to it through Trevor.
They would see through his position. He remained silent for a
long time, looking along the coast, along the line of cliffs to
Sutherland, at the three closest oil rigs. Further out to sea he
could make out a dozen more.

He was finished. It was a matter of time.

'I guess you know what you're doing.'

'I'll walk directly down to the compound from here. You go back the way we came. I'll be gone by the time you get back.'

Mac watched him make the first part of his descent, carefully at first down the higher steeper levels. He took his mobile phone from his pocket and pressed 3. Knowing James Swann was on his way would not repair the mess John Kelly had made but it would at least prepare him for the blast.

He stopped at the Ness Hotel for lunch, ordered steak pie, chips and tea, no alcohol, had to wait half an hour. After 10 minutes, he took out his mobile phone and pressed 1.

'Hi, Dad.'

'Hi Sweetheart. Where are you?'

'Just outside the school with Gillian and Mike. You?'

Mike?

'I'm in the Ness Hotel. What a dump. Ancient stags' heads with eyes missing, tatty tartan curtains, linoleum worn to the thread. Classic of a sort, I suppose. Hard to believe it can still exist.'

'Can I buy the new iPod? I'll be the last person I know to have it.'

This took no thought. 'You've got money so just go ahead. I'll make it up tonight. Listen, will you cook?'

'Dad, you have a responsibility to look after me, not the other way around. This is what Mum said.'

'What else did Mum say?'

'It's the age of equality. Women don't have to cook.'

'So be equal. I did it last night. Look in the freezer. Choose. Microwave! It's easy. Just set the table. And buy that music. We can listen together on the hi-fi.'

'I don't think so. It's modern and you'd hate it. But we can watch television. 6:30, remember you said.'

'Mike who?'

'Mike MacArthur. You know his Dad. You were at school together.'

That would be Colin MacArthur who had cut a swathe through the girls in their time. Why worry?

'Does he wear a leather jacket, Mohican haircut, ripped jeans, smoke dope.'

'Dad! I have to go.'

'Okay.'

'Dad, can I have contact lenses?'

'Ask Mum.'

'G'bye.'

The phone was heavy in his hand, but she wouldn't feel the aching hunger for him that he felt for her. It was too much to expect. He had to understand how it was for her.

The face of the mobile told him he had a voice message from Patricia. Well, that could wait until later. He ate his lunch in silence and paid his bill and, as he left, a breeze from the sea lifted some of the guff from the septic tank and poured it around him.

Back at the compound Kelly gave him a wry look but said nothing, continuing his untidy organisation of a construction site in the chaos of its early days. Mac took a box of drawings and documents from the boot of his car, the laptop from the back seat, the calendar, into the Agent's hut to enter each into its new space. In time he and the space would grow into each other. It would become the universal site hut he had lived half his life in. The pile of earth lumps, he noticed, had softened as the day wore on.

On his laptop he called up the works programme and checked materials required for the coming week against delivery notes, made the necessary call to the buyer to gee up the supplies. He took the folder of plant returns from his brief case and put it in the filing cabinet.

When the initial seting-out was complete he could hand all this over to Trevor. Not yet though; and the pegs had to be in the ground and checked before that side could be left to Paul. He phoned the electricity company, calling forward their connection. Both John Kelly and he were too much engaged in trivia, but that would stop when the major part of the labour force, dispersed from the Black Isle, was reassembled. That would be, he checked the programme again, half next week, the rest two weeks down the line. He made coffee and, as he sat down again, the phone rang.

Patricia.

'Mac, it's me. We have to speak.'

'Not a promising start. Where are you?'

'At home.'

'Ah yes. I remember.'

She would be in the kitchen of their house, under the new units he'd put in shortly before leaving, shortly before Ronnie. Her hair was shorter now, but the essentials would be the same. She would be wearing jeans and a pullover to work in. She would be finished for the day, article written and emailed to the paper. This call would be made after she was done, interrupting his work, not hers.

'How'd you get this number?' he asked.

'Sally at the office. Obviously you weren't going answer your mobile.'

'Ronnie there? How's he like my taste in furniture and paintings? Obviously he shares my taste in women?'

'The furniture and paintings are my taste, same as everything else in here. You don't remember? You were too busy with your valuations on site to notice the value of what was under your nose. Ronnie's at work. He has the sort of job where you go in at 9:00 in the morning and come home at half past five.'

'That's a real job? Okay, I'll take your word for it. What do you want?'

'I want to talk with you about Alison. I'm not happy about some of the attitudes she picks up from you.'

'What?'

'That's right, and there are other things. I think she's drinking. Have you been giving her drink?'

'She gets half a glass of wine topped up with lemonade, an introduction. That's not drinking.'

'I don't want her drinking at all and I'm her mother.'

'Well, I want her to have a responsible attitude to drink and not get ambushed by it when she eventually moves into the adult world and, by the way, I'm her father. Don't forget that, you and Ronnie.'

There was a long silence from Patricia, a great nothingness that had him taking the phone from his ear and looking at it until her tiny voice, now wounded, sounded across the gap.

'This is hurting us both,' she said.

'I guess so.'

'How's the job? Any better?'

'Same shit as last time we spoke. What I am thinking about is how we are going to lay the pipeline across the A9. One side at a time, I guess. Moving the traffic across to suit.'

'Think you can stick it?'

'I can try.'

'I know that tone. You still love it out there. You love the conflict. That side of your life always came first.'

'So, what did you really want?'

'I meant what I said. Did you know Alison is falling behind at school?'

'Really? She thinks about music all the time, and friends. Isn't that how it should be at fourteen? She seems okay to me.'

'I want her back early this time. Thursday.'

'Why? I see little enough of her. You want to protect her from my influence?'

'We're going to Ronnie's parents this weekend. It would be nice for them to meet.'

Now it was Mac's turn to make a silence. A9 traffic, men shouting, beep warnings from reversing vehicles, laughter, all went on outside the impregnable bubble of anxiety that had him for its centre.

'Is this a joke?'

'They asked to. They like young people. They have grand-children the same age.'

'It would be simpler if I wasn't here, wouldn't it? Better if I was dead.'

'Look,' she went on with effort, control. 'I can see I'm going to get no sense out of you. Try to think this through rationally for a change. We are already living together, the three of us. That's not going to change. It makes every kind of sense to ease the relationships. Think about Alison for once.'

'For a change? For once? Do you mind if we end this call now? Just leave it there. I have Alison until Saturday morning. That's not changing.'

'Look Mac, don't go into your martyr routine. You'll always be her father but Ronnie has his place too. Times are chan-ging.'

'Lets leave off there. Right *there*! I'm not going into any martyr routine and I'm not swallowing any of this guilt and responsibility stuff and I'm not budging on dates. Just leave it there.'

After two years it was no easier to get off the phone. They hung up together.

Well, he knew what Patricia was about all right, reducing his time with Alison on an 'it's-good-for-her' basis, building her into this new family. He was the lesser, no-rights, partner. So, who was he to stand in the way? Another stint in the Middle East would suit Patricia down to the ground. He would be out of the way. There would be more money. By the time he came back, assuming he didn't end up with his head in a bucket, Alison would be at University and a stranger. Ronnie would be her dad. Some day he would have to meet this Ronnie. According to Alison he wasn't so bad. Gratifyingly though, he wasn't so great either.

She still preferred her real Dad.

Outside he heard John Kelly shouting in irritation. The pipe bedding material had arrived a day early and he had nowhere to put it. He decided to let John get on with it and take the longer view, the programme, the gathering labour force.

If Swann was bringing in a grip squad the chances are they would be good. Almost certainly it was the beginning of the end for their full-timers. He would be obliged to back Healey's labourers, hard enough workers but slapdash and thuggish. Derek the steelfixer and his squad would, in a way, set off against them. In addition, and more to the point, Derek was ace at what he did and strong enough to keep his own men in line. Unlike most steelfixers he would bring problems forward as soon as he saw them. Most steelfixers just let the job run to a halt and turned the meter on. On a 'reward-what-you-want' basis Mac accepted Derek's higher rate. The good builder was already gone. Harry, the clerk of works, rated him but the time he took was unconscionable.

I see further than James Swann, he thought. Maybe I can wait him out. But no, Swann was as much Syme's man as Healey was Swann's. There was a programme of change for the company just as surely as there was a programme of works for the job and Mac was no part of it. To give himself a chance he had to keep his head in the job.

Later, as the light began to fade, he picked up the phone and called Paul's mobile.

'Light's going. Come off the hill now.'

'I'm packing the theodolite away now.'

'Will John MacKenzie be out tomorrow?'

'So he says. Two days to finish this.'

'Good, I'll bring Conn and his machine over day after tomorrow. He can start the soil strip as you start to come down this side. That should be safe enough. Later you can set out the profiles for Healey's men. They can start first thing next week. I'll see them later.'

'You're using Healey's men?'

'No choice. Let that go, Paul. Adapt.'

'Okay.'

Good boy Paul, he thought. Good teamwork beginning with Trevor. With Mac as Contracts Manager, Trevor as Agent, Paul moving up to sub-agent after he got that elusive qualification, it could be good. Good, but not what was written in the stars. James Swann was Contracts Manager and Mac was increasingly like the spare prick at a wedding.

He put his head back into his work and lost himself there until, outside, he heard John Kelly bringing the shift to an end, heard the troops piling into the minibus and leaving. John looked in.

'That's time, Mac.'

'Off you go. I'll wind up here and then head for the Black Isle. I'm bringing Conn over in a couple of days. That should please you.'

'Sure will. See you tomorrow, Mac.'

'See you then.'

'And good luck.'

Luck? Yes, the GF knew he needed some luck.

Mac called the Black Isle site hut and asked Conn to stay until he got there. He tidied up what he was doing and packed away his laptop and drove off in fading light that was soon black as pitch and as he drove both Patricia and James Swann kept invading his head.

The man was a bully. He would be Northern Director over Mac's twitching corpse. You had to be an animal to get on in this game. The civil engineering contract was the survival of the fittest, nothing more.

He drove the A9 under a low cloud cover, headlights sweeping the forest at bends. This was his land. He didn't want to leave. He didn't want to be sickened out of what was his own, his place in the construction industry in the Highlands. He wouldn't let it happen, by God, he wouldn't. He struck the wheel with the flat of his hand. He wouldn't.

It was after 6:30pm when he drove onto the site. Most of the old compound had been cleared and they were down to just a few troops. Derek's squad, with no reinforcement to tie, were tidying, repairing fences here and there. Healey's squad were struggling to get the sewer past Harry's tests. Conn stood by with his machine to lift old scaffolding, formwork, small items of plant, onto the lorry. Patience, a capacity for boredom, was as vital to him as his hands on the controls. A round man, his fair hair thinning on his ball shaped head, he was waiting in the hut for his instructions when Mac arrived.

Mac told him he was bound for Ness at last.

'There's no big lifts left here,' Conn reassured him. 'The labourers can throw what's left on the lorry without me.'

'They'll be following on as well.'

'No problems. I mind my own business.' This meant he didn't respect Healey's men either, although he was maybe afraid of them.

'What's the surface like out there? It's too dark to see.'

'Harry's happy enough. At least he will be when these last two pipelines pass.'

'They'd better. If we have to bring you back to dig them up again there'll be hell to pay.'

'They shouldn't have been backfilled before the test, Mac.'

'I know that. You know that. John knows that. Swannie said otherwise.'

'He'll be hoping for a claim against the contract? That's how we're working these days?'

'You can go home now, Conn. I'll lock up.'

Conn left and, as he locked up his machine and started his car, Mac sat and stared into space. The heating was off and it was cold but he sat unmoving, suddenly exhausted.

This was how it was. By now even the crane driver had the lie of the land, knew the new rule was haste and deception and claim, smash and grab. He could almost taste the sympathy in the man's voice and hated what he must become if he was to survive.

'The only answer,' he said to himself, 'is to stay and take it, adapt, or catch a flight east.'

So, struggle against it. Risk it all. He would have to work the weekend. Likely he would have to work every weekend. No hardship in itself because, never mind the cost to himself, he loved his work, the smells and sounds, the men, the demands on his foresight, his experience and intelligence, his leadership. Patricia was right about that, if nothing else. He went to the window and looked out, his hand against the thin plasterboard wall of the hut. There was a wind picking up. Conditions could change very quickly. As he watched, the clouds opened over the City and the stars shone through with their eternally cold, inanimate brilliance.

Across the water Inverness burned with electric light, the Kessock Bridge was strung with moving vehicle lights and along the Moray coast was all pinpoints of light, street lights, houses, the airport lights. Real constructs, they were the reality within which Alison would live her life. It had been his privilege to go to the basics of nature, the ground and the water and the energy, and turn them into the basics of civilised living. All along his life had direction and purpose he had never even considered. He had no inclination to leave. He would not leave. He would fight and he would lose, but he would fight. His mobile phone rang. Alison.

'Dad, you're late. It's after 7:00. I've made the dinner and it's getting cold. Are you coming home? I mean now.'

'Sorry, Ali. I'll be a while yet.'

'Where are you?'

'On the Black Isle, in my old hut that looks across the water at the city. As a matter if fact I'm looking that way now. You know I've played my part in building all this. That's really important.'

'I know, Dad. It's your job. I know it pays for the way we live and I know I'm lucky, but aren't you coming home?'

'Don't think it's just a job.'

'Dad?'

'Let me tell you what I'm looking at. Above the town the clouds have just opened and the stars have come out and it's as if the city is answering with its lights. I have this huge wonderful feeling of "home" that surged through me when I heard your voice and saw what I saw. It's an amazing thing, the City, because it's always growing although, just the same, it's always complete. Like you, Sweetheart.'

'Dad?'

'I've played my part in its making and as I sit here on my own I think I understand what I never did before. It was all for you, in some ways directly for you, in others not so direct, but all for you and Gillian and Mike and the rest and if there's a price to pay it's worth it.'

She said nothing but he could hear her breathing.

'And it goes on.'

'Does it?'

'And you will go on.'

'Oh, Dad.'

'I guess that's enough. It has to be enough.'

4

The specification is everything

The Resident Engineer's hut was split new and warm and smelled of plasterboard and paint and the scorched plastic odour an electric heater gives out in its first usage.

Behind his new desk, his new contract-purchased telephone/fax to one side and his new internet linked laptop square in the middle sat Allan Crawford, 26, two years out of University and also new. The three Contract Documents were open before him. The Bill of Quantities he had written himself, hastily, under Vernon Street's direction. The Specification and Conditions of Contract were standard except that The Russell Partnership insisted on the 5th Edition. He paused in composing an email to his girlfriend in Glasgow when a van drew up and Harry Gilfeather, Clerk of Works, entered.

Aged 63, Allan knew from the file, Harry was not new. Vernon described him as an 'old soldier'. Darkened by years of outside work, his face had been beaten by weather hard and cold and thrown at him by the winds on sites all across Scotland. A number of moles grew about it, each with its individual black hair sprouting and, below his right eye, the lid hung limp over a lifeless square inch that lay flat on the bone. Caution was perhaps required, Vernon had suggested, since Harry and GR had been together in West Africa before the Partnership was formed and while the great man was still was making his name.

Harry pulled a chair across and sat, removing his safety helmet but not his duffel coat.

'They're using Pat Healey's men again,' he said. 'Eight of them.'

'I heard.'

'Only skilled man on the Black Isle was the builder and they got rid of him.'

'I hear he was slow.'

'He did the work right. More and more it's about speed. Slap-dash and get it done and onto the next flaming mess. They've made some changes, got rid of most of the thugs, which will mean the new men have still to learn.'

'Some of them. Mac and Trevor seem responsible.'

'The Contracts Manager sets the tone. Swannie is different. First time on site?'

'No.'

'First time as Resident Engineer?'

'Yes.'

Harry made a 'what-have-they-sent-me-this-time' kind of look and nodded at the documents. 'The Specification is everything. You know *that*?'

'GR says it's the Conditions. He says it's our Bible.'

'If the job when it's done doesn't work the game's a bogie. Where's your Bible then?'

'Don't know.'

Harry gave him a 'what-kind-of-answer-is-that' sort of look.

'I worked with Sir Graham Russell long before he was a "Sir". In West Africa he knew the point was to get it done and make it work.'

Allan closed the lid of his laptop. 'Vernon told me you two go back a long way,' he said.

'What's this meeting for?'

'Mac says the wayleave on the hill is too narrow.'

'It's been widened for them already.'

'To carry materials topside they need to put an access road alongside the pipeline. That's why they asked for the first extra width. But to meet the landowner's requirements they have to strip off the topsoil and when they're done put it back. That means they can't just cart it away and free the space. Now they realise there isn't room for the pipeline work and the road *and* the topsoil storage they'd like to drop it outside the wayleave fence'

Harry shook his head in a 'you've-got-a-lot-to-learn' kind of way.

'All the space in the world won't stop these clowns cheating. They'll dig the trenches shallow to hasten themselves on. They'll skimp on gravel bedding to save a few pence, you watch. It's a game to them and you have to be up to it. You've to stand over them when you can and demand trial excavations where they don't expect them. If the job isn't to spec they've to take the whole line out and lay it again.'

'No room for compromise?'

'The Specification is all. Merciless with the lash.'

Together they stepped from the warmth and newness of the hut into the cold airs of winter and the stink from Struic's broken septic tank.

'They've parked you well out of the way of the main action,' Harry said. True enough, but it suited Allan to be out of the way. The sting should be out of any crisis by the time it reached him.

Thirty metres along the road the flow of sewage would turn and be pumped uphill, up to the right. Mac was already there, talking with an older man, his hair white, his forehead broad.

'Allan,' said Mac, 'this is Iain Sutherland acting for the Estate.' He opened the land plan and laid it on the roof of his car. 'Here's the amended layout we're proposing.'

'What's the dog leg for?' Iain Sutherland asked.

'There's an outcrop of rock,' Allan said. 'The Engineer thought it best to go round.'

'Did he now? And you've already asked for a widening?'

'For the access road. Yes.'

'And now you are looking for a further accommodation?'

'It's in everyone's interest,' Mac said.

'It should have been thought of first time round?'

'I guess so. We've gone through this merger. Turmoil. Sure, all the changes should have gone through at the same time.'

'That's honest enough. So what's it all about?'

'We're going to put an access road up alongside the pipeline, that's why we asked for the extra width. To meet your client's requirements we have to strip off the topsoil and when we're done, after we remove the roadstone, put it back. Now we realise there isn't room for the pipeline work and the road *and* the topsoil storage. We'd like to drop it outside the wayleave fence. We could go up and look?'

All four climbed as far as the dogleg and turned to look back. The surface was covered in thin spiky grass. Iain Sutherland put the heel of his boot in and scraped the thin soil back to the gritty pan below.

'Not much depth,' he said. 'All the more reason to keep top and under soils separate, of course. All right, Mr MacPherson. If it helps the job along and ensures a good reinstatement go ahead.'

'Financial implications?' Mac asked.

'We'll include, say, five metres to the side of the east fence in the reinstatement specification and increase my client's reimbursement on a pro-rata basis. That agreed you can get on.'

'That's between the Contractor and the Estate,' Allan said. 'No payment implications for the Client?'

Mac said nothing.

'I agree with that,' said Iain Sutherland. He looked at the sky. 'Think the weather will hold? The forecast is appalling.'

'We'll manage,' Mac said.

'No problems with this proposal though?' Allan asked.

'No problems,' Iain Sutherland agreed.

Harry and Mac looked at each other, looked at the slope and the lowering clouds.

5

The strength is in the gravel

Sitting in the cab of his tracked excavator at the top of the hill, relaxed by fan blown hot air from the engine, Conn looked down on the squad laying the gravity sewer up towards him. They were in a mess down there.

The ground was loose where he had tracked over it and dug it and the rain was carrying watery silt in rivulets down to the road drains. It would only get worse. Beyond them his eye travelled to the A9 and the compound and the shore and the oil rigs and as much of the North Sea as torrential rain and mist would allow and, ach, on to infinity.

The trouble with this job, he reflected, was it gave him too much time to think. He finished making half a dozen roll-ups, sealed five in his tin and lit the sixth

He placed the tin in his bag under the seat and fired up the excavator, tracking it back over the top of the hill like a giant fiddler crab. On the Struie side the troops were laying the pumping main and building the access road at the same time. They were better organised but it was still hopeless. When the pumping main and the access road were complete he would track the crane up the access road to work topsides on the culvert.

Now though, for the present, between the two squads and the road what they really needed was three machines, static at each pipeline and the road. This he knew. Skinflint Swannie was making do with one, travelling, and it was cutting up the ground everywhere for the rain to turn into a thin watery gruel. Getting a second machine into position now would be impossible.

At the top of the hill above Glen Struie he looked down on
the two lines of wayleave fence, the stone road that reached
about a quarter of the way up and the lengthening pile of
arisings he had dumped outside the fence. The hill above the
pipe trench where his tracks had spun was a sea of mud.
Beyond and below all this the River Struie was overhung with
alders and willows and a thin mist. Across the hill a few
bedraggled sheep stood with their green and slimy rear ends
to the wind.

Curtains of rain swept along the glen from the sea, thrashing
the door of his cabin, whipping at the four man squad in their
dripping oilskins. Off to his left the village of Struie looked very
small.

Not for the first time he pondered the economics of what
they did and shook his head and let it go past to just drive
his machine and continue to do what he was told without
question. When he opened his cabin door to lean back and
spit his rollup the wind blew it back and down against the
tracks.

By now the pumping main squad were nearly half way up,
laying and backfilling as they went, local drains neatly dug,
black polyethylene pipe and yellow warning tape laid out along
the line of the trench, bedding gravel spaced along the route.
The contrast with the Ness side was profound. This would be
the two with experience paying off, or else a brain had come
into play. True, they were working with bigger and heavier
pipes over there.

Also true though, with the access road, on this side there was
more going on to trip over. After Conn had cast the next three
metres of topsoil over the fence the geotextile had to be laid
and then stone would be carried up in dumpers and spread
and compacted. The pipelayers had to live with this and work
their trench. They had to lay bedding, butt weld pipe lengths,
lay pipe, cover pipe to 15cm, lay warning tape, backfill,
compact, and all this according to Specification, to Harry
the Clerk of Works' precious spec. The idea of compacting

the backfill when it was this wet was a joke. Put the wacker plate on that stuff and it just went – *brrrp* – down through it.

Healey's men, Trots and Jinkie who had survived from the Black Isle, along with JB and Tammas who were new, shovelled gravel bedding into the trench. They pushed it round the outside of the pipe and against the trench and filled up above it.

Back aching, JB looked up to see Conn's machine crest the hill and start downwards, up to the hubs in mud with a bow wave folding out in front and the weighted mass of the thing sliding from side to side as it descended. Conn behind the glass had a frown etched so deeply between his eyes JB could make it out through rain speckled glasses.

'What you looking at?' Tammas asked.

'A robotic dinosaur looking dangerously uncontrollable and it's coming our way.'

'Huh?'

Suddenly their hand dug drains were overcome as a flush of muddy water ran down and spilled into the trench.

'Out of this,' JB said, stepping on the pipe, the bedding and the first layer of backfill to get out and join the other two at the wayleave fence. Conn brought the machine slithering to a halt only two metres short and half stood at his seat to peer across at the new road.

'What's he looking there for?' JB asked. 'The troops are offski. Unlike us they know when they've had enough.' He took off his glasses and wiped rain and sweat from the lenses. 'Useless,' he muttered. 'I can hardly see.'

'We're paid on the metre laid,' said Trots. 'One more and we're offski too.'

JB was intent on the driver's face.

'He's going to strip the soil back? In this rain?'

'What if he is?'

'Ho, Conn! Are you going . . .? He can't hear me'.

JB stepped ankle deep along the wayleave, the mud deepening as he climbed, sucking on his wellies and through them to haul at his calves and thighs. He stopped when it began to spill over on to his socks and signalled to Conn. The driver climbed from his cabin and onto a track. Holding on to the door handle he leaned outwards.

'What?'

'Don't strip the topsoil now. By the time the troops come back it'll be saturated. I mean – tomorrow, overnight rain'

Conn waved his mobile phone. 'Kelly says.'

'Use your bucket here. Push the firmer stuff up into a bund above the trench.'

'Bund?' Conn shook his head.

'Bund, wall, dyke, I mean a barrier. Look, I'll show.'

JB waded downhill again and made shaping gestures with his two hands uphill of the trench. Conn nodded and climbed back into his cabin and fired up the machine. With JB directing him he used the bucket to push the drier loose material into a sort of wall that ran diagonally across the line of the trench. When it was complete it captured the flow of muddy rainwater that streamed downhill and directed it across to the side of the wayleave where it ran down onto Trots and Jinkie and round their feet.

'That won't last forever but we'll get another pipe length in and backfilled and then, as Trots puts it, we're offski.'

'Telling Conn was my job.' Unhappy Trots stepped out from the wayleave fence. 'I'm the ganger.'

'You didn't think of it,' said JB.

'You should have asked me first. Always ask me first.'

'It was JB thought of it,' Tammas said in his innocence. 'It's always him that thinks of things.'

'There's ways things are done.'

'And there's better ways,' Tammas said.

'Will I hit you with this shovel?'

The bedding was a round pea-shaped gravel that rolled before the backs of their shovels and tumbled down into the trench. Tammas and Jinkie jumped down to level it before the next length of pipe; now they stood below ground to their waists with the cold, saturated dirt sides of the trench still standing firm although oozing muddy water.

'The quicker the better,' JB told them.

They spread the gravel evenly across the trench floor first with their shovels then with the sides of their boots.

'Look down there,' said Trots. 'Harry. The last guy we need right now.'

At the foot of the hill the Clerk of Works was speaking to Trevor.

'Harry's pretty animated,' JB mused, 'At this early stage of proceedings he'll want to show who the boss is.'

Below them Harry took off his safety helmet and ran his hand over the back of his head. Tonsured and bare the stubble around it swirled in a bristly, natural circle.

'It's like a monkey's arse,' said Trots.

'A chimpanzee's,' JB corrected. 'Monkeys have tails.'

'Look you . . .'

'They're coming up. C'mon, let's get the pipe in and covered.'

Together they rolled in the next pipelength leaving its leading end curling up and out of the trench ready for the next butt weld. They shovelled in the top bedding, JB objecting when Trots wanted to skimp and get on.

'Make sure there's plenty on,' JB said. 'Look down now. They're close.'

Harry was leading the two others up hill, stopping twice to push in hand pegs.

'Know what the pegs mean?'

'Trial holes,' said Jinkie. 'Like on the Black Isle.'

'And they're still putting those pipes right,' said JB.

'No matter,' said Trots. 'We got paid and we're still here.'

Harry was fitter than Trevor in spite of his years. He arrived first.

'Aye right,' he said.

'These young guys,' said JB. 'They can't cut it.'

Harry didn't respond.

'You flaming well backfilled all this without me seeing,' he said. 'I don't think you've laid it to specification. I want trial holes hand dug down there. I want to see the bedding.'

'Hand dug?'

'Aye.'

'Now?'

'Aye now.'

'After we finish this backfill we're for the off,' said Trots.

Another curtain of rain and hail mixed blew in from the sea, a wicked whipping wave that stung their faces, that forced them to turn their backs to it and speak across their shoulders. Trevor arrived and faced it for just a moment and then gave in. As they faced inland to Struie and the Sutherland hills the rain lashed against their helmets and the upturned collars of their donkey jackets and ran down their necks and the backs of their legs.

Conn in his waterproofs walked past them and downhill on the other side of the wayleave.

'Enough is enough,' he said. 'See you back at the hut.'

'This weather,' Harry said to Trevor, 'is made for haste and corner cutting, and men make mistakes when they're this miserable. It all,' he indicated the pipeline, 'has to be proved'.

'Can't this wait until morning?'

'I guarantee there'll be the full 15cm all round the pipe in these positions come the morning. The spec has to be proved now.'

'You're saying these men will dig the holes before you get here and fake the bedding?' Trevor said angrily.

'Know how many minks in a mink coat?' JB asked Tammas.

'The full 15cm all round, is all I want. That and to be sure.' He kicked at a length of black pipe. This stuff's plastic, only the bedding protects it. The strength is in the gravel'

'You're saying we'd lie?'

'Don't come the injured innocent with me.'

'Between 80 and 100,' JB said. 'Mink I mean, not centimetres. Know how many donkeys in a donkey jacket?'

Trevor ignored JB and Tammas. 'We won't cheat you,

Harry,' he said, appeasing. 'All you have to do is be here for the excavation and you'll see for yourself. 7:30am.'

The muscles around Harry's eyes took a stubborn set.

'Tell you what,' said Trevor. 'I'll get John Kelly himself up here in the morning. Trots!'

'Yo ho.'

'Assign one of these three to help John.'

'Assign?'

'He means get one of us to dig the holes by hand while Kelly looks on meaningfully,' said JB. 'Just the one, by the way.'

'Just one,' Tammas repeated, at first puzzled. 'Donkey you mean.'

'Okay,' said Trots. 'You do it, JB.'

'Hard labour. Sure you want both holes dug, Mr Clerk of Works?'

'Don't speak back,' said Harry, too fiercely. 'You're not even a ganger.'

'I know it.'

'I'll help,' said Tammas.

'We're soaked to the skin anyway,' said JB. 'Why don't we do one now, the other in the morning? If it's okay that's it. Which it will be, is.'

'If the bedding is out of spec,' Harry held a warning finger in the air, swung it downwards along the line of the laid pipe, 'that lot is coming out and going in again.'

'There's a bus going to go over it?' asked JB. 'Here?'

'It's to be to spec. That's what's we're paying for.'

'Come back in an hour,' said JB. 'Tammas and I will have it exposed and we'll be standing to eager attention.'

'Now we go?' Jinkie asked Trots.

'Back to the hut.' To JB he said, 'You're full of ideas. This for your clever lip.'

'Just the friendly malice of a respectful underling.'

JB chose the topmost to dig at, half way down the hill.

'How come?' Tammas pushed the edge of the shovel into

the ground and pressed down with the sole of his boot. 'We know it's light on bedding here. Trots wanted to get on.'

'That's right,' said JB. 'Trot's commitment to the People doesn't extend to giving them their money's worth.'

He took his place beside Tammas, both with their backs to the wind and to the sea. He put his boot to the shovel and turned the first ground. 'You're a good bloke, Tammas,' he said. Funny how we get on. Opposites, I guess.'

The ground being already broken, and none too well compacted, the backfill moved easily for them. Their shovels went *hishsht hishsht* as they pressed the blades home, *shshloop* as the wet ground gave way. It stuck to the blades when they turned the shovels over so they had to shake it loose, the weight of clay straining across their lower backs and in their shoulders and thighs.

'Why show Harry the worst bit?' asked Tammas.

'Because it's also the shallowest and we can get down quickest. Because we can fake it up and fool him. Because he might insist on another trial and if someone else such as Kelly digs here he might not fake it, or might not get the chance because Harry will be standing by.'

'You never stop thinking.'

'I don't, but for all that I'm humble.'

'You won't stay in this game. Something better will come along and you'll go.'

'Hope so.'

'Take me with you.'

'I'll do that. You can be my driver, my chauffeur.'

'Great. Better than this.'

'We're down. Look, there's the yellow warning tape.'

They dug along the pipe length for a metre and across its width. Trots had only put in 5 or 6cm of bedding, well light of spec. They dug with the rain rattling on their safety helmets and the sweat running inside their oilskins, inside their donkey jackets and working shirts, running in rivulets along the natural creases of their bodies. They brought more bedding from uphill on the blades of their shovels held level and packed it down the sides of the pipe until the width was the full 15cm and more and then they spread it along the top.

'That's it,' said Tammas.

'Not quite,' said JB. 'Watch.'

Standing on the fresh bedding he dug into the trench at each end of their excavation, tunnelling over the pipe so he could pack more bedding in. Then he piled more earth around the opening. The new bedding was muddied by their boots and so didn't look fresh. Outside the trench again they had ten minutes to wait for Harry.

'If he comes back,' said Tammas.

'He'll come back.'

'Want a drink?'

'You got a drink?'

Tammas undid his oilskin and pulled a quarter bottle from his donkey jacket.

'Vodka,' he said. 'No smell.'

He took off his glove, unscrewed the cap and wiped the opening with the palm of his hand and offered it.

'Take it by the neck.'

JB looked at it for a long time.

'Ah God,' he said, took it and drank from it and handed it back for Tammas to drink from also and put away.

'There's a bit of you likes this work,' said Tammas.

'There's not a bit of me likes this work but there's maybe a bit of me a masochist.'

'What's a masochist?'

'No matter. I'm being punished for things I did in a previous life. Some ways it's good to be at the bottom of the pile. The only way is up.'

'There's worse places than this,' said Tammas. 'But you're going to bounce, JB. The way you can talk you won't stay here. Don't forget I was your friend.'

'I won't forget, Tammas. You're one of the best. Look, Harry's back on the hill. He'll be here in a minute.'

'Everything's okay. You thought of everything.'

'Yes? We'll dance for him though. When he whistles we'll dance. It's all about hierarchies really. We're below Trots and Jinkie although they're nothing because they don't think. Trots has grievance where his brainbox should be. We're all four of us below Healey and Kelly and Harry but for us it all turns on Kelly and the Clerk of Works and so we dance for them. They're below Mac and the RE and they're below Swannie and this guy Sir Graham Russell or whatever he's called and he's below whoever pays the bills and they all dance for whoever is above.'

'And whoever pays the bills is below the Queen and she's below God. That's how it's supposed to be, JB. We're the bottom of the pile. We're just shite.'

'Worse than that, Tammas. We are the heavy sediment of the shite. Verily we are the very *crème de la crème* of the faecal matter, except where it floats we have sunk. Here's Harry now. He can't like this any more than we do.'

Harry arrived and looked at the two half drowned wretches who had been washed up on the shoreline of his life. He looked into the hole and jumped down and scraped at the gravel bedding with the side of his foot until the warning tape was exposed. Seeing the tape JB remembered it should have been on top. He should have cut it away and replaced it on top according to spec. From this Harry would know they had filled above it with extra bedding.

The Clerk of Works kept scraping until he reached the top of the pipe. He took a wooden rule from his pocket and placed it on top, marking the top of the bedding level with his thumb. When he looked at it closely it was 14cm. Even allowing for the blunder with the warning tape they were still one centimetre short. JB drew in his breath. The cold must have addled his brains.

'That reminds me,' said Tammas. 'John Kelly says his prick is twelve inches long but he doesn't use it as a rule.'

'Funny? Don't try to be,' said Harry. 'Pass me that shovel.'

Harry took Tammas's shovel without looking up and dug into the wall of earth above the pipe at the low end of the trench. The bedding was the full 15cm where JB had faked it but Harry kept digging until he found the original 6cm. He leaned the shovel against the trench wall and crouched on his hunkers and looked at it.

JB ran his wet sleeve across his nose and thought about lifting and relaying the pipeline. The welded polyethylene, now a single unit, would all have to come out. It couldn't be just a length. With the ground turned over it would take twice as long or three times. There would be no extra money. The whole job would be set back by days, weeks if the Clerk of Works was going to be difficult. The wind cut through him but he shuddered as much with apprehension as with the cold.

Harry straightened up and kicked some of the backfilled earth down over the pipe. He looked into the distance, into the rain as it swept along the glen from the sea and then down the wayleave to the road and the mist above the river.

The wayleave was tidy enough given the conditions. Would having the pipe out make the job better or worse in the long run? He could stand on the spec, of course. It was the right thing to do, but the whole place would be turned upside down and no one would thank him. It would do no real good. Then there was the human factor.

JB and Tammas had tried to cheat him but so what? Caught out, they were that much less likely to try again.

He climbed out of the trench and looked at the two of them blue tinged by the freezing wind and soaked through and shivering. Poor sods, they looked half dead. Further up the hill the sheep still had their green stained rumps to the wind, taking it. The men were worse off than the sheep if only because they understood.

JB had been right earlier. There would be no bus running over this pipe. Standing on principle now was pointless. He had made his mark with the sub-agent. The job wasn't up to spec but it would be adequate. It would do. Like the men.

'That's okay,' he said wearily. 'Fill it in.'

'Okay Harry.'

'In future don't backfill without permission.'

'No Harry.'

'I want to see every pipe as it goes in.'

'Yes Harry.'

'You'd better get back to the compound. Get washed. Get something to eat.'

'Thanks, Harry.'

They made their way downhill together to the road and went their own ways. JB and Tammas went back to the compound to do as Harry had said and get away early. Harry went back to the hut he shared with the RE to tell him the pipeline was within spec knowing he had applied his own values to prove its adequacy. Everything was in its place according to the larger specification, the one that time and life had taught him.

It was okay because he said so, because his experience and humanity were truer than the printed word however legally absolute. When he reported to Allan Crawford he would give him his place and so prove his own. Allan would colour in his wall plan to signify the job was done and eventually let GR know through his reports.

First though, Allan would call Trevor and Trevor would tell Mac. Mac would include this length of pipeline in his next valuation. GR would recommend payment and the Client would pay. This way reporting and acceptance and reward would go along the line. Not as far as the Queen but possibly, yes, maybe, God.

6

There's a grip squad coming

Hovering about thirty metres above the site Mac looked down first on the Ness septic tank and the new pipeline leading from it towards the compound. He moved his eye southwards along the line until it came to the Collection Chamber and saw that it was the crux not only of the Works, when they were built, but of the Contract. Everything passed through this point, the untreated sewage from Struie which would come tumbling downhill from the new culvert, the sewage from Ness. Their work all radiated from this point because the combined flow entered a larger pipe and from there ran into the two circular settlement tanks that were being constructed now and, thereafter, to the sea. He blinked and the layout plan he had been staring down on became once again just a plan.

At the window of his hut he looked out on the reality. James Swann had pointed out that the Contract duration was eight months but that Strath Construction, under Ewan Matheson, had programmed for six. Sime Atwood would achieve substantial completion in four. Mac had learned not to protest. He had been humiliated in front of the men too often and the more experienced knew beyond doubt, as he did, that what was happening would eventually propel him down the road. Not Trevor though, still an idealist, nor Allan with the dew of morning across his whole being.

Now James had cranked up the site's resources to the point where they were falling over each other. The men were working under lights, Mac and Trevor were staying on late to decide the rapid day to day changes that had to be made in the light of events, to keep records up to date, and to project their thinking into the future.

Between here and Struie Healey's men had completed the uphill pipelines in torrential rain leaving a mess of enormous proportions behind them. This side was worse because the ground was steeper, the pipes were larger, and the squad was more slapdash. On the Struie side casting outside the wayleave had saved the day; that and the haul road which had a stabilising effect and the squad with the new man, JB, and his natural organisation in it. Conn was still up top, excavating for the first length of culvert, which meant that James Swann had hired in another excavator and driver for the pipeline from Ness. Six of Healey's men were working on it now with the Clerk of Works standing by their shoulders breathing fire and Trevor, at this moment, standing in apparent despair.

He had also hired in another crane to work on the tanks with the staff joiners. Derek and his boy were tying reinforcement steel on the tank bases now, glad to be earning again, keeping at it. The staff joiners were leisurely as ever, erecting the curved formwork that Swann had invested in, hopeful of the following Contracts. JB and Tammas laboured to them, JB impatient with their lack of urgency. Soon he would be a foreman, in time a general foreman, new as he was to the job and having made such progress. When the culvert was done Conn would come back to the main site and the other machines would be shipped out.

That left John Kelly and the nipper, Ikey, the only local start the Contractor had made and that to conform to the letter of the contract. Nip here, nip there, nip all about, he cleaned the men's hut as far as Kelly would allow, and went for messages. Not good for much what he did he did thoroughly, the wee man. Ikey limped from hut to hut avoiding John Kelly's eye, but with no worries at this time since John was receiving a load of steel piles for the Collection Chamber, calling the new crane across to lift them from the flat lorry to lie beside Paul's peg marking the Chamber centre. James was not bringing in a piling squad. Kelly could do it, he said. He's experienced enough. By the look of the piles they were far from new. All were rusted and dirty, some obviously twisted and unusable. John stood above them shaking his head.

Beyond the legalities of putting all of the A9's traffic onto one carriageway and then switching it to the other, no provision had been made for laying the pipes under the road, presumably in a deep, closely piled trench. When Mac asked him James had said he had not yet made up his mind about method.

Over at the Ness end of the job Trevor looked at his watch and returned to the hut for their valuation meeting with Allan. He entered and hung his helmet behind the door. A likeable lad, Mac thought, he had redrawn the programme and would present it to Allan later. 'There's a natural law involved,' he said. 'Deluge when you least want it. It can feel like a conspiracy.'

'But we're ahead of programme, even the new version.'

'We've pressured up on the programme, sure, but look at the hill on this side when you leave. A wrong step and you're in up to the thigh. It's going to take years to settle, and Conn couldn't separate the topsoil the way he should so it's mixed with the gritty stuff below. That means when we reseed it's going to grow in patches. We'll be coming back for years. Before then though, if it rains again like it did before, the surface is going to come sliding down onto the road.'

'The Authority wanted it done quickly,' said Trevor, enamoured with the idea of progress.

'And we're going even faster because James wants to impress and reckons speed and cost are the most persuasive arguments when it comes to winning the following contracts. That's where his head is now, pricing the Lochdon contract. If we'd waited three weeks we could have laid those pipes in the dry.'

'You couldn't tell how long the rain would last.'

'That's what James said,' said Mac, noting the echo. They

had been speaking separately, no doubt in Trevor's innocence. 'He called me this morning to say there's a grip squad coming to build the culvert. So, that's one mystery solved. You won't know what the grip is. The name goes back to when the tax man was more easily fooled and the grip was a lump sum paid on the QT. The labourer, joiner, miner, whatever, agreed a sum to do the job and did it, gripped the money and left. Nothing passed through the books. Often these would be the dirty jobs, or dangerous. They'll be quick all right. They'll also be hard, physically tough. They'll be uncompromising where money is concerned.

At that moment Allan Crawford drew in, approaching from the south. That meant he had been to Brora for the buns. Like his predecessor on the Black Isle job he had taken that responsibility. Punch the air.

7

A velvet glove

The chill was barely off the air in the hut when Paul arrived. Ikey should have turned on the bar at 7:30am, but twenty minutes later the window was still rimed with frost. Paul's first move was to check the kettle was free of ice and switch it on.

He undid his trousers and stepped out of them, folded them onto the end of the table and pulled on his cold working jeans. He took off his good shirt and pulled on the old one he was wearing on site this week and an old pullover that was holed at the elbow and frayed at the cuffs. Sitting down on one of the hut's two chairs he pulled his thick working socks over the socks he was wearing. He pulled on his wellies and turned the muddy socks down over the tops.

His jeans were stiff with the clay they picked up on site, clay that overnight had froze rigid. The wellies were worse because by the time he got back in to the hut, two days before, he had been too fed up to take a newspaper to them. Yesterday, Wednesday, he had been at day release in Inverness and spent the afternoon in the pub.

The kettle came to the boil and he poured hot water into his mug and dipped a tea bag. It was still dark outside. He checked his watch – 7:55am, almost start time – and sat down again, clasping the mug in his two hands against his chest, crossing his legs tight against the cold.

He looked around him at the broken down drawing table and the dented-in-the-middle filing cabinet, at the floor that was piled with dried clay from his boots and from John Kelly's. As long as Paul was working on the high culvert the place wasn't cleaned out. John should be taking a brush to the floor from time to time, except it was beneath him. That was Ikey's job, but Ikey was out of sorts since John had rousted him from his hidey hole in the cludge and called him 'a humphy backit wee shite', and John would accept such squalor before he would lift a finger. Paul drank deep from his mug and closed his eyes as the agent's car drew up. Inevitably, Mac looked in.

'You should be topside with old hookey-nose by now,' he said.

Paul got up and swallowed the last of his tea. He took the tripod legs from the corner and stood them on the floor, snapped open the theodolite case on the table and screwed the instrument to the top of the legs.

'If you're going to carry that out of its box you've to hold it vertical. Keep the weight off the screws. Fixing costs money.'

'Okay'.

'You might as well stay up there till the light goes. That should see you back here about 4:30pm. You can tackle the Plant Returns. That should keep you going until 5:30. Tell Jimmy Gillies he's to meet me here first thing in the afternoon with his measure.'

'I'll tell him.'

Mac went off to his own hut where the heaters would have been on all night.

Paul checked the left pocket of his donkey jacket to make sure his survey book was still there and dropped his iPod into the other. He took the tripod legs by the adjustment screws and hoisted them awkwardly so they leaned almost vertical against his chest with the heavy weight of the instrument at the top. Carrying this way meant he would have one hand free and could shift the weight from one side to the other as he went. He swung his shoulder bag round back, plonked his safety helmet on his head and set out across the compound, across the road and onto the hill to climb the wayleave.

The gravity sewer had already been laid to the top where,

eventually, sewage pumped across from Struie would spill in from the culvert the grip squad was building now. Paul walked close to the fence that kept the hill sheep and the cattle out of the works and the troops in, but whenever he was forced away from it he would sink into the churned surface and mud would squelch up over his boots, dirty water splashing as high as his face. Counting fence posts he forced himself to cover ten metres before resting and changing shoulders until, at the top of the slope, the view opened out on to the mountains and the ground was still unturned and firm underfoot. It was almost 9:00am.

He stopped by the wooden peg he had established on the centre line of the culvert and looked across the hill to the mounds of earth and the excavator and the crane. On either side of the wayleave were patches of snow that had caught the windblown dirt and was streaked by it. He set the instrument up over the peg and focussed the telescope on the excavation.

Beside the excavator was the compressor that fired the concrete vibrators that were used during concrete pours, and the lights and generator that hadn't worked for the whole duration of the job and that Mac had so far refused to replace in spite of Paul's reports.

Willie Quinn walked into the crosshairs from behind the crane, waving his arm and shouting, the telescope bringing him up close. Paul couldn't yet hear him, only recognise the joiner's powerful build below his check overshirt, his impatient expression below his woolly hat.

From the far side of the hill, the Struie side, the haul road ran to the top and along as far as the works. The grip squad would have set out from the bottom about the time he arrived at the hut. They would have come up along the haul road with torches, timing their arrival at the culvert for just before first light.

Paul aimed the telescope past the excavation to where he had established another setting-out peg, driven it deep and con-

creted it in place. He focussed the instrument precisely on the
nail head so that it made a little grey 'tee' in the cross hairs.
That done he turned 45 degrees to a boulder he had marked
with a yellow chalk patch. The pencil mark on the patch
matched the cross hairs perfectly. Pegs, instrument and line
were all okay and could be trusted.

'Where you been, wee man?' Willie had reached him,
slightly breathless.

'It was like walking on a sponge.'

'Give me that thing. I'll carry it now.'

'Are you stopped?'

Jimmy Gillies wouldn't like it if they couldn't get on.
Normally Paul would give the next day's seting-out before
he left, but he had been in college, or should have been.

Willie picked up the instrument, hoisted it on to his shoulder
in exactly the correct way and set off along the hilltop. Paul
half-walked, half-jogged beside him, his unburdened feet
springing on the firm turf. When they reached the excavation
Willie opened the legs over Paul's temporary peg, allowing the
instrument to lean over at an almost jaunty angle. Paul righted
it quickly.

'No time for that,' Jimmy Gillies called from below. 'Give us
this mark now so I know we've got it. You might get called
away.'

Paul stood on the edge of the excavation and looked down
on the gang leader's lean frame. As thin as Willie was wide
Jimmy was nonetheless strong. His forehead was broad above
cavernous cheeks, his huge nose, said Willie behind his back,
like the prow of an ocean liner. As usual he wore an old khaki
jacket from Army Surplus over his boiler suit. He stood on one
leg with the other knee bearing down on a length of two by two
and a wooden frame. Guiding the blade of his saw along the
knuckle of his thumb he made his first cut of the day. When he
looked up their eyes met.

'Called away?' asked Paul.

Jimmy jerked a thumb behind him at the concrete culvert.

'Called away, down the road, sacked, call it what you like. This is taking four times as long as it should. Swannie's breathing down Mac's neck and he needs a scapegoat. What will you do if you lose this job?'

Paul shook his head.

'Who knows?'

'You'll end up with one of these round your waist.'

Jimmy Gillies shook his apron so the nails rattled together.

'You'll end up working outside in all weathers, always looking for the next job. Believe me, you don't want that.'

As a matter of fact, he did. The grip squad was happy in the teeth of foul weather and set backs. They worked for each other and looked after each other and when he was with them they looked after him as well. He liked them and admired then more than he respected Mac or John Kelly or even Swannie, although the Agent and the Contracts Manager should be his models, and the GF should be his guide.

In the excavation they were preparing for the next wall pour. They had cast the base Tuesday and stripped the shuttering Wednesday, while he was away. Three double lines of starter bars stood up from the two wall kickers. Jimmy had cracked the previous wall shutters, ready to move them forward. Cammy, the third joiner, was untying bunches of reinforcement steel and checking the labels.

'Get your body down here!'

'What's your hurry?'

Jimmy Gillies pursed his lips and shook his head.

'Don't ask stupid questions. You've got a brain. Use it!"

Down in the hole Paul looked into the culvert at the props holding up the roof shutter. There, in the dark, tucked away behind a spare sheet of plywood was the level box, folded down legs and staff. Less sensitive than the theodolite, also less expensive, it could be left out overnight. Paul took it topside and set up. Conn climbed out of his cab without being asked and carried the staff down to the seting-out peg by the fence.

Paul took his first reading from there and checked a level mark he had made on the roof slab after the pour. It hadn't moved. The joiners' work had been sound.

'How is it?'

'Near enough,' said Paul.

'Ho!' said Willie. 'It's spot on.'

Paul closed his survey book and shouted joyfully.

'Spoteroonie!'

He looked past the excavation and the backfilled section of culvert to the two lines of fence running towards Glen Struie and the haul road. It had a sort of beauty. Conn was a craftsman with the excavator bucket; the way he dropped the clay back and rammed it into place and then carefully replaced the topsoil. The way he broke the lumps down with wide sweeps of the bucket and combed the surface with the bucket's teeth, leaving it harrowed and ready for seeding come the spring. He had it down to a fine art.

Conn took the staff into the hole and placed it on the kicker for Paul to level. Jimmy shouted up to him.

'Height to the first bar?'

Paul walked to the edge of the way-leave where he could think. He turned to the back of the book where he had already worked out the true level of the first bar at this point. He subtracted the level he had just taken.

'185mm to the centre.'

Jimmy put chalk marks on the vertical starter bars that stood up from the base. 'Now measure down to the top of the slab,' Paul called down. '235?'

'Spotto both sides,' said Jimmy, folding down his rule. 'Okay, let's get the steel in place. How's the time?' He looked at his watch. 'The day's getting on. When the job gets idle the idle get going – down the road.'

Conn climbed back into his cab and Cammy cut the first set of bars loose. He and Willie carried them one at a time to the wall. Starting on the outside face of the north wall they tied one of the bars to the first vertical starter, and the top horizontal to the starter coming out of the existing wall. Paul checked the lap length that had to be 40 times the diameter of 6mm, 240. It was 250, okay. The joiners worked on.

All Paul had to do now was make sure they used the correct bars and that the spacings were right. When they came to move the wall shutters forward in the afternoon he would check the line with the theodolite. The walls would be spaced just the right distance apart and, when they made their adjustments to the north wall the south would come into place as well. In the morning they would place nails and string lines for the concrete gang to work to and the pour would start about 11:00am Friday. The dumpers would charge up and down the haul road feeding Conn's skip and it would be over by about 1:00pm.

Paul would check the wall position after the pour. If it had moved a few millimetres they could bring it back with the props but no adjustments had been required to date. This was why Swannie had brought them up from Glasgow. This sheer *effectiveness* was why he paid them so far above the rate. Already the local troops sensed what the squad's wage packets were like. There were rumblings.

Paul poured a cup of tea from the first of his two flasks. He took out his iPod and fitted its earpieces to his ear and turned it on.

Cammy took his snips and a length of wire along the mat, tying every second crossing.

Jimmy and Willie took a bar at either end and heaved it up. As they lifted Jimmy looked at Paul and said something but all Paul heard was the *thud-thud-thud* of the music.

Thud-thud-thud!

Jimmy spoke again but Paul turned his eyes up in his head and started to bounce up and down.

Bounce-bounce-bounce.

When he got to the top of his flight he headed the air like a centre-forward.

Thud-thud-thud.

Bounce-bounce-bounce.

Head-head-head.

He danced round in a circle while Willie laughed and Cammy shook his head and got on with tying. As they picked up another bar, Paul shouted *'Yeah'*.

'Yeah!' Willie repeated.

'Don't encourage him,' said Jimmy as they heaved up the second bar, Cammy working his way along, tying as he went – leave a length free, pull the wire round this way, round that, round again, pull it tight, twist the ends with the pliers, snip it off. Next bar!

Bounce. Bounce.

'Yeah! Yeah!'

Jimmy came over and signalled that he should take the earplugs out.

'Don't you know you're the company man around here? You're supposed to be in charge. What's Mac going to think if he hears?'

It didn't matter what Mac thought. Paul and Mac had lost touch weeks ago. Paul hung his head, but it had nothing to do with Mac. In his heart of hearts he knew he would follow Jimmy Gillies anywhere but it could never be said. It wasn't necessary for it to be said.

'Ho, boys!'

John Kelly ran down the slope of the excavation.

'Ho, John!'

For John to have walked all the way up here there must be something on, some change, and it wasn't likely to suit Paul or the grip squad.

Jimmy rubbed his hands down the seat of his boiler suit. 'What goes?'

'We're pouring here tomorrow at 9:00. Mac wants the roof slab at the Pumping Station poured in the afternoon.'

Willie scratched his jaw. 'It'll be dark by 4:00. What's he thinking about?'

'We won't be ready,' said Jimmy, 'not by 9:00. 10:00, maybe – at best. 11:00 is what we said.'

'9:00 is what he says now. Trevor's ordered the concrete. The first truck will be here by 8:30. The dumpers are on their way round the hill now.'

'Healey's men?'

'We've got to use them somewhere.'

'You could get rid of them.'

'Tell that to Swannie.'

No, they couldn't get rid of Healey. He was part of Swannie's great scheme, as was Jimmy Gillies himself.

'Okay,' said Jimmy. 'It'll be dark at 4:00. We'll need all that time to get the shutters down, to clean them off and get them ready. Get Derek up here, he can finish the steel.'

John Kelly shook his head.

'He's on the Pumping Station.'

'How am I supposed to get this done in time?'

'That's up to you.'

'I'm supposed to meet Mac this afternoon.'

'He'll see you tomorrow.'

Jimmy went over to the shutter where he hung his jacket on a bolt and took out his mobile phone. He tried Mac's number but got through only to the message box. Then he tried Swannie's number but still made no connection.

'Right,' he said, 'we'll do it.'

'How do we manage this?' asked Willie.

'Just by doing it,' Jimmy replied. 'Conn!'

Conn turned the crane on its tracks and looked down from his cabin door into the excavation.

'Paul?'

Paul had already put his iPod back in his pocket and thrown his jacket in a corner.

'Five of us,' said Jimmy, 'all willing. Willie and I will put the chains on the west shutter. Conn, you get the crane to take the weight. Then we can get the bolts out more or less safely.

Cammy, you and Paul tie the rest of the south wall steel. Let's get cooking.'

Jimmy and Willie picked up their spanners and climbed onto the wall head while Conn swung the crane's jib across. From the end of the jib hung two hawsers and chains. The hooks on the end of the chains made a long slow swing as they travelled.

When the swing had settled Jimmy and Willie grabbed one hook each and hauled them out to the ends of the formwork. Jimmy made a spiral-down gesture with his hands and Conn extended the hawsers until Jimmy made his 'whoa' gesture. He and Willie fed their chains all the way round the endmost uprights so the hooks could turn back and clasp the chains. That done he made an open-and-close gesture with his hands.

Conn drew the chains up until they were tight and the shutter was just drawn away from the concrete. He locked the jib and cut the engine. The two joiners went to work with the spanners, loosening and removing the top bolts, dropping them carelessly on to the concrete base

'You tie, Paul,' said Cammy. 'You haven't got the hands to carry. Too soft'

'They are not.'

'Aye, they are,' said Conn, climbing down into the excavation, taking the first horizontal bar at its opposite end from Cammy.

Paul took the snips and tying wire to the bars and made the first knot – free length, round this way, round that, round again, tighten and snip while Cammy and Conn lifted the next bar.

'How many pies can you eat, Paul?' asked Cammy, not looking at him.

'Pies?'

'Yes, pies.'

'One at a time?'

'One, two, three at a time, any way you like but how many at one go.'

'I don't know.'

Tight, snip.

'Three – four, maybe.'

'Ho!' Willie called from the wall head.

'He can eat fourteen,' said Cammy admiringly. 'Fourteen at one go.'

'Fourteen,' Willie called out triumphantly.

'I could manage that,' said Paul. 'Fourteen.'

'Ah, but I'm an old man of forty – when I was your age I could manage twenty-six. That was my record. Twenty-six.'

'This was when he was on that big pyramid contract in Egypt,' said Cammy.

'Nah,' Willie said. 'Neffartootie's tomb is where Old Jimmy served his time. This was on the Caledonian Canal.'

Jimmy Gillies worked quietly away and steadily.

'The Caley Canal,' said Cammy. 'Leaking to this day.'

Paul, Cammy and Conn continued on the south wall, Paul chalking the bar positions, Cammy and Conn lifting the first bars across.

Jimmy and Willie dropped the last of the bolts on to the concrete base and climbed back down to place wooden pads and wedges to support the shutters after they were moved. Conn fired up the engine and eased the first shutter from the wall.

Thuck!

The low end swung heavily out from the green concrete, out and across the channel, its slow grace eloquent on the subject of mass and motion and what amounts to unstoppable force. Everyone acted at once; Paul moving in to grab the edge, trying without thought to halt the swing into the opposite wall, Jimmy's arm going out to stop him, Cammy also grabbing him by the shirt, the two of them hauling him back.

'Careful, son!' Jimmy said sharply. 'What would I tell your Dad?'

Paul turned away as if he had been struck.

The shutter clipped the east side lightly and swung to and fro without hitting again. Jimmy and Willie waited until it was almost steady in the centre of the channel and moved in to take a hold of each end.

'We can fix the shutters,' said Cammy, 'but we can't fix you.'

'Don't call me "son" '.

Jimmy nodded to Cammy and Cammy signalled up to the crane cab and slowly Conn lifted the shutter, slowly swung it out and laid it gently on the haul road with its facing side up.

The face of the shutter was stuck with lumps of concrete and streaks of mortar. Without removing the chains the two joiners set about knocking it away, beating it with their hammers and brushing the loose material off on to the road stone. Willie dipped a mop into the bucket of lubricating oil he had brought topside from the culvert and ran it all about the plywood face. That done they dropped back into the excavation and Cammy held his hand up, circling it in the air, opening and closing his fist, guiding Conn and his jib as he moved the shutter through the air. Slowly it came down to land at the wall kicker, Jimmy and Willie putting their shoulders against it to push it in the last few centimetres.

'Hold it there!' Jimmy shouted.

Cammy made a flat palm towards Conn while Jimmy and Willie propped the shutter up with sturdy timbers. This done they went through the process again with the outside shutter but this time the concrete was more stubborn. The joiners hammered away all the harder. They banged and brushed and scraped with the edges of their hammers and, from time to time, straightened to ease their backs. Suddenly Willie shouted at the top of his voice.

'Your hole, getting your hole, that's the best'.

He bent down again and continued beating at the concrete lumps. Jimmy shook his head.

Willie straightened again.

'Then again,' he said. 'I once got a wank with a velvet glove, which was better than a shag come to think of it.'

'That's a mountaintop view,' said Cammy, also straighten-
ing, looking inland to the Sutherland hills. 'No one can explain
why it should affect us as it does.'

'Cammy was a minister of the church before he joined us,'
Jimmy said to Paul. 'He had a crisis of faith.'

'Still have,' Cammy volunteered.

Conn leaned out of his cab and spoke to Willie.

'I got that once as well. It was a green velvet job, a long
evening glove such as Princess Margaret used to wear. She
pulled it on slow, like this.' Conn made a show of running his
hand along his forearm. 'Then the young lady pressed down
between the fingers to make sure it was on real tight.'

'She was teasing you,' said Willie. 'She didn't want you to
take too long.'

'I didn't!'

Jimmy had one eye on Cammy as he bent to the shutter.

'Just get on with this,' he said. 'We've only got today.'

'Where was this?'

'In the Gorbals,' Conn said. 'It was 78 Oxford Street, in the
stairhead lavvie.'

'Hey! Same address.'

The two men raised their fists in mock salute.

Paul looked at Jimmy, more than half expecting him to bring
this banter to an end. Instead Jimmy made the only conscious
joke Paul ever heard from him and uttered the only strong
word.

'Bastards!' he said. 'That was my sister.'

'Everybody,' said Willie, 'needs a wee hand from time to
time.'

'*Enough!* Cammy, back in the excavation.'

By now the sun had moved to the other side of the hill and
what little heat the air had taken from it was already departing.

With the second shutter on its pads they pushed the bolts
through and tightened and the two shutters stood unsteadily,
but independently, in place.

'Okay,' said Jimmy, 'we'll eat while you three tie the rest of the steel. Then we'll steady it.'

Jimmy and Willie took out their flasks and sat on some loose timbers. Now Willie had a question for Paul, the bosses' man among the men.

'Why this concrete culvert? Why not a big pipe? It would be cheaper and quicker.'

'The Engineer wanted to give Mister Crawford a reinforced concrete design for his professional qualifications. He has exams to pass. When he does that his rate goes up and the Engineer charges accordingly. Also, the Engineer is paid on a percentage of the price. When the cost goes up his fee goes up. That's the way it's done.'

Paul felt uncomfortable talking this way, as though he was giving away a secret of his Craft. As though he was saying: this is our way, but I prefer yours. I would rather be in your Craft. It's more honest.

'Harry told me,' he said. 'He's pretty hard on his bosses, pretty cynical, except for his ultimate boss, GR.'

Jimmy shook his head.

'This is how it is,' he said. 'Between this kind of thing and the Healeys of this world, this is how it is.'

'It would be better with a big, fat pipe,' said Cammy. 'We're wasting our time.'

Willie put his flask back in his bag, pieces finished.

'No we're not. We're here to make a living. Somebody else has to worry about what's best. Jimmy's got to worry about getting that girl of his through University. I've got a mortgage to pay and kids to feed. You're single, Cammy; so you have to think about it.'

'That's right,' said Cammy. 'I don't matter. What about you Paul? What are you here for?'

'Paul matters because he's the future of this game,' said Jimmy. 'At least, I hope so.'

Paul said nothing to this but put his flask away and climbed topside. He checked the set-up of his theodolite over its peg.

'We'd better get on or it'll get too dark to check the line,' he said.

'That's the way,' said Jimmy. 'Do the job in front of you. The rest will take care of itself.'

The three joiners set about putting the metal props in place and tightening the bolts, connecting the two sets of shutters and making them firm. Again and again Jimmy and Willie checked the wall widths. Again and again they measured across the gap to make sure the distance was correct and consistent and, when they were ready, Willie took Paul's levelling staff and held it outright, horizontal, from the north wall's inside face. Paul knew his offset size was 600mm. He checked the reading through the telescope of his theodolite.

'15mm north,' he called down.

Cammy slackened the props on the north side while Jimmy tightened those on the south. Willie put the staff back in place.

'Too much! 5mm back.'

The joiners went through their slackening and tightening process again. As they completed the movement the sun dropped below the horizon and it was suddenly dark.

'No use – can't see.'

Willie stepped back and found the torches in the culvert. Back on the shutter he shone his on the 600 mark.

Paul checked the reading and called out, 'Okay! Now, how am I going to check back?'

Cammy picked his way carefully down the haul road and climbed the fence.

'Don't go off the wayleave!'

Who's to know?'

Cammy went to the boulder and shone the torch on the mark and Paul focussed as best he could.

'Spoteroonie!'

'Levels,' said Jimmy, when Cammy got back. 'Cammy, shine your torch on Paul's book for him.'

Paul worked out the correct reading to the top-of-the-wall level, took the actual reading on the shutter head, worked out the difference and called down to Willie, '138mm'. Willie measured

138mm down the inside face of the shutter and drove a nail halfway home. He put the staff on the nail for Paul to check.

'Spoteroonie!'

They repeated this for all four shutters at the halfway points and the ends. All were correct.

'Just as well,' said Conn. 'It's too dark to lift safely.'

Paul took down the level and put it in its box for Willie to stash in the culvert. The theodolite would come with him down the hill.

'It might snow in the morning,' said Willie.

'They'll pour anyway,' said Jimmy. 'That's Swannie for you. He's driving this, not Mac. However strong and ugly Mac seems to you, Paul, he's nothing against Swannie.'

'Harry will find something wrong if he can,' said Cammy. 'He'll stop the pour if he's able.'

'He won't find anything. It'll be all right,' said Jimmy.

He shone his torch on Willie, Cammy and Conn, one after the other. 'We'll get here early. John Kelly's saying they'll pour at first light, but they won't. There'll be something, late concrete, frozen diesel, Harry being awkward, something. We'll get it all checked again and be ahead of the game. Paul, can you make it up here for 8:00am? I mean up here on the hill.'

'I'll be here,' said Paul, 'if I've still got a job. Mac wanted me back to do plant returns before this. He won't like me coming out here first thing and not checking with him, but I'll be here. We'll get it done.'

'Come down our side of the hill,' Willie said. 'We'll give you a lift back to the compound. It'll be safer than going down that slope in the dark.'

'I'll get back myself. I'll be okay.'

'You're sure?'

'Sure I'm sure.'

'I don't want you getting hurt,' said Jimmy.

'I'm sure.'

'Cammy, give Paul your torch. You and Willie can share.'

Paul took Cammy's torch and found himself staring at the

circle of light it cast at his feet. He folded the tripod and lifted the instrument carefully against his chest, holding it with just the one arm.

'I'll walk you along the hill,' said Jimmy.

The two set off with their torches lighting the ground before them while Conn locked the cabs on his machines and the others gathered their tools. Very quickly the job was out of sight behind them and the hill was silent. They got to the edge, to Paul's setting-out peg and the beginning of the churned ground where the pipeline had been laid.

'You'll have to go on yourself now. This is as far as I can take you.'

'I'll be okay.'

'You're a good boy. I'm sorry I said what I said about your dad. If you were mine I'd be proud. But listen, go easy on the drinking.'

'Okay.'

'And stick in at college. You've got it in you to be an Agent, maybe even a Contracts Manager.'

'I'll do my best.'

'That'll be good enough. Don't drop out; hang in.'

'I'll do that.'

'You can't choose your family but you can choose your friends. Be careful there. Your employers too – once you get qualified you can move about. Do that until you find somewhere you fit. Stay there. Don't worry about the money; you'll get by. Make sure you're comfortable.'

Jimmy offered his hand and they shook.

'Thanks.'

'See you in the morning.'

Paul pointed the torch downwards to bring his light in close. The going was no firmer underfoot than it had been when he came up in the morning. If anything it was riskier. He moved with care, growing fatigued quickly, and when he stopped to rest he looked back to see Jimmy's circle of light disappear on his own side of the hill.

8

The cludge and the portaloo

In the compound Harry watched as Derek unloaded a second load of reinforcement steel for the settlement tank bases. He turned his collar up, pulled down his safety helmet against the wind and pushed his hands further into his jacket pockets.

At last the high culvert was complete. Conn was removing the stone haul road and reinstating the ground. When he was done he would track his machine back here and Mac would lay off not one but two of the other drivers. No sooner had Jimmy Gillies, Willie Quinn and Cammy been transferred shoreside to the settlement tanks than the staff joiners were trooping one by one in and out of the agent's hut. The grip squad's big pay was exerting its inevitable disaffecting influence. Experienced Harry had seen it coming and socialist Harry didn't like it.

Ikey tugged at his sleeve.

'Beg pardon, Mr Gilfeather.'

'What is it?'

'Mr Crawford asks can you can come to his office as soon as is possible, sir. He says he tried to call but your mobile phone is turned off.'

'Communication is best a one way thing with the likes of Mr Crawford. From me to him and not t'other way round. What's it about?'

'He wouldn't tell me that, no sir, but I heard something.'

'What did you hear?'

'GR called him to say that you've to go down to Newton-more and sort something out.'

'Sort what out?'

'Don't know, sir, but I heard on the radio that someone left a valve open in the new works and the Spey is running with sewage.'

Another joiner went in to see Mac. This was the fourth. Each stern looking tradesman entered with a frown and come out happily jingling the nails in his apron.

'See this, Ikey?'

'Sir?'

'The troops want off the books and onto the grip. They'll find themselves working longer hours under worse conditions but, because they aren't real grip men, they won't make more money. In fact they'll make less, but greed and pride beat common sense every time. So they'll get unsettled again and ask to get back on the books. Swannie won't have this. He'll move them to other sites and eventually they'll get out themselves. Until then, he'll get more out of them for less. He'll have this kind of deception down to a fine art. I told them he wants rid of them and to stick together whatever. Deaf ears.'

'How long will you be away, sir?'

'If I know GR – and I do, Ikey, I do – until the natives are purring.'

Harry climbed into his van and drove off to speak with Allan Crawford and receive his instructions. Ikey limped into Stores to pick up a brush. With Harry in Newtonmore for a few days, or weeks, the site would become that bit slacker. Just the same he would get on.

In the compound he worked with a perpetual smile, sweeping out the men's hut and tidying the ground between. The troops did nothing for themselves in this way but it wasn't that they were uncaring, only accustomed to it. Filth accumulated on the floors and litter around the huts because they didn't have time except when they were rained off, and then everything was too wet to brush or lift or even shovel, the mud they trailed inside, the oilskins they peeled off, their hair and hands.

There were two toilets in the compound, a wooden shack for the troops, and for Mac, Trevor, John Kelly and Paul a portaloo. The difference between the two was marked. The three cludge bowls had no toilet seats. Strips of wet newspaper took the place of toilet paper. The u-bends were always blocked and the bowls always full. The portaloo was spotless and clean but never used. Whenever Mac or Trevor felt the call they would drive to the Ness Hotel, but still the men never ventured into the portaloo. As a status barrier it was recognised and its purpose shifted to being a focus of discontent.

Ikey brought a space heater into the cludge and lit the gas. He raised a tin of barrier cream, a bucket and disinfectant from Stores. He went down on hands and knees among the pools of urine and the stink and set to deep cleaning the floors. One of the toilet bowls was brimming and floating with turds. He rolled up his sleeve and coated his arm with barrier cream to the shoulder. In to the elbow he felt around the u-bend and scooped at the soft faecal matter with his hand, in and back to make a suction until the blockage cleared and the water level dropped to his wrist. He cleaned inside the bowls and resolved to bring in toilet paper if only John Kelly would provide the money. He brushed out every corner and changed the only light bulb. When he was done the cludge was usable, no more than that.

Kelly on his way to the tanks excavation stopped to stare at him when he reappeared.

'In there again?'

'Cleaning it up as ordered, sir, as part of the compound.'

'Look at the state of you. Get some of that swarfega and get yourself properly cleaned.'

'I'll do that.'

'3:30pm and the light's near gone. There's no working day this time of year.'

'No sir.'

'Let me take a look in there.'

Kelly stepped inside the cludge and came out again frowning.

'All well, sir?'

'Enjoy your work, Ikey?'

'I do, sir.'

'Well listen, don't do this again. Not only is it too clean in there, it's getting on to being warm and dry. It's too comfortable.'

'Sir?'

'I don't want the troops hanging about in there. Just keep the u-bend clear so it's more or less usable.'

'Can I use it now, sir"

'Yes.'

'Thank you, Mr Kelly.'

Ikey returned inside the cludge and into one of the wooden cubicles. He hung his jacket behind the door and sat without dropping his trousers. From his jacket pocket he took his book and joined Raskolnikov in prison. Some people's troubles, he reckoned, were worse than his own. At the start he thought he could identify with the man but now he thought otherwise, although he understood about keeping his own essential character within himself and secret.

With a place of his own on site, made comfortable and private and perfect for his own use, he would finish this chapter by going-home time. After he had given mother her dinner and done the washing up, he would join the Dostoyevsky Appreciation Group on the internet and discuss today's reading. His fellow dreamers, some were educated people and some not, and some could see the shape of things to come while others never looked forward at all.

9

An executioner's wind

Almost forty years away from Ireland John Kelly had not thought of home for at least thirty, not until now. Hands on hips by the A9 he was oblivious of traffic noise, his eyes ranging south and north along the Ross and Sutherland coastline – a rocky escarpment distinct with the quality of edge. It reminded him of Kerry. It had about it a familiar, isolating feel, a floating island that drifted into his life from time to time bearing different names, Alaska, Libya, Colonsay where he had worked on the new pier. It had been an itinerant, restless sort of life that had given him a tidy enough nest egg but little else, no family and few friends.

He reached down to the wooden peg by his foot and gave it a shake, working it round and round until he could pluck it from the ground and toss it to one side. Paul had placed it to mark the centre of the new collection chamber. From that and the two lines of pipe to set out the four sides of the cofferdam. Now its job was done and, that being so, it could go. Two massive concrete and steel frames stood beside the stack of steel sheet piles. A ladder with a rope tied to the top rung leaned against the compressor. Beside them again were the pile driver and four square timber beams he would use as guide rails. Beams, frames and compressor were all massive. On the other side of the dual carriageway another stack of steel piles lay waiting where the second chamber would go.

In the compound Conn had lowered his crane's jib to the ground and was speaking to Paul while the fitters tightened up the extension. The piles were seven metres long, two metres to be driven below the bottom of the four metre deep excavation, a metre to stand proud of the surface and act as a barrier. The piles would have to be lifted their full length above the guide rails. This meant the top of the lift would go to about twelve metres. The pile driver was almost two metres long, hence the extension. Conn gunned the engine and, in a moment, the jib was up and the machine tracking slowly uphill.

Kelly nodded his head. They were about ready to start driving the cofferdam piles.

'I hear Swannie's thinking about tunnelling under the road,' Conn said from his cab.

'So Mac says,' Paul agreed.

'It's going to be tunnelled all right,' said John Kelly. 'That's for certain.'

'Hear that, Paul? Swannie never moves without asking John.'

'Otherwise this cofferdam's twice the size it has to be. Four metres square with the walings in, not just the bare size of the chamber like on the Black Isle; that's two, three men working down there with room for air hoses and scaffolding and whatnot. It's decided.'

Conn waved his roll-up in the direction of the A9. 'Why not shut one carriageway at a time and go in from the top? Do it in two halves as per usual. Move the traffic from one carriageway to the other.'

'It's to do with reinstating the road surfaces, according to Mac,' said Paul. 'Also the Roads people want least-disruption so there's a time penalty built into the Contract. Swannie says they were trying to be clever and they've tripped up.'

'He'll have to shut a carriageway anyway,' said Conn as an articulated lorry ground past, tyres flattening on the bitmac. 'You can't have beasts like that running over a working tunnel. They'll stove the roof in. Tunnelling costs a fortune; makes no sense.'

'Never mind,' Kelly interrupted. 'C'mon, let's get these frames up.'

Conn moved his machine into position and turned the tracks from side to side beneath him, forming a flat area almost as a dog would lying down in a field. From here he would position the frames and lift the piles into place and drive them into the ground. An excavator would take the bulk of the earth from inside the cofferdam and the arisings shovelled into a skip.

Conn would work both machines, digging with the tracked excavator and lifting the skip in and out with the crane. If Swannie decided to tunnel he would skip for that too, and lift in the pipes. He would lift in the blinding concrete for the troops to work from and the bricks for the Chamber. Only then would the machine be free again. He wasn't likely to stray for weeks. Occasionally he would get out and use a shovel. It was important to appear willing with Swannie and Mac around, but most of his time would be spent sitting and waiting.

He rolled another cigarette and looked down at Kelly. Never a big man, of late he had developed a stoop that made him seem quite small. The years of alternate soakings and burnings had eaten away at him. He had become forgetful too, but when he straightened his back you could see the strength that had been in him in youth.

'You're getting on in years, John,' he shouted down.

'Never mind that, you ignorant Paddy. Just swing your jib over here till we get these frames in place.'

Concrete blocks a metre wide and almost as deep gave the piling frames stability against the weight of knock they were likely to take. Two steel I-beams stood upright from each block with between them, top and bottom, two cross pieces. With the frames in place and the timber beams spanning the width to kept the piles in place John Kelly would be required to drive his four lines of piles to closure round the square of the cofferdam, moving the set-up for each side. That meant working within a tolerance of 8mm. He would work from right to left.

Conn lowered the chains from his jib so Kelly could wrap them around the top crosspiece of the first piling frame. 'How come you're doing this, John, and not one of Healey's men?' he asked. 'Shouldn't you be walking round the site making a nuisance of yourself?'

'Swannie's cutting corners,' said Paul.

'Never mind all that!' said Kelly, lifting his hand in the air, slowly opening and closing his fist. 'Stand back, Paul.'

Conn eased the lift handle back and the chains drew slowly upwards and tight against the heavy frame.

'That's it,' said Kelly, still making his hand signal.

Gradually the frame was lifted upright and off the ground. It made a swing of about half a metre, no more.

'Good man, Conn'. Kelly showed an open palm, halting the lift. 'Now take her across easy like.'

Conn turned his cab on the machine's tracks and lifted the jib to bring the frame in closer, slowly swinging it across to the marks Paul had made on the ground. Kelly made a turning, downwards gesture with his hand and the frame settled in position, looking like a crude guillotine. He put the ladder against the frame and climbed up to loosen the chains. In minutes the second frame was in place, looking at its companion across the width of the cofferdam.

Between them they wrapped the chains round the end of the first timber beam and Conn lifted it across to the frame. Carefully he placed one end on the loer crosspiece and they shifted the chain and dragged it through to the second frame. Kelly shifted the chain round the upright and had Conn drag the beam through to the other side. By the time they repeated the process with the second beam half the morning was gone.

'Tea!' said John Kelly. 'Fifteen minutes.'

Conn took their bags from his cab, leaned against the tracks of the machine and looked at Paul sitting beside Kelly on the block.

'I wouldn't sit on that cold concrete' he said. 'You'll end up like him – piles down to the backs of your knees.'

'They're cured,' said Kelly. 'Willie Quinn whipped them off with a Stanley knife. The great thing was to do it quick.'

Paul climbed off the block and took his tea standing.

'Will you travel when you retire?' asked Conn.

Kelly shook his head. 'I'll work till I drop. What for would I retire? I've seen the world and the best of it's here. The rest would freeze your bum off, or burn you to death. There's places you have to carry a gun; other places they cut your finger off if you get the change wrong.' He drew his thumbnail across the base of his pinky. 'Listening, Paul? Don't travel; stay here. Stick in at that college and stay here.'

Every time Paul turned some older man was telling him to 'stick in at college'.

'Home then?' Conn asked. 'Back to Ireland?'

'D'ye know the size of their minds over there? One time I went back, long ago, and I said something about the bombs that were going off in the North how it looks different from out of Ireland. I said there must be other ways. When I went to pee two of them followed me and told me if that's what I thought I should maybe go home. Home? One showed me . . .'

'His prick?'

'He took a gun out of his pocket. Can you imagine that – what it is to be shown a gun in that way?'

'You've told me that story before. You could live in Dublin. You don't have to go all the way back.'

'What's the point unless it's all the way to Shannon, and who's left there now? The men I knew are all dead and the women are as ugly as me. And what am I to the young ones? There's a few Gods-Owns I've been, not many; places I've thought I could settle. This is maybe one. I think I could stay along the road there in Ness. It's quiet. It's like Ireland without the priests.'

'You won't go back to any of these places?' asked Paul.

'Never. D'ye hear me, Paul? Never go back. Mind though,

when I've left these places there's always a part of me stayed. This one will be no different,'

'Don't give us that sentimental *ould* Irish bejabers.'

Kelly looked at his watch.

'Time up!' he said. 'Back to work.'

With the two top guide beams on their cross pieces Kelly leaned the ladder and climbed up and tied the top rung.

Conn shouted up from beside the piles. 'Shouldn't we put the scaffolding up?'

'Hsst,' said Kelly. 'I've done this a thousand times. The ladder will do. Now, Paul, get the first pile spoteroonie and all the rest will follow.'

'Take a look at these.' Conn was kneeling by the piles, picking red clay out of one of the clutches with a screwdriver. 'They've been used a hundred times. No chance they'll drive true.'

Kelly looked down at the piles from the top of the ladder. They were old and rusted and hadn't been cleaned when they left their last site. Swannie had bought them on the cheap. At least the ends, where driving had flattened them out and bent them, had been cut away. The centimetre wide steel shone silver and hard where the winter sun caught it.

Conn ran his fingers along the cold edge, from the bulb of the male end to the receiving clutch at the other. From pile to pile, bulb would enter clutch and the wall of piles would stand strong and true, although not if the piles were twisted as these were. The cut edge was dead smooth except for a few black balls of smelt that came off to his fingers.

'No matter,' Kelly shouted down. 'We'll just have to do our best. I'll speak to Mac. Maybe he can replace them. Now let's get on.'

'Mac can't change anything,' said Paul.

They all knew the sub-text. Swannie wasn't just being cheap. He was making life difficult.

'Never mind all that,' said Kelly. 'Let's get going.'

Paul already had his theodolite up. He took a back sight on the offset peg he had established before and turned the instrument 180 degrees to the cofferdam. He looked past it on to the road and half way uphill to a peg on the wayleave. Everything looked right: the lines of his fences, his centre lines and profiles, his seting-out, all looked good.

Conn climbed back into his cab and lowered the chains over the piles.

Kelly passed the clamp bolt through the hole at the top of the first pile and screwed it tight. He lifted a thick wooden block and tucked half a dozen wedges under his arm and carried them to the top of the ladder and placed them on the wooden guide. Taking a nail from his pocket he looked down, his arm draped around the timber beam.

Paul checked his line and sighted his instrument upwards, guiding the nail into position, indicating left and right with his hands.

'Near enough!' said John Kelly, making a scrape mark across the wood. He turned on the ladder to look at Conn.

The driver fired up his engine and lifted the first pile off the ground, lifted it and moved it slowly through the air until it hung over the frame. As Kelly made his downward, turning gesture Conn eased the brake off the hawser and pushed his stick forward, braking again as the pile descended closer to Kelly, quickly responsive to the older man's gestures, the opening and closing fist, the spiral down, the quickly opened palm that meant stop *now*. When the pile stood on the ground between the four beams Kelly indicated that Conn should lock the jib and come over.

'Put your rule against the side of the pile for Paul to read,' he said.

Paul read Kelly's rule at the top and Conn's at the bottom. 'It's about right at the top, 15cm out at the bottom.'

Kelly nailed a piece of timber across the top beams and had Conn lift the pile again. He climbed down and pushed the bottom end of the pile across until it was about right and made his spiral down gesture for the driver. When they checked the pile head again it was out, but not as much as the bottom end had been before. Five repeats of the process had the first pile sitting dead plumb in the correct position. Kelly pushed the block of wood into the belly of the pile and chocked it tight at the top.

By the time he had it secure at the bottom as well, Conn had attached the pile driver and lifted it across. John Kelly climbed upwards and stepped off the ladder and on to the first beam, standing upright and unprotected as he reached to guide the huge mass on to the head of the pile, again turning his hand as Conn lowered it into place, now pushing with his shoulder to get it locked on to the pile edge.

A gust of wind pushed against his back. He straightened and looked out to sea, counted four oil rigs, two of them flaring off gas. Beyond them clouds were gathering and rain was sweeping across the North Sea towards them. Below the compound, in the settlement tanks excavation, the troops had just finished pouring the first segment of the first tank base. The grip squad were gathering their tools and Healey's men were working the top surface, levelling it with the backs of their shovels before taking the wooden and steel floats to it. An hour should see them through.

He untied the ladder and climbed down to turn on the compressor. The hammer drove against the anvil, the anvil against the pile head – once – twice – and a deafening *thang-thang-thang* echoed from the hill opposite as the pile went in the first, the easiest metre. As Conn placed the piledriver back on the ground the first of the rain reached the site. Kelly looked at his watch.

'Dinnertime,' he said.

They made it into the hut as the heavens opened.

Paul cleared his drawings off the table and switched on the kettle. The electric fire had been left on as usual. Rain lashed against the window.

'Know what they call that east wind,' Kelly asked Paul, taking his seat.

'What?'

'The executioner's wind, because it cuts right through you.' He looked around. 'This place is a midden but at least it's warm.'

'Ikey does his best.' Paul made tea in the pot and poured for all three, not mentioning that John Kelly did nothing to keep the place liveable. 'I'll make more for the flasks,' he said. 'How's progress, John? Frames up, first pile in. Good enough? Will Swannie be happy when he gets back?'

'Good enough, but Swannie won't be happy,' said Kelly. He nodded at the window and the rain. 'And that won't help.'

'Especially if it freezes on the ladder – or on the beams,' said Conn. 'Mr Swann wouldn't want John to fall off, Paul. It could mean a serious delay.'

No matter,' said Kelly. 'When did you last check the hawser? It's frayed where it's attached to the clamp.'

'All the checks are done. Harry looks at the papers every week. He's not good for much, but he does that.'

'We don't want the pile driver to fall, or one of the piles. It could cut young Paul here clean in two.'

'C'mon,' said Paul.

'Except it wouldn't be clean.'

'Aw!'

'Don't think accidents can't happen, son,' said Kelly. 'There's things I've seen would curl your hair.'

'Don't call me son.'

'One time I was working in London,' said Conn. 'You know these tower cranes? Seen one yet?'

Paul shook his head.

'Like a big letter 'T,' tall as hell. The cross on the 'T' has a long arm, that's the jib, and a short arm, that the counter-weights slide back and forward on – big concrete blocks, big as this room.'

'The most dangerous plant on the site,' said John Kelly.

'Especially when they're being dismantled. The counter-weights have to be moved back and forward to suit the length of the jib. What happens is the jib comes away in pieces so you have to be careful with the blocks. You have to watch how they're moving against the downward pull of the load over at the other end. It's a constant balancing act.'

Both hands round his mug of tea for the warmth Paul stood and listened.

'This day I was in the cabin with the fitter out on the jib undoing the bolts when, all of a sudden, the end of the thing fell clean away. The fitter went with it – killed. I was thrown back in my seat. Looking at the sky I thought I was for a quick cheerio as well. The weights ran along the lever arm and shot off into space and, next thing, the cab flipped over and I was looking at the ground, near sick with the fright. They had to talk me down.'

Conn had the floor. He drank slowly and opened the paper.

'Tell him the rest,' said Kelly.

'You sure?'

'Tell me,' Paul said.

'What people down below saw was two concrete blocks like two cabins, and it looked like they were hovering in the air.' Conn looked up at the roof of the hut. 'Yes, it looked like they were just hung there like two balloons. Then all of a sudden they got bigger and down they came on the site. *Whoom!*'

'Anybody hurt?'

'I don't like to say.'

'C'mon.'

'There was this steelfixer working below. Somebody called out and he stood up saying 'what?' and suddenly there was this huge concrete block where he used to be – drove him into the ground like a nail. The paramedics had to take a week off.'

'Tell him the rest,' said Kelly. 'He has to know these things.'

'He has to sleep at night, John.'

'Don't leave me hanging,' Paul said.

Conn continued reluctantly.

'One of the setting-out engineers came across his fingers.'

'His fingers?'

'Four of them.' Conn held out the four fingers of his right hand, thumb tucked behind the palm. 'The edge of the block must have come down across the knuckles. The shock threw them half way across the site.'

Paul was conscious his mouth was open.

'What did he do?'

'I'll tell you what he did. He put his foot on them and turned them into the ground and as far as I know they're under that building now.'

'C'mon!'

'What should he have done?' asked Kelly. 'Put them in a fag packet and taken them to the widow? "Here missus, have one of these." Listen, I'll tell you another.'

'There's more?'

'There's more all right. I was concrete ganger on this bridge in Glasgow, years ago. We were pouring the columns that were to hold it up. I can see the Clerk of Works now; finicky type, looked like a dead body heated in an oven. I remember he had a smile like a dog's. What was his name? We used always give him something to find, steel not tied, a wrong bar near the top where we could get at it. He'd go away happy and we'd get on with the pour.'

'And?'

'This time we dropped a fag packet between the steel and the formwork. When he spotted it we sent the nipper down and he went away and we got on.'

'A nipper? Like Ikey?'

'Just like Ikey, but no one thought to check he'd come out again before we poured. Next day we stripped the shutter and, by God, there were the backs of his nails and knuckles, flush with the concrete down at the bottom – three of them. He must have crouched down and got them through the steel to get at the fag packet and got stuck. His ring will have caught in the tying wire. He must have been shouting up to us when we were pouring. Pulling away at his trapped fingers and shouting.'

'What a terrible, terrible end,' said Conn.

'What did you do?' Paul asked.

'You haven't heard the worst yet,' said Conn. 'You'd better tell him, John.'

'I don't know if I should.'

'You said yourself, he has to learn.'

'We were staring at the fingers,' John Kelly continued, 'when they started to move. Not much at first, but then they started to wiggle and straighten out from the concrete, slow as you like. It was as if he was still alive in there and begging us to get him out. I tell you my blood ran cold. One of the labourers started to cry.'

'He'd be dead,' said Paul. 'It would be nerves.'

'My God boy, I hope you're right.'

'How did you get him out?'

'Taking that column down would have held us up for a week. No, I got the cement finisher to lop off the fingers with the edge of his trowel, one – two – three, and fake the wall up with grout. He'd no family, poor man. No one ever asked.'

Paul stared at the lumps of dried mud scattered across the floor of the hut.

'Looks like the rain's easing,' said Conn.

Cold rain had filled the ruts in the compound with puddles, some shallow, some deeper than the leg of a Wellington boot, gleaming drops distended from the fence. The wind had gone but somehow the air seemed even colder. Kelly beat on the men's door with his fist.

'Out!' he shouted. 'Back at it!'

JB was first into the light, Trots last, trowels in hand.

'Joiners, get some kind of tarpaulin rigged over the base so Healey's men can finish it off. Boys, what you've done will be all speckled with rain. Go over it all again.'

One by one, and with different levels of reluctance, the men picked their way through the mud back to their jobs.

John Kelly stood close to the top of the ladder again, one arm draped around the top beam, as he guided the bulb edge of the second pile over the clutch of the first. He held out his free hand, shaking it to the left and right to direct Conn and his jib. Rain had made the beam slippery. For balance he held the first pile that much tighter, leaning his shoulder against it. The executioner's wind cut into him.

When the second pile was in position he took the edge in his left hand to make the final, slight, adjustment. Whatever condition the rest of the pile was in the end cuts had been done to perfection. The steel across the centimetre thickness shone as if new, except where the little black balls of smelt had formed at the edges. Not that it mattered, but he ran his hand across the smoothness to pick a few of them away before giving his downward spiral to Conn. The pile lowered slowly until it was engaged, then still slower until it was past the first beam. Kelly made a quick horizontal cutting gesture with his arm and Conn let the pile drop, running metal against metal – *hissshhhhttt!* – to the ground.

Paul checked the line and Kelly and Conn, between them, shifted and chocked and wedged the pile into position.

John Kelly moved the ladder, again tying the top rung to the beam, and waited for the third pile to steady above his head. Again he reached up and took its edge in his hand and directed it into position and again – *hissshhhttt!* – the bulb slid down the receiving clutch to the ground.

Kelly unbolted the clamp and, without descending, indicated Conn should attach the pile driver. He waited for it to swing over the piles and climbed back up on to the beam. Grasping the machine he looked down between his legs at the lower beams. His eyes refocused on the ground still further below and he felt his head spin. He gripped the frame to steady himself and looked round at the churned wayleave on the hill across the road. It was soaked and ripped beyond redemption and now subjected to more torrential rain.

The two piles were hammered down their first metre and Paul looked from John shifting his ladder, to Conn in his machine, to the men working below them on the settlement tanks and, for the first time, felt part of something greater than himself. The Contract had its difficulties, externals like weather, like traffic controls, and internals like Swannie's workings against both the Engineer and his own staff, and the tensions between the men, but he felt part of it. It was something like a family, something like a team or an army, but not quite any of these things. He wanted it to work. When the job was complete he wanted it to be good. Today it had become more than just a job.

Now the day was wearing on and the light beginning to go. With the worst of the rain blown past the temperature dropped. The wind continued, ice formed in the ground ruts and the sky began to darken. Conn lowered the piling hammer and released it to fit the clamp to the next pile. Unlike Kelly he could not see any sign of wear in the hawser. He climbed back into the heated cab and away from the cutting wind.

'Watch yourself when you're up there,' he shouted.

'I've been doing this since you were driving a pedal car.'

Conn lifted the pile and swung it slowly across and above where John Kelly clung shivering to his ladder, one arm draped across the beam.

As the pile came down John took it with his left hand, steadying the heavy sheet metal as he made his spiralling down gesture to Conn, guiding its bulbed edge above the receiving pile's clutch. The two cut faces were shining all the more brightly, he noticed, after the rain – except for just a few black beads around the rim of the clutch. He made his open palm gesture and the descending pile halted in the air.

'Can you see properly?' Conn called up. 'We could do with having the lights on.'

Without thinking Kelly moved his hand around the clutch to pick a few of the beads away. These were more stubborn. 'Just a minute,' he called.

'What's that, John? Will I get the lights on?'

'I said just a minute!'

Paul, cold and tired and rapidly becoming more so, looked up from behind his instrument.

'Can I put this away? Will we need it again?'

Engrossed with the beads of black smelt Kelly stood upright on the ladder to tug at them, moving his arm back and forward, pulling at them and, one last time, tugging.

Conn peered up through the machine's rain speckled window at Kelly's arm moving back and forward in the cutting gesture that meant 'let go'. The movement looked impatient, urgent. He pushed the handle forward to release the lock on the hawser and the pile descended neatly into the receiving clutch where it met nothing that offered a moment's resistance, nothing that remotely prevented it from running down between the guide beams.

Hhissshhhttt!

The sound drowned John Kelly's cry that was more of despair than pain as his three severed fingers dropped on the other side, and rolled into the narrow space between the driven piles and the ground they had opened and were lost, the fourth pile quivering and shaking as he reeled from the ladder and fell.

10

The phone like a gun to his ear

Ikey pulled up the site van between the Struie Pumping Chamber excavation and the Resident Engineer's hut. Less deep than the two A9 chambers Trots and Jinky were shoring up the sides with trench sheets, propping the sheets with metal frames top and bottom. He peered down at the tops of their heads. Holding a metre long spanner between them they cranked the frames into position and tightened the box into shape.

'Cigarettes, sweets, newspapers wanted, sirs?'

'Don't give us that "sir" stuff,' Trots said. 'You're a working man, not just an ugly wee monkey. Show some dignity.'

'Dignity, sir? Not me, sir. Want anything from Brora? I'm going there after I wash the RE's floor.'

Jinky unbuttoned the top of his boiler suit and rolled it down. From the back pocket of his jeans he took a small leather purse and from that some change. The change he rolled in a handkerchief and tossed up to Ikey.

'Fag papers.'

'That all, sir?'

Silence.

Ikey took a brush and shovel from the back of the van and poked his head round the door of the RE's hut. Allan was seated at his desk, the phone pressed to his ear like a gun. His eyes were distant with concentration and anxiety.

'Sir?'

No response. Ikey entered and began to brush.

'Mac went this morning,' Allan said to the phone, 'after Health and Safety left. That's right, down the road. Kelly broke every safety rule in the book but he's paid the price. It looks like Mac will be held culpable as well.'

Silence.

'. . . and a broken hip from the fall. Yes, expensive errors.'

Silence.

'No Vernon, it won't. What's GR saying; furious?'

Ikey brushed out the four corners of the hut and dropped to his knees to reach under Allan's desk. He gathered the dust and dried mud to the centre of the floor and scooped it onto the shovel, took it to the door and dropped it to the ground outside.

'Watch that!'

Trots wasn't as angry as he sounded. Leaning against the site van he was taking tea from a flask, eating a roll. Jinky was rummaging in his bag, eventually finding his flask.

Ikey took a bucket from the back of the van and filled it from the urn of hot water he had topped up at the compound and dropped in a wet cloth. A second cloth he draped over his shoulder. Again he knocked the door and poked his head round.

Allan was still behind his desk, listening. His head was down and his free hand stroking the top of the desk was trembling.

Ikey squirted washing-up liquid into the bucket and again went down on hands and knees. He took the cloth at the bottom of the bucket in both hands and leaned back and forward, persuading the mix to foam. Starting from the two corners behind Allan he dipped and scrubbed with the cloth, pulled the remaining grit towards himself and made sure it was all lifted in the cloth and then floated off and left in the bucket. He worked in circles, making them larger as he leaned back and forth, moving along, joining them to cover the whole floor within his reach.

'James sent Mac to the Black Isle job, what's left of it. That's right, a non-job, a temporary arrangement. Mac himself reckons he'll be sacked. Meanwhile James has stationed himself here in the Agent's hut. Yes, Trevor is acting Site Agent and they are going to manage the site themselves until something gets sorted out. New people on the way.'

Silence.

'Yes, James still has to be away a lot.'

By the time Ikey reached the centre of the floor the water in his bucket had turned a flat murky grey. He went outside and poured it onto the river bank, rinsed his cloth and refilled from the urn. Jinky was straddling the trench sheets and reaching with his foot for the top rung of the downside ladder.

Back in the hut and once again on his knees Ikey listened to the RE with one ear, only half wanting to know. He began at the remaining two corners, leaning on the cloth and drawing it back and forth. From the corner of one eye he watched Allan flicking through the Contract Document as he spoke.

Silence.

'The two cofferdams are ready now,' Allan said to the phone. 'The tunnellers arrive the day after tomorrow. Yes, traffic plans have gone past Roads and Police.'

Silence.

'No full time General Foreman for the present. Any sign of Harry coming back from Newtonmore?'

However Vernon Street replied Allan paled at it. 'The cables?' he asked. 'They're going to support them. That's all they've said. They're leaving it to the tunnellers. There's no more detail.'

Silence.

'To a fine art, Vernon. Yes, as we say.'

Silence.

'Okay, I'll find out.'

Ikey finished washing the floor as Allan hung up. He took the bucket of dirty water to the door and looked at the RE. Allan looked past him blankly, stunned.

'Couldn't speak while you were on the phone, sir. Mr Williamson says he has the line pegs re-est . . . re-estab . . .'

'Re-established.'

'On the line of the pipe, sir. On the hill, sir. Can you check it, sir.'

'Check it?'

'At least take a look, sir.'

Allan looked through the eyes of a frightened child and nodded slowly.

'Anything from Brora, sir? I'm going there now.'

The Resident Engineer did not reply. Lost within himself, he looked like one who would rather be anywhere but here, who wished that the time was any time but now. Slowly his head descended into his hands.

Trots was still topside when Ikey came out. He took the bucket from him and cast its contents down the river bank.

'Get them to give to give you a mop,' he said. 'You shouldn't be on your knees for any man.'

'Wasn't, Mr Trots, except to scrub the floor.'

On the drive south he reflected on how things could be worse. He could move around in his head better than most, if not so well in his body. Like Raskolnikov in Saint Petersburg, like Mr Crawford in his contract and John Kelly in hospital, or for that matter like Trots in his beliefs, he could be a slave to the decisions of others and his own nature and trapped.

11

What we think about when we can't straighten

Beside the busy A9 Paul stood with the head of the Tunnel Gang, Eamon Bowles. The nearside lane had been coned off for the width of the drainage channel, and signs laid out for scores of metres to the north. Still the southbound traffic thundered past with undiminished speed, cars and vans and huge articulated lorries carrying livestock out of Caithness bound for the slaughterhouses of the south, cod and haddock from the remnant fishing industry and dry goods from whatever ships had berthed at Scrabster. Eamon, a man no higher than Paul himself and not much broader, had a powerful, mostly silent presence. Of this Conn had warned.

'The strongest men you'll ever come across. There's lots think it's the big boys, the muscle men that can tear telephone books in two. Most see past all that and say it's the whippet types with pound for pound leverage that leaves the big boys far behind although it can't touch their sheer physical power. Both wrong. These men are neither big nor small but when you look close you'll see there's no excess flesh or excessive leanness. It's not even hardness, or toughness, not as you would think of them. It's a tightness they have, especially across the shoulders and the front of the chest and in the thighs. It seems to hold them together. And they come as a type; don't speak much. It's the noise. Tunnelling doesn't lend itself to conversation so they hold their thoughts in.'

Paul looked down the road embankment at Conn in the cabin of his machine beside the completed cofferdam. The square had closed neatly along the top and below, where the ancient piles Swannie had supplied had come apart, there was water peeing in although the clutches were welded as far down as possible. The flow of water that couldn't be shut off was at least 'controlled'. The base was blinded with a massive 10cm thickness of concrete with a sump hole cast in and channels running to it. From the sump the water was lifted and cast into the burn by a 4' diaphragm pump. A relic, Willie Quinn said, of that 'big pyramid job in Egypt'. The cofferdam on the other side of the road, at the foot of the hill, was also complete but dry. Conn raised a hand in salute and went back to his Daily Record and his roll up.

At their feet, Paul's and Eamon's, two of the tunnel gang were busy with shovels, up to their hips in a track of their own digging. They had exposed the four concrete surrounded ducts that ran along the verge, two for communications, one for power and the other spare, for a metre on either side of the centre mark Paul had given them by chalking the kerb. The track was 3.2 metres in length to allow for the 60cm concrete pipe and its 30cm drymix bedding all round, the width of the tunnel with an additional metre to either side. They looked down now at it together. It seemed more organic than manufactured, Paul thought, part of the great beast they served. The RE appeared beside them.

'Yo ho, Allan,' said Paul.

Eamon looked to neither left nor right but kept his eyes and his counsel for the men in the ground.

Allan's eyes went continually to the traffic, back and forward from the trench, as if he might be tempted by some inner demon to step into its flow.

'I have your sketch,' he said, taking from his pocket an A4 sheet with the tunnel drawn in cross section, the ducts above it with their wooden support system, and the kerb. Eamon hunkered down to speak quietly to the men in the ground, so they could hear him against the traffic noise.

'Take out another 25cm either side. Just that depth,' he said, holding his thumb and forefinger apart. 'We'll put a longer length on the underside of the cable and that will be more support.'

'Excuse me, the drawing doesn't show that,' said Allan.

Eamon stepped down the slope of the verge and lifted the first two wooden slats that would be placed top and bottom under the ducts, and the metal bander that would be used to tie them together. He handed both down for the troops to tie into place with string.

'Excuse me,' said Allan, 'that's additional to the drawing.'

'Now this longer piece,' said Eamon. 'Up here on the surface. We'll peg it down later.'

He handed down the bander for the men to secure, first, the top and bottom protection, then all three to the top piece that spanned the trench and a metre to either side to support it.

'Give it a shake,' he said. 'That's not going anywhere.' He straightened. 'Right Paul, show me the notches you've made on the piles. Gerry and Mike, come down the slope behind us. Take a breather there.'

At the cofferdam Allan stood in a silence that matched the tunnellers' own and watched while Paul took Eamon to the upstream side of the cofferdam.

'Here,' said Paul, pointing to a nick he had made in the pile top, the pile standing a metre above the ground and making a sort of barrier to the excavation.

Eamon ran his finger across the top of the pile, lingering on the nick as if to be sure it was really there, as if feeling was the only reliable sense.

'And here.'

This was on the downstream side near where the acetylene and oxygen bottles and the rest of the burning gear had been left. On the other side of the cofferdam stood the generator and lights. Beside them was the compressor and beside the compressor the breakers and coiled air bags, the bogie and rails, and a pile of stacked railway sleepers already cut to length. Below both nicks the welder had blown a small circular hole in the piles.

'How many times did you check the line?'

Eamon asked this question with his eyes looking beyond the nick, over the piles and down at the narrow, two-stage scaffolding and ladders that descended to the cofferdam base four metres below.

'Twice from this side, then again from high up on the hill with the laser.'

'I checked it from the hill side,' said Allan.

'Both cofferdams?'

'Yes.'

'And the four nicks are a perfect line? This is important.'

'Yes,' said Paul.

'Yes,' said Allan.

'The level nails down below? You've checked them as well?'

'Same number of times,' said Paul.

'You didn't cheat and do it together?'

Allan folded the sketch he still held in his hand, put it in his pocket and walked away.

'No,' said Paul. 'We didn't cheat.'

'Okay. You can leave now. Come back in about an hour with the welder. He can start burning then.'

When Paul was gone Eamon lifted his satchel from where it lay on top of the sleepers and took out a roll of piano wire. He passed one end through the hole that had been burned beneath the nearest notch and tied it over the top of the pile. Making sure it passed through the notch he walked around the cofferdam and performed the same operation on the upstream side, pulling the wire tight with hands toughened by more than thirty years of labour and hard weather. Although he couldn't work the Face any more, his back long done for, he could do all the rest. Tight he pulled it, tight, through the notches until it sang in the breeze. Then he took two more lengths from the bag, and two plumbobs to be hung front and back.

'Gerry,' he said. 'Down we go. Mike, go back to the compound and help Tony and Pat set up the caravans.'

From the bottom of the excavation he looked at the water as it peed through a single open clutch half way down the piles. The flow was less now than it had been when he first saw it early in the morning, but still running along the channel to the sump where the pump rose sucked and spluttered on a mix of water and air. He held out his hand to take some in his cupped palm as it fell, tasted it and nodded.

'Clean,' he said. 'Probably rain. We can use it for the tea. But what are we going to find when we go through the piles? Here, Paul, gimme a hand.'

Paul had cast into the blinding concrete wooden stobs and calculated from the design gradient of the pipeline the level of the pipe's middle produced at those positions. He had placed his nails exactly half a metre above to allow Eamon to eye through provided he took the piano wire around the tops of the nails and not the bottoms or, worse, one above and one below. Eamon stretched the next line of piano wire between the nails closest to where the opening would be and made it tight as he could but down here there was no breeze to make it sing. When he had done the same with the other he took his spirit level from the long pocket at his thigh and held it at the middle of each span in turn. The bubble was dead level on both wires.

'Good man Paul,' Eamon said to himself. 'If you can do nothing else in life you can do this and you will have your bread.'

From his pocket he took a piece of chalk and handed it to Mike, signalling that he should go to the cofferdam wall where they would make their opening. He stood behind the furthest vertical line and closed one eye, finding with his monovision the other vertical and moving his head until the two wires made just the one line. He lifted his hand and Mike put the chalk against the piles and moved it back and forth until he put a mark on the piles that was in line with the two wires. Joining the two marks they had the vertical centre of their pipeline.

With this vital line on the piles Eamon put his eye behind the two horizontal wires and they put two more marks a metre to either side which was the pipelines horizontal centre. In this way they sketched a cross in chalk on the piles and from that they drew the square shape of the bedding that would surround the pipe and was the size of the tunnel opening. 1200mm square, a space to crouch in and break your back with the work but better that than lying on your gut in the mud. No kind of a space to be trapped in, it was the bare size they had to remove, to take out more for the sake of comfort was to increase the duration of their task greatly and that was to reduce their rate of pay since they were paid by the metre dug and secured.

On the lowest stage of the scaffolding they located their gas rings and kettle. Mike filled the kettle with ground water and they had tea in the last ten minutes before Paul came back with the welder.

Conn lowered the burning gear into the hole.

'There,' said Eamon, pointing at where his first two lines crossed. 'About an inch.'

The welder pulled his mask down over his eyes and turned on his two gas bottles, lighting the mix into a puff of loose flame at the point of the burner. Turning the tap he altered the mix and the pressure and the flame hardened into a straight line first red and then blue and roaring. This he put to the chalk mark and held it as the steel reddened and turned to liquid, dripping and running and hardening again down the face of the pile. A spout of water jetted from the newly cut hole and fell on the blinding concrete to run into the channel and be sucked away by the rose-like intake of the thirsty pump. Within a minute the stream lessened like a small boy's stream of urine and came to an end.

'Local then, not the water table,' said Eamon.

'*Couldn't* be,' said Paul and Eamon looked at him silently, informing him in that way about the difference in what should be and what proved to be and the need to test when it is your own life under consideration. Also silently informing him that now in his life was the time to learn.

'Now welder, cut the piles along the lines given.'

The welder held the hard flame steady against the chalk line until the steel pile started weeping molten metal and then cut slowly along the four 1200mm lines. When the metal square fell away they hooked it to Conn's cable and stood within the scaffolding until he had lifted it clear above them and placed it by the generator to be taken away eventually, whenever. Now the earth lay open before them in the corrugated shape of the outside face of the piles, four metres below ground level at this point and with the road rising two metres above that, a dry glacial till studded with boulders that had been rounded by the very sea that stood behind them and that answered to the same tidal pull those many thousands of years ago as it did now. The face of it was wet with water running down the outside of the piles and that spilled onto the concrete floor from the younger, softer material sitting on the till and that held the rain.

What they called that visible section of ancient ground from this time on was the Face. Even as it receded before their efforts and travelled under the road, the Face.

The welder left them and Conn lifted his burning gear away, replacing it with the small skip they would remove all the arisings from the tunnel. With the skip and in it was the pneumatic breaker. Conn threw down the air hose for Mike to connect and, when that was done and the broad bit secured in its place, turned on the compressor. Paul watched Mike's ease with the weight and bulk of the breaker knowing that he, Paul, could only lift it with a great effort.

Mike hefted it and gunned it and, at Eamon's nod, put it to the Face with his hip pressed behind it and all his weight. When he pulled the trigger the cofferdam filled with sound and his body shook, his whole body from his boots up. The bit sank in to half its length and he levered the breaker up and down until the first chunk of till fell away.

'Hard digging,' Eamon said to himself. 'Nor will it get any easier.'

He signalled upwards to wave Tony down and soon the

younger man was shovelling the broken lumps into the skip with Eamon at his shoulder.

'Are Gerry and Brian here yet?' Eamon pronounced the second name 'Bree-on'.

'Just arrived. They're setting up the second caravan now. Should be ready for the shift change at 6:00pm. Patsy and Deek won't be here until about midnight.'

'Pf.'

'Don't look that way, Eamon.'

'You know Deek. Drink?'

'He's with Patsy. They'll be okay.'

'They'd better,' Eamon told him. 'Paul! Upsides.'

At ground level the compressor was roaring alongside the echo of the breaker as it reverberated up the metal piles and up again still further into the cold air.

'Come further away,' said Eamon.

They stood at the toe of the road slope where they could hear each other speak.

'You know what's happening?'

'24 hour working in three eight-hour shifts. We put all the traffic onto the northbound carriageway and fourteen metres takes us to the middle of the central verge. Then we lay the pipes back the way and concrete them in and close the tunnel this side. We change the traffic over and go in from the other side and meet in the middle.'

'That's how important your work is. Think if we don't meet in the middle, or if we come in six inches low.'

'We won't.'

'You're sure?'

'I'm sure.'

'Okay. Tell Swannie to get the traffic across on the other side now, today, this minute. We'll be here,' he pointed at their feet, 'in two days.'

Depth of winter, 4:30pm, and the floodlights were filling the cofferdam with light far brighter than day. The rest of the site was pitch dark but for these lights and those in Conn's cab and in the Agent's hut where Trevor was working on the next valuation. Paul had spoken to him about the traffic diversion and Trevor had activated the plan with the Roads Department right away. The adverts had been placed weeks before and all permissions arranged to allow them this suddenness. Only then had he called Swannie and that way shown both Paul and himself that he would have more freedom in his actions than Mac. The clock rolled round to 6:00pm with no change other than the clouds that alternately hid and revealed the stars and blackened the sea

Paul and Eamon looked down into the cofferdam at Mike and Tony working the Face. They were half a metre in and Tony was still able to stand to work the breaker but his face was against the piles now, and his whole body juddered with the vibration of the heavy machine.

'Make sure they know,' Eamon told Paul. 'I made my deal with the other fellow and I don't like this change. We will work three eight-hour shifts changing at 2:00am, 10am and 6:00pm. That way we'll avoid the rest of the starts and finishes. There'll be no more than two days notice for shifting the traffic onto the southbound lane. He has to make that okay with the Roads Department and the police and all the rest else we'll be held up and that's more cost. Understand?'

'I do.'

'You here full time?'

'Yes, if a nail gets knocked out or whatever I can put it back. And I've to take notes, changes in ground conditions, accidents, whatever happens.'

'Ground conditions? You know that's the name of the game? Swannie will want to know all about changes in ground conditions all right so he can hit the Engineer with one of these contractual claims he is so expert in. That's how he'll make this job pay.'

They held their heads close together against the sound of the compressor.

'And tell Trevor he's to keep an eye on that pile of cut sleepers. There's no telling but we might have to use extra and if we run out we're stopped and that's more delay as well. He's to make sure there's always plenty.'

'The RE wants you to take the sleepers out before you concrete round the pipe,' said Paul. 'He says if you don't they'll rot and create a void.'

'Then he's more stupid than he looks. You tell him that. Look though, temperature's dropping. There's ice forming on the puddles.'

Ice on the puddles, and steam rose out of the cofferdams from the men's sweat and from their breath. Like horses, Paul thought, but wouldn't say. They're beasts of burden, he thought where do their minds go while they work: Mike's as his body was battered by its hard push against the breaker, Tony's as he shovelled and brushed the concrete base clean, the two of them silent and purposeful.

Below them Tony hooked Conn's chains to the full skip and clenched and unclenched his fist until Conn had taken up the slack. When the chains were tight he signalled for the lift and climbed the scaffolding until he was on the surface to tip the skip onto the pile of arisings growing by the cofferdam, the grey earth and the round boulders.

Downside again Tony helped land the skip and unhook the chains and waved in more or less dismissive fashion that Conn should lift the chains away. Mike had stopped work, leaning against the piles while he wiped the sweat from his eyes, his face tense and worried.

'You've not to think about it,' Tony told him. 'I know it's not easy but you'll hurt yourself. Besides, it might not be what you think. She might . . .'

'Of course she . . .' Mike said. 'Work is best. I'll get on; nothing else for it. Look you, it's time to get bent down and inside the tunnel. I can't get a bite on the Face any more, not from this angle.'

'Will I take over with the breaker? You've done your hour.'

'No.'

They shifted the bit and the air hose across to the small breaker and Mike got down on his knees. Feeling his jeans tight across his thighs, his shirt tight across aching shoulders he edged in under the piles to look at the shape of the unsupported void he had made in the till. It was clean enough and hard, safe ground.

What was it Eamon said about 'safe ground'? Men got killed in it. No one was ever killed in unsafe ground. Meaning you only got into it if you thought it was safe, or if you didn't think at all.

He put the bit against the Face and his shoulder against the rear end of the breaker and pulled the trigger. His head shook on its stalk until he tensed his sinews like a body builder and leaned even harder.

Safe ground is what I thought I was on with her, he thought, remembering her voice as it was the first time he heard it. Just off the boat, a horse of a man and proud of it, what he didn't understand was how ignorant he was of the ways of the world and of women. Was it possible for him to believe, he wondered now, that when she did what she did that night he wasn't the first? So ignorant was he then, he didn't even have the frame of reference within which to consider such things. He did now though, and a wider reference beyond that. The boy though, how would he relate? Where would he be in his son's life? He would have no say. He'd gone along without a word of dissent. He should have married her. No, he shouldn't. It would have been a disaster, but he would have had rights.

They were getting beyond the first metre, hollowing it out. It was beginning to look like a cave. What had Eamon said? He was to look out for something. No matter. He leaned all the harder until the bit jumped across the face of a boulder and into the hard compressed silt that time and pressure had turned near to stone. Like her heart, he thought, the family running back into generations of uncaring people and the weight of time exerting this intolerable pressure to be like them. The mass of it, the gravity, she would be helpless against it and as unknowing of any wider reference as he was that day they met. Why, she wasn't responsible at all! Not she. It was history that did it. Deek would say it was the system behind it all. It would come down to the bosses and the class system.

He slung the breaker behind him and away and felt the relief not so much in his shoulders and arms as in the small of his back. Another thing Eamon said; five years to learn, six years to harden, seven years to make your money before your back goes. Make sure you don't squander it, Eamon said. Not on drink, not on horses, not on women. There's men can make it grow for you, and there's women can run it into the sand especially if first they've staked your heart to the ground with a child.

That's what he had to look out for, sand.

Worse would be sand and water mixed.

He reached for the clay spade where it leaned against the piles.

Why call him 'William'? He had conceded that without thinking. Now he remembered the way she and her parents had looked at each other when he suggested 'Dermot,' his father's name, and 'Michael,' his own.

Tony took hold of his shirt, pulling it. 'I'll do that. Let me do that.'

'No,' he said. 'I'll finish.'

The clay spade was of Eamon's making. He had taken the shaft from the blade and cut it to half its length and asked the welder to burn the edges of the blade away to only half the width. So now it could be used when you were on your knees with the walls holding you in and the roof so low it had you doubled over even then. With this spade he scraped the base of the first metre clear of lumps and stones and tossed them behind him for Tony to shovel into the skip and now in his head there arose the memory of her coming home in the morning looking like she had been dragged through a hedge backwards. How could he not have known she did it for money? That however much he made it would not be enough? Drink and that other stuff she took were more to her than him and the kid together.

Her parents were no better.

The floor of the tunnel and the walls and roof were smooth and hard and unyielding except at the Face, but he'd had enough. He put the spade against the wall and crawled in and turned and sat with his back to the Face with his own face in his hands.

As though she'd been dragged through a hedge backwards, that's how she looked when she came home after staying out all night.

He worked all day and looked after William while she went out and fucked for money, and he, poor clown, believed she needed to get out after being in all day and that he it was had the easier time. Poor clown? He had asked for it and, by Christ, she made sure he got it. Now he had to pay. Now he had to pay near every penny and no recourse to anything because he didn't marry.

There was always death. No, don't think that way.

Ho! There's a laugh, even death was a no go because of William and William was the knife she stabbed him in the heart with. For a moment he thought he was going to be sick but then there was a hand gripping his trouser leg and shaking it. He looked up and this time it was Eamon down on his hunkers looking at him, his whole body bathed in the white light of the floods. He was like an icon framed in the 1200mm square opening, a statue on a church windowsill, and his eyes were blue as Christ's and old beyond belief for a man not yet fifty.

'C'mon,' he said. 'Get out of that hole. You're taking too much on. This is your life, boy. If you want to survive you have to share it. When Tony says it's time for him to go inside you've to let him. You've to come out while it's his turn. Look at you burning yourself out. There's a hole appearing right through your middle I can see through. *Hear me?* Out!'

Mike crawled silently out of his cave and stood up, his weightless head whirling under the lights.

'Bring the sleepers over,' Eamon told him. 'It's midnight almost. We'll frame up and be ready for Gerry and Brian at 2:00am.'

The sleepers had already been cut to length and sections of marine ply nailed into place and the centre marked with a pencil by Paul. Mike put the first of them down on the floor of the tunnel outside the cofferdam, hard against the piles, while Eamon went upsides to slowly lower the plumbs. When they had ceased their swing he sighted through them and centred this first sleeper.

'Now the verticals.'

Mike sat inside with the first vertical sleeper, toeing it behind the horizontal, leaning it against the wall, repeating this on the other side with the third. The fourth sleeper went on top, all of them spaced by lengths of marine ply that had already been tacked in place. Finally Eamon had him stitch the corners together with single six-inch nails. 'Just to hold them.'

With a tape measure and a nail Eamon marked the next location one metre into the hole and they went through the exercise again, the two frames sitting one behind the other in progressive symmetry. 'Now the six by twos.'

Tony brought them over from the scaffolding in pairs and backed into the hole on his seat to take them one at a time from Mike and feed them between the frames. Neither the sides nor the roof were visible now, only the floor. It was ceasing to be a cave, becoming a tunnel, a sort of home for them.

'Now the wedges.'

Tony took the wooden wedges one by one from Mike and pushed them between the frame and each of the planks, pushing the planks hard against the wounded till. He nailed them into place.

'Ten minutes to spare,' said Eamon, checking his watch. 'Now tea.' He took the boiling kettle from its ring and dropped in two tea bags and gave it a minute and poured.

'You're done in,' he said to Tony. 'You were swaying when you came out.'

'I know it.'

'Mind where your head goes when you're in there, the bad things can easy take over.'

'I know it.'

'Don't just fall into your sleeping bag when you get into the big caravan. See you eat. Tony, will you cook? For you both I mean.'

'I'll do that.'

'I don't need any help,' said Mike.

'Ah, let Tony cook. He won't poison you.'

'Yo ho,' Gerry shouted from the top of the scaffolding. 'You'se can beat it now. The real workers are here.'

'And remember,' Eamon said, 'it's freezing up there. Don't mess about, get straight inside and fed and into bed. You're on again at 2:00pm and the time will pass,' he snapped his fingers, 'like that.'

As though to make a liar of him Gerry arrived at the base of the cofferdam wearing only a thin Celtic replica top and no donkey jacket.

'Far we on?' he asked, looking into the tunnel. 'Well, that's a start.'

Mike and Tony climbed topsides and Brian came down. He and Gerry were a pair, Brian broad and sturdy and the older of the two at about thirty. Gerry was 22 and lean under his Celtic top, his red hair cropped close in to the wood, a tiny frown locked permanently between his eyebrows. He pulled the top off over his head and threw it onto the scaffolding to reveal an upper body that was lean and hard and had the muscle definition of an athlete. He ducked down and into the tunnel, his crucifix dangling and his tattoos catching the light, the Sacred Heart, the shamrock and the huge Celtic cross across his shoulder blades.

'Put the plugs in your ears,' Eamon shouted. 'D'ye want deafened.'

The roar of the breaker began and Gerry's doubled over body vibrated in the tunnel like a tuning fork. After half an hour he was shovelling out the broken till.

'Not worthwhile,' said Eamon, looking at working space, depth of penetration, 'putting the rails down until the next frame goes up. That will be well into tomorrow. I'll stay an hour or so then you can get me in the caravan.'

He meant his own caravan. The others shared, hot bedding.

Not in bed and not wishing himself there, not wishing he was anywhere other than at the Face, Gerry put his knuckles to the ground and hoisted himself onto his hunkers to turn himself sideways. His head pressed against the roof and was turned down by it. His rear end leaned against a wall. All about him was that special odour of ground opened for the first time. This time with a metallic smell something like the smell of the acetylene before it took light. He loved the sheer hardness in breaking out the tunnel, loved the effort and how his mind could go where it willed, to the East End of Glasgow in pursuit of his heart.

Ireland, he thought, Celtic Park, but he was troubled because his love for Celtic was the love of an exile. Ireland had his heart but when he went there he felt as if he was a man apart. His village in the lowlands of Scotland had a statue to the famine victims but it was folk tradition to him, not family. His people had come from Dublin and shameful family memory held that they had laughed at such things. Of this they did not speak aloud for Irishness was their essence and the famine a national grievance.

As a boy he had wanted nothing more than to play football for Glasgow Celtic and go home a hero to the village or, better still, all the way home. His talent had not been great enough but the anthems were never far from his mind and below his breath he would sing as he dug, *The Fields of Athenrigh* and *Soldiers are We*. He sung them now in the constrained, confining narrows of the tunnel which he extended, his back bent and his shoulders round under the weight he was carrying, an exile not completely Scottish, Irish or British.

The breaker was biting deeper now, so heavily did he put his weight behind it. His head would be going round when he came out. His arms would be tingling and his back would ache with the good ache that hard work gave it. Inside the tunnel the temperature rose and the sweat stood on his skin like glass beads. Drops ran down the length of his nose and fell to the floor as again and again he plunged the bit into the Face.

He took the flat of the bit across the walls, smoothing them for the wedged boards to come, took the clay spade to the root and chipped away at the boulders that might be loose. He made it all as perfect as he could and called to Brian to be ready with the sleepers for the next frame. It would be up for Patsy and Deek and that would show them who the best workers were. Good that would feel because Deek was hostile to all that Gerry longed for, a puritan of a different stamp.

The thing was the beauty of movement in green and white. How do you tell those who can't see it, or see beauty at all, of the great thing behind it. Those who could not be told what it was to be made larger by the skills of a footballer who stood, whether he knew it or not, for what Gerry stood, a nation where he would always be an honoured guest.

He hit the Face again, feet back against the previous frame and his whole weight thrust against the Face even though he was doubled at the neck and the base of the spine and couldn't straighten, but he was strong as well as young. He loved to use his body and if it wasn't to run free in the green hoops of Glasgow Celtic, well, he would wear the colours where and when he could and otherwise exchange his sweat and his time for money in this way.

They shared their shift in such a manner that Gerry did two hours at the Face and Brian one. It had nothing to do with fairness or relative power only what worked and what they wanted between them. It was the way they had done it for the whole two years they had been together. They rarely talked because of the noise but when he was on the shovel, not the breaker, Gerry would sing his sentimental songs and his patriotic songs and they would arise out of the cofferdam to address the sky.

What few words they spoke were to the point.

'That's enough, Gerry. Isn't that far enough? Don't go too far in without support. If the roof comes down and you get crushed Eamon will give me a terrible telling off.'

'Well that won't do.'

'I'd have to do the rest of these shifts myself.'

'Okay, okay. We'll get the frame up. What time is it?'

'It's 9:00am and it's getting lighter up there. We'll get the frame up and let them put the boards in place but here's Eamon on the scaffolding. By God Gerry, we're shifting ground. We're moving this Face.'

Paul came down behind Eamon and spoke in his ear although Brian could not hear what was said and, indeed, only guessed he was the setting-out engineer.

'Swannie called me in. He wants me on twelve hour night shifts starting tonight.'

'8:00 till 8:00?'

'That's it.'

'What if I want something through the day?'

'Trevor will be down a couple times. He's doubling on his own job and mine. You can always speak to the RE, Swannie says.'

'The RE?'

'The RE.'

'Pf.'

Trevor had called Paul into the office as he came out of his car. There was a steady intensity about the site now. Numbers were spread more thinly in the absence of Mac and John Kelly but Swannie would not go backwards. This intensity was of his making and was how he wanted the place to feel. Trevor could handle the setting-out through the day, he said, and keep the records up evenings. What did he do in the evenings anyway? Watch television? Half the time, he told Paul, you're standing around anyway.

'I didn't know what to say,' said Paul. 'He was sneering at me.'

'Pf! It's your place to be standing around, but better be silent with Mr Swann,' said Eamon, 'although you'll find the words if you have to, Paul. I can tell. If you have the words; they'll carry you through life. You'd better go now. Before you do you can tell Trevor to get the traffic onto the northbound carriageway. We'll be under the embankment later today. Check everything with the Police and the Roads.'

'I'll get it done before I go.' He didn't tell Eamon about the way Swannie had looked at him from the desk with a look that spoke from another world, the world Paul would have to own eventually.

He didn't repeat what Swannie had said. That Eamon was a thick Mick.

'Okay,' Eamon told him. 'Don't sleep too long. You're breaking your rhythm. Just put maybe three hours in if you can manage. It'll take a couple of shifts to get used to it. Here's Patsy and Deek.'

Patsy and Deek materialised at the foot of the scaffolding, Patsy the tallest of the gang at nearly six feet, Deek being Paul's own height and wearing a red working shirt and a cloth around his neck that might have been red before it was stained and rinsed out by sweat, washing and weather. Deek was the oldest of the diggers at nearly forty.

'Yo ho,' said Patsy for them both.

'Yo ho,' said Eamon.

'I'm going,' said Paul, and climbed topsides and got away.

Gerry came out of the tunnel and straightened up, hands against the small of his back.

'You're grinning like monkeys, you two,' said Patsy. 'What have you done?'

'Second metre's dug, frame's up.'

'Second metre's not complete until the boards are up too,' Eamon said. 'There's a lot of work in that.'

'Is this a competition?' Deek asked. 'We're in this together. We should be doing the same every shift, the same distance.'

'As fast as the slowest?' Brian asked.

'That's fast enough.'

'Brian and Gerry, you two get into the caravan and get some sleep.' Eamon interrupted, always impatient of argument. 'Paul will be on same time as you for night shifts now and right through. Gerry, get that shirt on. You'll freeze.' He looked at Patsy and Deek. 'Who's going in first?'

Deek took a deep breath and crouched onto his hunkers and crabbed inside the tunnel, his eyes slowly adjusting.

'Tunnel needs lit now. What are they two thinking about working in the dark?'

'They were just used to it and wanting to get on,' Eamon called in. 'Here Patsy, bring them lights over.' He pointed to the corner where they were coiled. 'Take the end topsides and plug it into the genny.'

Patsy dragged the rubberised cable topsides and in a moment the bulbs lit up, barely visible in the strong white light that came down from the two floods. Eamon grabbed the end and handed it in to Deek.

'Hammer,' said Deek. 'Nails.'

Eamon passed them inside and Deek put a nail in close to the top of each of the left side verticals, stringing the lights across the first two. When they had the boards in, top and sides, he put a third nail in and extended the line and there it hung like a colourless Christmas decoration, the line of 40 watt bulbs and their black cable. Deek looked along the tunnel, along the lines of the boards, the frames, out into the cofferdam at the other men's legs. Already he had pain in his back. Already he was wondering how long he could keep going at this kind of work, but knowing that when he was in his shift and properly digging he would forget the pain until he had to straighten again.

'Now we'll need the rails down. There's no shovelling out at this distance.'

Patsy pushed in the first of the narrow steel rails and the second and then the wooden spacer that gave them their distance apart and Deek used six-inch nails to fix them to the bottom sleepers. Patsy and Eamon extended the line a rail's length back into the cofferdam and together lifted the bogie into position. They lifted the skip onto the bogie.

'Half the bloody shift's gone,' Deek said as he came out of the hole. He straightened, hands on the small of his back but with a look, Eamon observed, that was far different from Gerry's, the difference between the sharp pain that needled into the nervous system and the dull ache that preceded it by who knows how many years.

Patsy picked up the small breaker and gunned it once before putting his plugs in and ducking and entering to do his hour. The roar of the breaker broke out of the tunnel like the roar of the Minotaur.

'At least,' said Eamon to Deek, 'you two don't sing.'

'Not often.'

'D'ye know, you'll never walk alone? That's Gerry's favourite.'

'No, but I'd mean it if I sang it.'

'Pf.'

When Patsy was near to finished Deek put his hands on the end of the bogie and placed his feet well back so that his head was low and pushed the bogie into the tunnel. Patsy put the breaker down and used the clay spade to shift the arisings into the skip. When they hauled it out between them Eamon was in Conn's cabin and the lifting hooks were already down. They attached them and signalled for him to lift and Patsy went topsides to upturn it over the heap.

Deek put his earplugs in and took the weight of the small breaker across his two forearms and into his belly. He bent his knees until his thighs were on his heels and crouched his upper body under the first frame to crab walk into the tunnel on six-inch steps. By now the floor was wet with the water the four who had preceded him had dragged in with their boots and with their condensed sweat and had begun to soften and puddle. He reached the Face and gunned the machine once and then put it down again. Reaching behind him he took the nearest light from its nail and dragged the line forward to hold it against the Face.

'Wet,' he said. 'Eamon!'

'Yo ho.'

Eamon came in on his hands and knees to look. Side by side and doubled over they pressed against the walls with their sides and against the roof with their heads, lifting such of their weight as they could from their thighs and backs. Deek took the plugs from his ears.

'Hold the light up,' Eamon told him.

The Face glistened. Eamon touched it lightly, then ran his fingers firmly round and across the broken ground, rubbed his fingers together.

'Doesn't feel like sand. It's not all that gritty. Might be stuff you've loosened.'

'Why is it wet?'

'Might just be your breath.'

'Think so?'

'Keep going,' Eamon instructed, 'but not so fast. Take a look at the Face every time you pull the breaker away. Keep an eye open for sand. Watch especially if it runs. If it even starts to move get out. Don't wait.'

'I will.'

'I'll keep the bogie well back from the entrance just in case.'

'Do that.'

'If the worst comes to the worst we'll stop the job and get some air on it. A few pounds.'

'Compressed air? Swannie won't like it.'

'Unexpected ground conditions? He'll love it. It's what he wants. The Engineer will hate it. And that sapsy RE will hate it even more because he'll have to come down here and look from time to time and if you ask me he's scared.'

'He's a worker like the rest of us. He'll do his best.'

'Pf.'

Eamon backed out of the tunnel and Deek put the plugs back in his ears to address the Face. Tensing the muscles in his lower back and his buttocks, feeling them almost as if they were adhesions to his skeleton and not part of a whole body, he lifted the breaker, put the bit against the Face, leaned and gunned it into the till.

Good to have Eamon between him and the bosses, he decided. He was better than the foremen at any factory he'd ever worked in.

Who was the worst, the Bosses or the gaffers, the shepherds or their dogs? Come the day. Nowadays the revolution seemed very far away. His father had marched. His grandfather had fought. Both of them had struck and in times before that, before Deek's time, there had been the opportunity to use a gun, to use it on a recognisable fascist. What would he give for another Spain, to wear the red bandanna?

What was Swannie beyond being a Boss? A mason? Some loyalty other than the People that was for sure, driving around in his big car while the Workers were jumped through hoops, crawled through holes in the ground, broke their backs with shovels as he was doing now, hammered and sawed for him. The People will rise of this there is no doubt. The circumstances would reach such a pass the People would throw off the cult of the individual they had been taught to love, they would throw off the guilt and complicity of capitalism and rise out of their own spilled blood. All those still living would become as one being, the People, and advance from feudalism through this present phase, capitalism, to socialism. So strong was his emotion at this that he wanted to stand, but his closed environment prevented it.

He put down the breaker.

'Patsy!'

'Yo!'

'Wheel in the skip.'

'What's that Face like? Is it running?'

He had forgotten about the water. Tugging the light bulb across, he again held it close to the Face.

'Drier. It's drier.'

'You sure?'

'Sure I'm sure. Will you roll in the fucking bogie?'

'No need for that language.'

Patsy's feet were moving at the opening, Eamon's voice that he couldn't quite make out. The opening darkened and the bogie and skip appeared, Patsy's head showing behind it.

'Eamon says you've to come out. Fill the skip and I'll take over with the gun.'

Deek dug the clay spade into the pile of arisings, levering his forearms across the bones of his thighs. When they were all on board he pushed the bogie along the rails at Patsy.

'I've more time to do,' he said. 'I won't shirk. The load has to be even.'

Studded in the Face was a boulder larger than the rest, as big as Swannie's head. He put the bit to where it was embedded in the Face and gunned it hard, prising and twisting until it fell away. Now he had access to a greater depth than he could have reached directly. There's always a way, he thought. Even granite has a seam that if you hit right you get it away without breaking your back except there was no rest in a world run by the Bosses. Never would be. Always there was this struggle with the rate of pay while they rung the deepest penetration out of the cheapest labour. He had the bit in behind another boulder that was showing in the hole the other had left. With the right leverage he could get it all out together. Why, he was almost at the depth now. A sucking 'thock' sounded even through his earplugs and a huge lump fell away from the Face and onto the floor almost striking his knee. He hit it with bit and breaker and turned it into spadeable lumps.

'Now,' he shouted, 'the skip again!'

'Already?'

'Aye, now!'

The bogie and skip appeared and he cleared the arisings with spade and hands.

'Now, Patsy. I'm out of here. The breaker's waiting for you.'

'I'm ready,' Patsy said, the two of them between them hauling and shoving the bogie out into the white light of the cofferdam.

Once again the tunnel opening was clear. He looked along the nearly three metres, along the lines of the planks and bulbs to Patsy's feet and Eamon's and dropped forward on to hands and knees and crawled clear of the tunnel. Out in open space again he crawled across the cofferdam in the direction of the scaffolding until he could take hold of a steel tube with first one hand and then the other. The others knew not to look. It had been Eamon before and eventually it would be Patsy. This is what it was to be a digger.

Slowly he climbed the tube with his hands, the stretch reaching deep into his back, into his spine between the prolapsed disks. He straightened in his pain, breathing heavily and with small moans drawn from deep in his inner being. When he came upright at last the hurting was so severe he cried aloud and staggered back and almost fell, his head swimming. This would be the last tunnel, he knew. He was slowing. He couldn't take this for much longer.

He felt Eamon's hand on his shoulder, felt it squeeze but could not look around for the pride it would cost him to show his despair. He was losing. He had kept going while he waited for the People to rise and soon would not be able to keep going any longer. He had nothing because he had chosen to have nothing and soon the Bosses would discard him. He took the plugs from his ears and put them in the breast pocket of his sweat soaked shirt.

'Good man,' said Eamon. 'You've a great heart. Now take it easy. I'll wheel in the skip when Patsy's ready.'

So they worked the shift away and dug their distance and placed their frame. And the few daylight hours passed, and the

longer 24 hour day, to the sound of compressed air released
and the generator running and the men crying out and sometimes singing their loyalties and their anguish and their pain
until night returned but made no end to working. Mike sang
his torch songs and Gerry the songs of Old Woman Ireland
that lived in the collective memory of his tribe and nowhere
else and Deek sang the People's Anthems of equality and
revolution. Day after day they went on digging and eating and
hot bedding and returning to the Face that retreated continually before the breaker, the clay spade and the skip. Trevor
came down the ladder daily to check on progress and on what
might be required. Paul stood by all through the darkness
hours and took notes and measurements and checked the line
and levels with Eamon.

Eamon Bowles was happy with progress but always a
worrier. That was his nature and it had served him well for
many years, through more tunnels than he could remember
and only one of his men dead in all that time. Yes, it went well
until they were eleven metres in and so under the southbound
carriageway.

Paul found himself alone in the cofferdam with silent,
morose Deek. Patsy was working the Face, the compressor
roaring every time he struck with the breaker. From the road
there was only the occasional thrum of traffic and that from the
far carriageway. Paul checked the thermometer that hung from
the scaffolding and saw the temperature was six below zero.
Topsides would be even colder. He noted the time, 3:00am,
and jotted it into his book.

Inside the tunnel Patsy put the breaker down and called for
Deek to push in the bogie and skip. Another half hour and
Deek had lifted it out, driving the crane in Conn's absence, and
on to the pile of arisings that had now grown large enough to
obstruct other site traffic. Tomorrow a lorry would arrive and
Conn would load it using the excavator to be taken to coup and
dumped. They were more than half way by length of dig, half
way because the Face was now under the central reserve. Now

they could place the pipes and concrete surround on this side and transfer across the road. They would tunnel from the north cofferdam to meet the new pipe and inside himself Paul felt such a thrill of achievement in prospect that it might capture him to this form of toil for life.

Deek loaded the bogie with sleepers and pushed it inside, hauled it out again empty.

'Line,' Patsy shouted from inside.

Paul looked in along the eleven frames that were already in place and along the line of bulbs that cast a light that flickered with the irregularities of the ancient generator. Patsy was crouched, doubled over in the void he had dug into the till, three of the sleepers stacked behind him, the fourth laid horizontal in position. He held a nail upright on its top surface, roughly in the middle.

'Hold on,' Paul shouted in. 'I'm not ready.'

'You should be! Get up there.'

Paul was already half way up the scaffolding. He stretched the piano wire again between the nicks, tight as he could, not as tight as Eamon with his leather palms but tight enough, and eased the plumbobs down to minimise swing. Downside again he steadied them with his hand and sighted through them to the nail.

'Left a centimetre,' he called into the tunnel. 'Left. Smidgeon. Smidge. Spoteroonie!'

Patsy swore and shifted the whole sleeper to the right.

'Again,' he shouted.

This time it all fitted.

'Send Deek in to give me a hand with these three.'

Deek was still topsides and Paul knew, as Patsy knew but wouldn't say, that the pain in his back was too great. He would linger up there and hope for the salvation that comes from unspoken human sympathy translated into action with no questions.

'I'll get it,' Paul shouted back, already on hands and knees and entering the tunnel that way.

Crawling towards Patsy he took himself up onto his hunkers under the last frame, there accepting one end of the second sleeper. Now he could neither rise for the low roof nor go properly down on his knees for the leverage it would put on his back. The weight of the sleeper transferred from shoulder to hips to knees to ankles and he took the shock, that way, through the muscles of his thighs.

'Prop it upright,' Patsy told him. 'Hold the bottom end in place while I push the top over. That's it. That's it.'

Patsy backed further into the unsupported tunnel to let Paul get his shoulders into position and between them they got the sleeper vertical and in against the wall. Paul still couldn't get a proper purchase.

'Hold on,' he said. 'I'll lie down. That way I can pull the toe in.'

'Do that.'

Paul lay down and pulled on the base of the vertical sleeper, his head resting on his arm. Behind him the lines of the planks receded, the line of bulbs likewise with their dim light casting shadows from the sleepers and the rails and beyond the tunnel opening the skip on the bogie lit from above by the fierce white light of the floods. Then it happened and the dread unexpected became, without warning, real.

They saw the movement in what was a sort of slow motion to them, so quickened by the run of adrenaline were they, the wild uprising of blood with no time for fear, he and Patsy both. The top wedges distorted, the wedges between the frames and the roof planks crushed and splintered and the broken pieces forced out, dragging their six inch nails with them, spat onto the floor by a sudden massive increase in pressure while the planks between the frames buckled downwards but held.

Patsy moved in silence. At once his whole body was over Paul's, his hands and feet scrabbling for purchase and finding it first on Paul's body, then his arm. Paul cried out in pain and struggled to turn in the narrow low space of the tunnel. Without thinking he tried to stand but was stopped and buckled by the roof that might come in on him before his next breath. He dropped to his hands and knees and crawled like an athletic baby for the light of the tunnel opening and there Patsy took his arm, grasped his donkey jacket and hauled him bodily into the light of the floods and the cold air of winter.

'What kept you? I thought you were dead!'

'I'm okay.'

'I thought you were dead!'

Paul looked back along the tunnel and saw nothing that had changed but for the splintered remains of half a dozen wedges.

'Did it really happen?'

Deek called from above. 'Y'all right down there!'

'We're okay' Paul called back. 'What happened? What hit us?'

'Some kind of huge truck; a monster. Come up.'

Paul followed Patsy topsides, his legs scarcely able to carry his own weight for shaking, and the three of them stood in an uneasy triangle in front of Conn's machine, illuminated eerily by the cab light.

'What was that?'

Eamon came running from the compound, fastening his trousers as he ran, his bootlaces flapping.

'What was it? You okay, Paul?'

'I got up the slope in time to see two red lights disappearing,' Deek said. 'He can't have seen the signs, must have ploughed through the concs.'

'Come on,' Eamon said. 'We'll look.'

There was no traffic to either side when they reached the tarmac, no lights but the wintry stars and the moon. They walked to the north and found their traffic controls had been smashed through. Two of the signs were crushed and bent and thrown onto the verge by the force of collision.

'What was he thinking of?' Eamon asked. 'Do you have your phone, Paul?'

'I have.'

'Call the police. Let them know. Patsy, Deek, we'll put this lot back together as best we can. Then it's back down the cofferdam.'

The troops were quicker with the traffic controls than Paul
was, calling the police. He rejoined them at the mouth of the
tunnel as they looked in.

'Wait here,' Eamon told them, and went inside on hands and
knees to feel around the frames and look at the roof planks.

'Deek!'

'Yo ho.'

'You're the most expendable. Bring me half a dozen
wedges.'

Deek did this without comment, steeling himself before
entry. The two men first re-wedged the spaces where the
old wedges had been destroyed utterly, then replaced the
others one at a time. That done they crawled to the end of
the tunnel and completed the frame that Patsy and Paul had
begun and placed the planks. When they came out Patsy had
mugs of tea waiting for them.

'The planks were bending down,' Paul said. 'That's suicide
in there.'

'No,' said Eamon. 'It just looked that way.'

He bent and looked into the tunnel again.

'That's this side dug. We'll make sure Swannie knows about
what happened and the whole thing is recorded. Driver must
have been asleep.' He looked at Paul. 'We'll begin piping in the
morning. You'll come off night shift, Paul. I think they'll agree
to that. At least until we cross over. Everybody okay?'

'Okay, Eamon,' said Patsy.

'Okay,' said Deek.

'Okay,' agreed Paul at last, with them but still not of them.

'Now, finish,' Eamon said. 'The beds are full so get your-
selves a room at the Hotel, it's a dump but it's warm and dry.
Paul?'

'Yo ho?'

'See you at 9:00am.'

Paul was home by 3:00am for four hours sleep. In the morning
his mother made sure he was fed, made sure he was clean

going out however he might come back. At their front door she took him by the shoulders and looked him over before letting him go. When he rolled onto the site and parked by the huts her eyes were still burning holes in his head. How they showed concern, puzzlement at this commitment to long hours and night working without additional reward, commitment that didn't run to working, really working, for a qualification.

He knew, because she told him, that in some ways he was like his father. What were these attachments to the wrong things? Where was the future in his thinking and where were the girlfriends? Not that his father ever had any difficulty finding those. Did she not know this hurt her? Did he know she wanted grandchildren? Not now but eventually. Say in five years time. What was he all about anyway? Her questions punched him in the heart each one.

Come home safe, she said over and over in his head. Keep on coming home.

Stepping out of the car his skin felt tight on his face and his eyes heavy in his head. The sky was overcast and it was cold and rain was on the way. Patsy was already shovelling sand and aggregate and cement into the mixer in the compound. Deek sat on the dump truck ready to carry the mix across to the cofferdam. Gerry was attaching the concrete skip to Conn's chains.

Eamon caught his eye and waved him on. He dashed into the hut and changed quickly, dashed out again and across.

'Where you been?'

'I'm on time.'

'Pf.'

Beside the cofferdam fourteen one metre long 60cm diameter concrete pipes without chip or crack on any part of them sat on wooden boards that kept them from the ground and unmuddied. Brian and Gerry were clearing the area of stones.

Eamon ran his hand across the nearest of the pipes.

'Went through the stack,' he said, 'with a fine tooth comb. They have to be perfect. Did you hear the clerk of works has reappeared?'

'Good.'

'Think so? Think we need our quality controlled? It's in his interest to find fault. Anyway, these are perfect. He can come down the cofferdam whenever he likes but you can bet he won't enter the tunnel.'

'Mike and Tony?'

Eamon nodded down into the cofferdam where Mike was stooped, looking into the tunnel. 'Tony's inside loosening the far end rails. When they come out we're ready to go.'

At that Mike reached into the tunnel and hauled out the first of the rails, placed it in the corner, then the second. Gerry ran a scaffolding tube through the centre of the first pipe and signalled Conn to swing his jib across the cofferdam and lower the chains. When they were down he wrapped rags around the tube where it would meet the concrete and signalled for Conn to lift. Downside Mike and Tony landed this first pipe beside the tunnel opening and signalled Conn to lift the chains clear and back across to where Brian was waiting by the concrete skip.

'Okay, Paul,' said Eamon. 'Everyone and everything is in place. Patsy's on the mixer. Gerry's driving the dumper because of his back. Brian at the skip. Mike and Tony placing the pipes and the concrete and taking it in turn. You and me, Paul, on line and level and whatever else comes up. Listen, there's no stopping once we start.'

'I know. We don't want any cold joints. Mister Gilfeather wouldn't like it.'

'Neither would you, Paul, because it would be a weakness in the pipeline. And neither would I. It's to be right.'

'Nothing to do with rules, specifications, contracts but just for its own sake. I know it.'

'Now, downside.'

Eamon strung the piano wires across the cofferdam and tightened them while Mike and Tony handled the first pipe onto the bogie. Mike disappeared into the tunnel and Tony pushed the bogie to the end of the rails and both, together, used all their strength to manhandle the pipe off the bogie and into rough position in the confined space. With the bogie out again Paul crouched on his hunkers and looked along the line of light bulbs at Tony lying on the muddy floor of the tunnel at the pipe's near end, Tony at the far end and the two of them red in the face with pushing short lengths of sleeper under the pipe and pushing wedges in between.

'Now,' Mike called urgently.

'Take a breath, man!' Eamon called back. 'Put the traveller on.'

Mike took a short wooden tee-shape from where it leaned against the wall planks and stood it on top of the pipe.

'Now.' Eamon positioned himself behind the piano wires and sighted through them and saw the pipe was 2cm high. 'Down two,' he shouted up the tunnel.

Mike knocked the wedge delicately with a hammer, taking the pipe down at that end. 'Again.'

Eamon sighted again and nodded. 'Now Paul, check that,' he said.

'Spoteroonie!'

'Y'hear that, Mike? Spoteroonie. Now you, Tony.'

Tony took the traveller from Mike and held it at his end of the pipe.

'Up one,' Eamon called again.

Tony took the hammer from Mike and shifted the wedge.

'Spoteroonie,' Paul said.

'Now, Mike again.'

It took three rounds of sights and shifts to get the pipe in position just so and by that time Deek had delivered the drymix concrete from Patsy and Brian had directed it into the concrete skip. Out of the tunnel again Mike and Tony dropped it into the bogie and pushed it inside and shovelled it under the pipe until they could remove the supports without the pipe moving. Then they filled all round the pipe from the Face end forward.

'Here now,' Eamon called in. 'Don't come too far this way without using these.'

He handed in a fence post to Mike who passed it along to
Tony who took it with two hands because it was so awkward
and heavy and used it to push and stab at the drymix until it
was as hard compressed against the walls and roof as powerful
shoulders could make it. Now all the end of the tunnel was
filled with pipe and concrete around the pipe. It was 10:30am.
An hour and a half had passed since Paul arrived on site.

'As usual,' said Eamon. 'The first is the most important.
From here on we only have to sight one end in.'

There was no time for reply. Conn was already lowering the
second pipe and Gerry, up at the pipe stack had begun to sing.

> *Now Mary this Scotland's a wonderful place*
> *We come here to work by night and by day*
> *We don't dig for barley. We don't dig for wheat.*
> *We're digging for gold far under the street.*

'D'ye hear that man?' Eamon said. 'He's daft. If it's not the
Celtic it's Ould Erin, and if he's not loving he's fighting. He's a
fool. You can't tell them by sight. You have to know their
thoughts.'

Mike from inside the tunnel heard and he too raised his
voice, not in harmony but as an assertion of difference, a
spurious sort of independence.

> *She may have a face you can't forget*
> *A moment's pleasure brings regret*
> *No matter what you do or say*
> *A lifetime's toil's the price you pay.*

Then from above came Deek's voice joining in but not joining,
being his own unique man by refusing independence.

> *The worker's flag is red with blood*
> *Blood the People spilled for love.*
> *Let the Bosses fear the day*
> *The Revolution's on its way.*

With the first pipe in place the work went more quickly and Mike and Tony took it in turns at the receding Face. In nine hours, better than a pipe length an hour, they were at the cofferdam opening.

'Deek,' Eamon called up.

'Yo ho!'

Deek was leaning over the piles.

'Clean out the dumper and the mixer. We'll finish here and see you topsides.'

'Yo ho!'

'Look at that, now,' he said to Paul. 'These boys know how to work.'

Tony and Mike had come out of the tunnel, back into the cofferdam, shovelling the last of the dry mix around the last pipe, Mike pushing it home with the blunt end of the stob, Tony smoothing it with the flat of the shovel. Eventually they were done and, after the course of a single shift, the tunnel was no more. The four of them climbed topsides and walked to the compound, the troops to their caravan and Paul to the hut he had to himself now John Kelly was gone.

'Don't leave right away,' Eamon told him at the gate. 'Go in and see Trevor. You might get a lie in tomorrow while they move the signs and the traffic cones and get the traffic onto the other carriageway. You never know what might happen.'

The hut was like an oven after the freezing outside temperatures. Paul shook his muddy trousers out of the door and hung them over a chair. He took off his pullover and washed his hands and face in cold water and put on his jerkin. He changed his socks and put on his jeans and his shoes and leaned back in his seat very tired. Relaxed at last it occurred to him that he was happy. His energy was almost spent and there was nothing of anticipation in the feeling, more that he was for the first time in his life in some way fulfilled. This first part of the feat they had set out to do was achieved. It had taken part of him away but although that was true yet there was more. That seemingly lost part would recover. His head spun from lack of sleep and from physical exhaustion and there could be no accurate tracing to the source of this passive joy.

In the Agent's hut he found not only Trevor and Eamon but the tunnellers standing round the four walls and Swannie seated behind the desk. The men were all holding cups and holding them not by the handle as with hot tea but round the body as with a glass tumbler. Deek had a bottle of whisky, half empty, in his hand. He pressed a cup on Paul which he three quarters filled and shuffled on, pouring into the outheld cups. It looked like an everyday normality of no more importance than tea.

Paul looked down into the cup and when he looked up saw that the bottle had rounded and almost returned. He swallowed his whisky down and took his refill.

'We're topping out the first half,' Gerry told him.

Paul looked at the men with a new eye. They were cleaned up, spruced. They had managed it more quickly than he.

'Brora is waiting for us,' Mike added. 'The fleshpots, Paul, will you come?'

'Ah no,' interrupted Eamon. 'This lad's to go home. He's a mother waiting for him and you lot and Mister Swann have been pressing on her patience. You driving, Paul?'

'Sure.'

'Not any more.'

'Are you telling my staff how to behave?' Swannie asked provocatively.

He had a cup of whisky in front of him that he never touched.

'I'll give such guidance I think is right.'

Swannie looked at Trevor and nodded towards the filing cabinet. Another bottle of whisky went round and Paul only barely noticed that, aside from Deek, the others had slowed down. Like Swannie, Eamon held a cup but never took it to his mouth. Paul drank another off and another before the first had properly found its way to his head.

'You'll have the traffic switched in the morning?' Eamon asked Trevor.

'I will.'

'We can start at 9:00.'

'Say 10:00,' Swannie said. 'We want the police on our side.'

'Look at that night,' said Mike at the window.

Together they gazed out and up at the sky. The clouds were gone and the stars were out. The moon was full and shining.

'Jeez, cold though,' said Gerry. 'You'd die sleeping out.'

While all their attention was at the window Paul slipped through the door. Eamon didn't want him to drive, but he was fine. Yes, he was fine. His head was clear and filled with great thoughts about men and work and the ways of the world. On the drive home he intended to bring them forth and go through them and be wise but when he reached his battered old hatchback the notion that he should return to what had been the tunnel overwhelmed him. He walked on across the hardening mud to the cofferdam and checked the temperature on the thermometer. It was eight below and falling.

He climbed down the scaffolding and onto the concrete base. The last pipe protruded from the cofferdam wall like a stubby phallus. He put his hand on it, ran his hand lovingly over the concrete and thought how good it was, how well done, how bloody fucking well done. He touched the concrete surround and wondered that the beautiful tunnel that was laboured for so hard could be so quickly gone, its purpose served. When he looked up Orion hung in the sky directly over his head and it too was beautiful. He stared up at it and almost toppled over. Yes, it was beautiful all right, but he had realised at last that everything was beautiful, all we do, all we see, all we are part of, and he hummed the words over and over under his breath.

Everything is beautiful.
Everything is beautiful.

Wasn't there a tune to go with it? Gone, but no matter, everything returns in time. The stars themselves go round.

Topside he headed for the compound and the car but changed his mind again as he approached the lighted hut. He wanted to see the beautiful sea with the beautiful stars reflected in it. He continued downhill to the shore and the North Sea where the wind blew chill across Europe from the Russian Steppe. There he kept walking into water that was so cold it would be ice were it not salt and perpetually moving. Yes, it was beautiful. Ankles, knees, up to his thighs and now the cold was biting into his very heart but he kept going until he felt strong arms under his own arms and around his chest and himself being drawn backwards and out into the dry.

'Back you come, Paul,' said Eamon in his ear. 'Out of this and home.'

Paul insisted on walking unsupported to the huts but didn't resist as Eamon helped him change out of his wet jeans back into his working trousers.

'Sorry.'

'S'okay.'

'What now?'

'You gonna be sick?'

'No.'

'Now into my car and I'll get you home. Stay awake long enough to give me directions.'

Paul fell asleep in the car but was awake enough by Dingwall to give directions. He accepted Eamon's arm that took him to the door and there saw his mother's face again. Strangely, strangely, she was not looking at him so much as Eamon who was holding him up. They went inside and Paul could re-member little after that, only Eamon assuring her that 'it could happen to anyone' and that it happened to most although this she certainly knew. The last thing he heard was Eamon telling her that she should please go easy on him in the morning and that there was no need for him to come in to work at all since he, Paul, was likely to be more dead than alive by that time. He remembered later how his mother looked very carefully at this Eamon she had heard about and nodded and nodded and thought behind her eyes. She was a woman of harsh judgements when it came to men.

He fell asleep in a chair and wakened in bed with the light on and, it was true, felt more dead than alive. There was a pungency in the room and with a shudder of horror that almost took his head off he realised he had been sick. He sat up and looked around. The first flush was across the duvet and the rest had flooded the carpet. How could his body have held so much stuff? Outside the window it was still dark. Through eyes shuttered by pain he watched the dawn slowly break.

That morning on site Eamon had Mike and Tony move all the small plant across the A9. Moving the crane and the mixer and the lights and generator required a police presence and would be carried out later in the day. He had Brian and Gerry cut sleepers since the supply was by now low. Deek and Patsy he ordered down the cofferdam to tidy up. It was 9:45am, almost time for tea. He was leaning against the piles, looking at Paul's hatchback rusting in the salt coastal air, looking at Trevor's company saloon and Swannie's beamer beside it when a newer hatchback turned in off the road and into the compound.

From the passenger side there emerged the remorseful Paul. Whiter than a glass of milk, thought Eamon, he looked 100 years of age. Without speaking or gesturing or acknowledging any other presence he made his way into his own hut to his donkey jacket and level book. The hatchback's engine gunned as it turned and advanced to the compound gate and there halted as though it had the power of thought and knew doubt.

'Well,' Eamon said. 'We'll just watch what happens now.'

A moment later it reversed back into position outside the Agent's hut and Paul's mother emerged and knocked at the door, entering without a pause.

'What is that?' Mike asked.

'A handsome woman in her forties,' Eamon told him, not taking his eyes from the door of the hut. 'Her name is Mrs Eileen Williamson.'

Patsy had already brought the gas bottle and ring out of the cofferdam and set it up topsides near where Brian and Gerry were sawing. Eamon put a match to the ring and the kettle to the flame.

'I would have guessed something of the sort,' Eamon went on.

As the kettle came to the boil Trevor emerged from the Agent's hut, pulling on his jacket and shaking his head. Eamon dropped four tea bags into the kettle and gave Brian and Gerry a shout. All three watched the hut as they drank. All three were silent, all waiting for something without knowing what until Paul's mother emerged grim in her dignity and, as all men could see, her beauty.

'Now he knows,' he said to the others. 'Now Big Swannie knows and my guess is he's slumped over that desk of his and the wall behind is running with whatever cold fluid does the work of blood in the Swann veins.'

'That'll be right,' said Deek.

'Oh, that'll be right all right.'

Eamon caught Mrs Eileen Williamson's eye as her hand grasped the handle of her car door.

'And Paul is at his work right on time, even if half dead and good for nowt. As I guessed he would be. As I knew.'

When Paul's mother took on his eye he raised his helmet in her direction and received a shy smile in return and at that moment Paul came out of his hut and saw both his mother and Eamon with their eyes locked and for him the world of men and women could never be quite the same again. Mrs Eileen Williamson in her hatchback bumped out of the site and on to the road and was gone and not before then did Eamon allow his helmet to return to his head.

'Did you stay long?' Deek asked.

'For some small measure of time.'

'Get anything?'

'Beyond a digestive biscuit do you mean?'

'Aye.'

Eamon made a great show of looking at his watch. 'Tea's over,' he said, 'back to work now. Honest toil never hurt no man.'

Mid afternoon, when the A9 traffic was lightest, they laid rubber mats on the road and tracked Conn's machine across with the police standing by. In the course of the day they moved the saw, the sleepers and all the appurtenances of tunnelling. Brian and Gerry slept in the caravan from 4:00pm to start digging at 10:00. In that time the others made the set up and Paul and Eamon marked the cofferdam wall.

Under a lowering night sky, with the temperature plummeting, the welder blew a hole in the cofferdam and found the ground was dry back there. He cut the piles as he had done on the downstream side and Conn lifted them clear. Brian was first at the Face, gunning the breaker and hitting the till. The going was harder this side but they made their one metre over the first twenty-four hours.

When Trevor asked him Paul moved back on to twelve-hour night shifts and it never occurred to him, not even then, what the strange happiness he felt could mean. College, home, old friends, these were other worlds he grew less attached to. He lived within the cofferdams and the tunnel and the diggers were his brothers. Eamon was what he supposed a father should be. They completed the ten metres in eleven days.

'Not bad,' Eamon said, 'but now the pipes, the concrete.'

They organised as before, same man, Mike, in the tunnel, same men on the mixer, but this time with Patsy clearing up. Eamon wanted it all quick now. Speed without haste, but speed. They had to be away as quick as they could when they were done.

'Away?' Paul asked.

'To Oxford,' Eamon told him.

Paul looked around the cofferdam, at the scaffolding, at the shovels. Why this hole inside?

Mike and Tony pummelled the drymix in around the last pipe at 3:00 in the afternoon and cleared the base of the cofferdam for the bricklayers. Paul watched them climb the scaffolding ladder, watched them with the grey clouds flying above them and ached with the knowledge of their soon parting. He turned to look at the pipe sticking out from the Face into the cofferdam and touched it and crouched on his hunkers and looked through.

The far end was a perfect circle that perspective had centred within the near end circle. Inside it was white and smooth. Between the two ends twenty-three pipe joints each made its concentric ring and the line of them was perfect. This was the only word, perfect. His own early seting-out and care, Eamon's precision with piano wires and eye, the troops' brute labour, all were justified by a perfection of line and joints that was built for the sole purpose of carrying human waste.

He went topsides and crossed the road to the compound, knocking on the Agent's door and entering as he had been instructed first thing. Swannie was sitting at the desk with Trevor busying himself at the filing cabinet looking very young and oppressed.

'In,' Swannie instructed.

'You wanted me?'

'I'm paying these guys off now. You might as well learn.'

'I'm learning.'

'I hope I didn't hear any kind of tone just now. Don't forget you're one of us, or at least you're shaping up so you might be.'

'Eamon . . .'

'I told you before. He's a thick mick.'

Swannie didn't look at Eamon when he eventually came in, not at first. He went on with his notes, forcing the head of the tunnel gang to stand in attentive silence. When he was ready he put his notes away and instructed the gang leader that he should sit.

Eamon sat opposite Swannie at the desk. Trevor leaned on the filing cabinet behind. Paul stood to the side, half way between the two and watched Swannie go into his brief case and take out a brown A4 envelope.

He opened it to Eamon Bowles to show it was stuffed with notes.

'Want to count?'

Eamon shook his head.

'You'll have to sign for it.'

'I'll do that.'

From a desk drawer Swannie took a sheet of paper and put it on the desk between them so Trevor and Paul could both see. He turned it round to Eamon and pushed it forward, holding the top down with one finger. Trevor placed a pen on the desk close by.

Paul looked on, understanding this tableau had been created at least partially for him.

Eamon looked down for a long moment before picking up the pen.

The paper had a title, Ness and Struie Drainage Project, and a sub-title, A9 Tunnel. It had a paragraph of words and below that a listing of the troops' names; Michael Clark, Brian Fairlie, Patrick Gallacher, Anthony MacMahon, Gerard O'Brien, Derek Watson. Below the names there was a blank space and then the words 'for the above and myself, Eamon Bowles'.

Eamon took the pen and put his hand to the paper. Both Swannie's hand and his own hand were on the paper. He turned his head as though he would somehow see the blank space more clearly that way and, with two sweeping strokes, there he placed his mark.

12

It's all about survival

Harry donned his hard hat and duffel coat to make the walk up the hill from Struie and over towards the works at Ness. This way he could look over the surface reinstatement, give the fence posts a shake and himself time to think.

Mostly the slope was holding and the flatter surface along the top, when he got there, was well nigh perfect. It hadn't gone totally to pot while he was in Newtonmore. This was what a driver such as Conn could achieve, a man who could roll an egg with the bucket of his excavator not so much as cracking the shell, who had the whole thing down to a fine art.

A spattering of rain rattled on his hard hat. He drew his collar up, walked quickly across the top and looked over. This was much, much worse. In the centre of the wayleave a stream had formed, running down to find the road drainage below and disappear in a whirling pool into a drainage chamber at the foot of the hill. Rain quickened topsoil, already turned to mud, dropped in from the side and was carried with it. Half the area's topsoil was already gone.

Allan Crawford was sitting on a boulder about half way down, leaning on his elbows. Descending cautiously because of his bad back and painful knees Harry made his way to join him. Left foot first, right to follow, always leading with the left.

'Yo ho!'

'Hoo!' Allan jumped to his feet. 'You startled me.'

'Thinking time? You can have too much of that.'

'Look at this,' Allan said.

At the side of the A9 the Roads Department had parked one of its cleansing wagons. Two men in bright yellow waterproofs stood holding the vehicle's hose, steadying it in the drainage chamber. Close by, Paul and Trevor were deep in discussion at the nearside cofferdam.

'The drains blocked again yesterday.' Allan nodded at the shifting topsoil. 'That's the third time since you've been away and it's getting worse.'

'Contractor's responsibility, not ours.'

'Think so? They say this angle of slope couldn't hold the soil, that it was bound to run. They say we should have allowed for this in the document and given them the chance to price.'

'The slope was there to see when they flaming well priced.'

'The Area Roads Engineer goes off like a gun every second day. He calls first of all Mr Swann then the Glasgow office. I get it here from both sides.' He pointed at his ear.

'Nothing is going to keep this material on the hill. It's too steep this side and it's too mixed. In addition, Healey's men made a pig's ear of it, as per prediction.'

'Roads send their bill to the Contractor and Trevor puts it on the monthly valuation with an additional service charge. I strike it off but it comes back. They're very insistent. Trevor says they have principle on their side.'

'Just keep striking it off.'

'Trevor says eventually some kind of compromise will be made. I suggested a 50/50 compromise but GR didn't like it. He says the Contract is a pure moral thing and absolute amounts don't come into it but he didn't like the idea of additional spend on the unforeseen.'

'This is how it's been since the beginning of time.'

'Since that big pyramid job in Egypt?

'And the Hanging Gardens before that.'

'What's to be said for this game, Harry? It's cold, miserable, rewards are low and stress is high. There's never enough money and no one wins.'

'It's all about survival,' said Harry. 'You love it or you don't.

Mac loved it, and I'd say he did his best, but he didn't survive. Look down.'

Below them the site was a hive. The Roads lorry stood beside the nearside tunnel chamber, now up to ground level with concrete rings, not bricks. The decision had been made while Harry was away.

The pipeline from Ness was almost complete. Another day would do it. Trots and Jinky had already started on the Collection Chamber. In Harry's absence Allan had agreed that concrete rings could be substituted for bricks. Trots and Jinky were building them ring on ring. A further week would do them, not only to construct but also to seal the chamber, surround it with concrete and cut away the tops of the piles.

Further towards the shore the Settlement Tank bases were complete and the joiners were working on the walls. JB and Tammas were labouring to them. Conn's crane stood unmanned beside the excavation. He would shift locations come the concrete pour. Paul stood by with his level, ready to give his marks and check levels when required.

'He's quieter since the tunnel closed,' said Allan. 'It's changed him. He even looks bigger. More filled out across the chest.'

'Paul also loves this game,' said Harry, 'although he maybe doesn't know it yet. He still thinks about things he might be doing elsewhere but he loves it. In time he'll travel with it. Take a nail's end to his skin and his blood will run thick with cement. I bet there's building in the genes, not that I'd ask, and the tunnel matured him. Now the game has him in its gut it won't let him flaming well go until it's done with him and farts him away.'

On the wall shutter Willie Quinn straightened and shouted across to Paul. From the hill they could not make out what was said but there was laughter in it.

'Look at that,' Allan said. 'It never stops. The weather is vile and the boredom is like a wall. We've already had a serious accident but these guys just get their heads down and get on.

They were laughing about who could eat the most pies the other day, with the rain whipping round them. I just don't get it.'

Harry understood that Allan just did not get it.

The mist that had blown in from the west, from the Atlantic, settled on the hill behind them and reached out towards the North Sea and the oil rigs. He drew his donkey jacket tighter about his neck.

'The days are drawing out,' he said. 'Don't think it will get any easier for that. The shifts will get longer and it's still freezing, still wet. I hear there's a new GF starting Monday.'

'Someone from the parent company in Leicester.'

'Flaming typical!'

Swannie's beamer turned off the road and into the compound. He got out and went into the Agent's hut without looking round.

'There's the man that wields the whip,' said Harry.'

'*Wields* the whip or *is* the whip?' Allan asked.

'Both.'

'The Lochdon contract is just about ready to go to tender. Look down, Harry. It isn't Strath Construction any more, not even a half way house. Mac and John Kelly are gone. Half of the staff joiners are already away; the rest can be laid off when James Swann chooses, or retained if they cut the mustard. We are looking at Syme Atwood now, pure and unadulterated. Swannie has reduced his overheads, increased output, and has the advantage of having this whole shebang in place. No one is better placed to win the next job.'

'It was always going to be that way.'

'Trevor tells me that Swannie is preparing a claim on the tunnel and will go to arbitration if he has to. Apparently he never loses.'

'Take it from me, GR never budges.'

'So, one of them must fail?'

'That's the nature of the game, Allan. Merciless with the lash, it's always on someone's back.'

13

That it should flow the way it does

Healey's men tumbled out of the van onto mud frozen overnight into ridges and curlicues that turned their ankles and cracked the stiffness of their joints. Cold air invaded their lungs and drew out moans and grumbles of unfocussed grievance. When they piled in to the hut, all eight, it was filled with steam from the urn. JB took off his glasses and wiped them on his pullover.

'Did I see Ikey dotting between the GF's hut and the Agent's? Hard to say when it's so dark. It might have been some animal. Shouldn't we be his first priority? The place is like a Turkish bath. What's he thinking about?' He turned the gas below the urn to a peep.

'Dunno,' said Tammas.

'Higher things most likely. I've told him reading will lead him astray but he doesn't listen. All he'll get is a lot of stupid ideas and disappointments.'

Scattered along the bench by the wall were copies of yesterday's Daily Record and Scottish Sun. There were no girlie pictures on the walls, religious Ikey made a point of removing them. JB hung his jacket in a corner and took the four stained mugs of the concrete gang and made tea. All took sugar spooned from the open bag, none milk. The first he gave to Tammas at the door opening.

'Mug for a mug,' he said. 'Must be a mug to be here.'

'You're telling me?'

Two cars drew up outside and one after the other dimmed their lights.

'Paul and the new GF,' said Tammas. 'What's his name?'

'Lammerton,' JB informed him, 'who hails Bolton. Bloont nawthnah, an old hand from the new firm. Notice the pattern? Our esteemed Mr Swann is replacing the former regime in instalments. Even we, *we*, shall I say Highlanders, are employed by his favourite Healey from darkest Glasgow. How easy we make his life. He can pick us up and put us down as he pleases, and does. Mac out in favour of young Sharp, defingered John Kelly gone and this eeh-bah-goom now in his place. Staff joiners sickened off and dispersed. The more paranoid nationalists will see Scots out, Angles in, but as Trots here will remind us it's really about social class. Isn't that right, Trots?'

'Shut up, JB.'

'Trots, this is an afterlife and you're part of my punishment.'

'I'll get our stuff from the drying hut,' Tammas said, meaning his own and JB's working clothes. Trots and Jinkie could get their own.

Only Tammas could stand JB's prosing. The other two worked in an atmosphere of silent reluctance they preferred left undisturbed. Tammas had his one talent to draw on: he could turn his concentration off when he chose. Not that it went on very powerfully, as he himself knew. From the drying hut he brought their two pairs of jeans, their socks and boots, their donkey jackets.

'How it rained yesterday,' JB reminded them, 'and how quickly we forget its awfulness. A miracle of the human condition; survival characteristic, I expect. Hunter-gatherers hunting and gathering across the veldt all those eons ago couldn't have continued otherwise. They would have sat down and died for preference, if they'd known today was destined to be much like yesterday and tomorrow would bring more of the same. But they were preparing the way for us, weren't they. They were conditioning the species to boredom and toil. What's this, Tammas? Flat pack togs for the workers?'

Tammas threw their jackets across the bench and held JB's

jeans out for him, caked with dried mud and stiff, icily stiff. He put boots and socks down by the bench and held the jeans in one hand. They were wooden and rigid, without sag.

'Flat as a witch's tit,' he said.

'You have a way with words. Sometimes you take even me by surprise.' JB at the door broke the hardness and scrunched them between his hands, watching as slabs of mud fell to the ground. He took off his trousers to reveal thin white legs, not strong, and stepped inside the jeans making an ostentatious '*ich*' sound. The others did the same but in silence.

JB sat on the bench beside Tammas to pull on socks and boots.

'Look outside,' he said.

Slowly the sun rose over the horizon to spread a pale wash of light across the surface of the North Sea, casting long fingers of shadow from the oil rigs and beginning its softening of the site's frozen mud.

'What?'

'Today will be less bad,' JB said, mostly to himself. 'We will come through. And who is this as if we didn't know, yo ho, but Swannie's pets?'

The grip squad, the only remaining joiners, drew up in Willie Quinn's car. From the boot they took boots that were cleaned and polished, and their tools. They put on leather aprons and made their way down to the settlement tanks.

Tammas was thoughtful.

'I think I know how they do it,' he said at last. 'They've got two pairs of boots each. They're not even company boots. They can afford their own. That's how much they make. *Two* pairs of their *own*.'

JB and Trots looked at him. This had gone in at last?

'Yes,' said JB. 'The joiners are better off than the labourers.'

'Their wives must clean them for them. Through the day I mean. The boots left at home that day I mean.'

'No way,' said Trots. 'Know what date it is?'

'Maybe though,' said JB wistfully, 'the *anno domini* and the fashionable ideas of the day can be overleapt by simple caring. Maybe that's what it means not to be alone. Yes, I think I remember.'

Lammerton, the new GF, thumped on the wall of the hut with the side of his meaty fist.

'A-aht,' he called. 'Pouring cawrncrete today.'

'What's he saying?' Tammas asked.

'I think he's telling us it's time to start,' JB said.

They put on safety helmets and protective gloves, and made their way down to the settlement tanks. Derek the steelfixer and his boy, also just arrived, were ahead of them. The other four labourers walked off to the pipe trench between the Ness septic tank and the cofferdam.

The two circular tanks were arranged side by side within a single excavation. The first, complete to base and walls, was ready for the plant contractor to fit scum boards and scrapers. The second base was complete, its wall arcing round only quarter of the tank circumference. That first wall pour was now a week past and the concrete surface had long since lost its green. The second pour had been twice delayed, once because the ancient batching plant had broken down, the second time because the fastidious Clerk of Works, newly returned to site, had something to prove. Derek had enough work to keep him going with the remaining wall steel but would not brook delay without extra payment and delay there would be if the second pour did not happen this day. Swannie, they knew, was trampling Trevor Sharp underfoot in his mania for progress.

The steel shutter was expensive but quick to assemble and not subject to damage from the concrete skip or the vibrating pokers. The investment, Paul had told them, Swannie had placed against the following contracts he intended to win along this coast. All the joiners had to do the day after a pour, was crack it free and run it along the rails. The rest was centring and levelling and procedural and so no problem to the grip squad and Paul with the teamwork they had developed. Now it was clamped against the first pour and shuttered at the leading end.

Cunning Swannie would win those other Contracts all right and the grip boys would be on them, JB thought to himself. He and Tammas could be easily replaced and, yes, likely would.

The labourers stood on the lip of the excavation looking down on the joiners blowing their hands and jogging on the spot. The scaffolding was already in place around the shutter for them to work from, erected yesterday when the pour should have happened and would have but for the geriatric batcher. Scaffolding poles for handrails; it was crude.

Lammerton appeared beside them.

'Raht, you lot. Dahn ole wiv pinch bars. Git them straps aht!'

The four of them ran down the slope and picked the heavy bars up from where they had lain against the wall. The base had four expansion joints built in, straps of wood cast to make space for bituminous sealant. That soft, black stuff Tammas called it and it was a full description.

They had to pinch out the straps and set to doing so while the joiners checked the shutter position again and Paul once again checked his levels. At 9:15 they heard the Clerk of Works' van pull up in the compound. If Harry found no fault, they would pour.

'It's all spoteroonie,' Paul called out.

The crane was already rigged with chains and concrete skip, ready to work. Conn looked down from his cabin in resigned silence, looked up to the compound and out across the North Sea.

'And it's spoteroonie off the centre nail,' said Jimmy Gillies.

'And the bolts are all tight and the props rock solid,' said Willie Quinn.

Derek turned from the wall steel he was tying ahead of the pour.

'Perfectos? Harry won't like that either. He'll want to find something so you'll know who the boss is.'

He took a twenty pack from his breast pocket and lit the last one. From the base he picked up a loose piece of aggregate and popped it in the packet to give it weight and tossed it up to Cammy on the wall head.

'Drop it inside. Give him something to find.'

Cammy dropped it inside and they waited.

'Aye, right,' Harry scowled from the top of the slope. 'Everything in place?'

'It is,' Lammerton told him.

'Everything still clean?'

'It is.'

'Okay, I saw it all yesterday. Just get on.'

He turned on his heel and left.

Cammy eased the stop end shutter loose and took out Derek's fag packet and dropped it outside the base. 'The thought was good,' he said.

The troops worked away at the straps in silence, knowing the next command was imminent.

'Raht, you lot,' Lammerton shouted. 'Let's get ahn. JB! Mix boocket graht and pour it dahn on kicker. I'll get on batcher.'

The troops climbed topside again and Trots and Jinkie dragged the concrete pokers across the platform looping their air hoses over the edge. Tammas fired up the compressor and Jinkie stepped into the stream of air that blew from the engine's cooling fan.

'Feel that, boys? Hot air.'

'We've got JB for that,' said Trots.

'Ho ho,' said JB, banging a shovel across the side of the skip, knocking loose concrete lumps off both. 'Start now, finish the pour by 11:00. Tea while the grip squad and Paul do their checks. Then we,' he looked at Tammas, 'finish off the wall head. Easy day if the weather keeps up. Grout, Lammerton asked for. *Gra-aht*, as Lammerton has it, meaning a thin mortar to facilitate bond between the hard concrete and the soft, wet stuff. That right, Paul?'

'Plastic. While it flows it's said to be plastic.'

'Meaning it doesn't snap back into shape. Paul knows these things. That's education for you. I'll get it.'

At the compound he put a shovel of cement and two of sand into a bucket and mixed in enough water to make a thin gruel to pour inside the shutter on to the receiving horizontal face. He swirled it in the bucket and listened.

The batcher broke down as soon as Lammerton fired it. Up went the revs and then it coughed and died. JB pursed his lips and back at the tank Trots and Jinkie cursed the day. Derek went on tying steel, mentally working out when he would be properly delayed and could start his claim time.

'Defer the grout,' JB said to himself, 'back to the straps.'

'What now?' Cammy asked at the shutter.

'Tea for us,' said Jimmy Gillies. 'If it's fixed for 2:00pm we might start and finish while it's still light. Three delays in a row because Swannie won't hire in decent plant. I'll put in a time claim.'

The concrete gang descended once again to the tank base and went back to prying out straps. The grip squad went back to their car. Derek and his boy kept on tying.

'We're idling,' JB said to Tammas. 'As with a finely tuned machine just turning over it can only go on so long.'

'That right, JB?'

JB pushed a lump of concrete against the pinch bar with his foot, used it for a lever. The strap splintered. He dug the bar in again and again it splintered.

'More crap. This simple job,' he said, 'is going to take forever.'

'Ahv'n trooble?'

Lammerton appeared from nowhere. He was taller than JB and wider in the shoulder. Across the tank base Trots smirked momentarily. He knew the score. The new GF would have to prove himself. Tammas was too easy a target and JB had to be a black sheep because of the way he spoke, because there was some part of him that was undiminished in spite of everything and it sounded like pride heading for a fall.

'No trouble Mister Lammerton. I'm just pinching away, pinching away.'

JB pushed the concrete lump against the bar again and again the strap splintered.

'Ah expect yih'll ahv advice to offer Mister Swann abaht materials.'

'Mister Swann rarely consults me. When he does I give such guidance as I can as honestly as I can.'

'Yir talk funny, don't yir.'

'I do indeed.'

'Yir doan't lahk me, do yir? I know your tahp. Yir doan't lahk me cause ahm English.'

JB looked down on the pinch bar where it met the strap.

'Now let me see,' he said. 'I don't mind you being English any more than I would mind you being French or German or for that matter black as a lump of coal, and that's something you couldn't say. Right?'

'Wot?'

'I'll try again. I don't mind you being English but I'm not keen on the way you put on the accent when you're talking to us. You're making a point Mister Lammerton. You're telling us you're different and keeping yourself apart and in a funny kind of way you're making yourself superior. I bet you don't speak that way at home. I bet you don't speak that way to people who don't have to defer to you.'

'Yir wot?' Lammerton's hands came out of his pockets, fists clenched. 'You saying Ah'm putting it on? You can talk abaht putting it on? The way yir speak? Think Ah doan't know why yir ere.'

'Making a living.' JB weighed the heavy bar in his hands. 'That's why I'm here. I'm getting by, and there are worse jobs. It's less boring than most. I like the people, usually. Fascinating discussion on all kinds of interesting topics, you should hear Trots on the late Princess Diana.'

'Careful JB.' Forgotten Tammas was standing nearby, Trots and Jinkie glancing warily from the other side of the tank base.

'You lahk this work?'

'Hard labour and I were made for each other but I admire also the organisation and foresight the likes of Mister Swann and yourself demonstrate day by day. How do you do it?'

'You're being sarcastic.'

'Bought the next job yet?'

'*Bought* it? Think you'll be on it?'

'Now I had no difficulty understanding that,' said JB. 'You can do it if you try.'

He pushed the pinch bar under the strap and prised it upwards and again the strap splintered.

The fitter didn't appear until 2:00pm and it took him an hour to get the batcher working. Trevor called the troops back into their own hut.

'Swannie's breathing fire,' he told them. 'We're going ahead right now.'

'We'll finish in darkness,' said Trots. 'It'll mean overtime.'

'You'll get paid. When the pour is done Conn will drive you all back to Inverness as per usual. JB and Tammas can stay on and finish the top surfaces.'

'In the dark, and how do we get back?'

JB as usual asked the questions, Tammas being an accepting sort. Trots and Jinkie were diplomatically silent.

'Paul will stay on. He'll sit in Conn's cab and shine the headlight down.'

'The headlight? The one headlight?'

'That'll be enough. Then he'll drive you back.'

'Lets start,' said Lammerton. 'I'll get the batcher going. Jinkie can help me. Trots!'

'Yo ho.'

'You drive the dumper.'

Back at the settlement tank JB and Tammas stood by the crane, ready to step across the gangway on to the steel shutter. Conn sat in his cab smoking. Chains hung from the jib to the elbow shaped concrete skip resting on the ground in front of his machine. From his high position he could see Trots driving down from the batcher, the dumper bouncing from side to side and the first batch of concrete swilling about.

'Bloody dangerous machines,' he mouthed.

Trots parked the dumper by the crane and hauled back on the tipping handle. The dumper skip lifted and concrete poured into the concrete skip. JB and Tammas held the backs of their shovels at the edge, directing the sides of the flow, preventing spillage as best they could. They stepped on to the shutter and when Conn had swung the skip across JB steadied it with his shoulder, grabbed the handle and opened the chute.

Wet concrete, plastic, flowed downwards into the shutter opening. He pushed the handle down again and cut off the flow. Tammas banged the poker against the side of the shutter and it started up with a high-pitched whine. He dropped it into the shutter and saw the concrete slump downwards, watched while air bubbles rose to the surface and a thick grey cream formed on top. JB opened the skip again and let the rest of the load flow out. 'Beautiful in its way,' he said. 'Right down to the bottom with the poker, Tammas, we don't want honeycombing at the joint.'

Tammas let the hose run through his hand until the poker met the hard. Another moment and he drew it out to drop it again further along. By now Trots was coming back with the second load and when that was in they got both pokers going.

They worked through what was left of the afternoon and into the dark, watching the sun pass low in the sky to eventually disappear behind the hill. It might have been descending into Struie and on to the RE's hut for all they could tell. The temperature plummeted and Paul went back to his hut for a second pullover. At these times he was worst off of them all since he had to stand by his level and couldn't move and burn energy and so be warm. They all knew this, although they also knew he had a future or at least the possibility of one.

When the shutter was full and the concrete vibrated into place with all the trapped air freed and the smell of cement everywhere Jimmy Gillies and Paul checked the shutter's line

and level by torchlight. Willie and Cammy made the few
necessary adjustments to the props and were finished. Trots
and Jinkie also were finished. Conn left the keys of his cab with
Paul and drove them away and then Paul and JB and Tammas
were alone. The compressor was off and Conn's machine
barely turning over for the sake of the light although the moon
was out for once, and stars so bright they could almost have
done the job under natural light alone.

JB had brought the trowels and floats down in two buckets.
Their job now was to level the concrete top of the wall and
make it smooth and finished to Class C as Harry the Clerk of
Works would agree conformed to spec. They had to use the
metal trowel to dig away the excess concrete and make the first
surface, then the wooden float to bring up the cream and then
the metal float to smooth and polish.

JB and Tammas got down on their hands and knees while
Paul looked on, digging and flicking with the trowels making
thik and *tuk* and *tch* noises and not speaking to each other until
they were properly going. The night air was still and there were
no other sounds but occasional passing traffic on the road and
the sounds of the shore below, waves on the shingle, oyster-
catchers, a curlew.

The two of them worked their way along the wall head
taking the concrete level down, chapping it with the trowel
edges to leave it like a ploughed field viewed from the air and,
when they were done, taking the wooden floats and starting
again, pushing the wooden plaque down flat on the wet surface, using the natural suction to draw up the mortar, sand and
water mix, the cream.

'How long you gonna be?' Paul asked.

'About an hour,' JB told him from his knees. 'Hear that,
Tammas? The lad wants home. Must have a home to go to.'

'Same as me, JB. I've got a home as well.'

JB straightened up and rubbed at his back.

'Just me, is it? I guess.'

He went back to pushing the float down and pulling it up

again and now the air was filled with *shloop* and *thup* noises. Paul looked down on the two backs lifting and falling, the shoulders and arms working.

'Why'd you rub the new GF the wrong way,' Paul asked.

'Lammerton? What's he trying to prove?'

'John Kelly thought you could be a ganger. Maybe even a GF. Mac had his eye on you.'

'Before he got whacked? Not much of a reference.'

'He said you see further than most. Sometimes, he said, further than John Kelly.'

'That would be difficult?'

'Nothing wrong with John. He's a good guy. Good to me. I don't like to speak about him after what happened.'

'Wake up, Paul. He broke every health and safety rule in the book. Worse than that, he showed no common sense. He was pressing on the way they do in this game. He took risk to keep Mac in with Swannie and now he's lost three fingers and won't be back and Mac is off the site and as good as down the road. And Swannie's still king of the castle.'

'You see further than most. Mac thought you could have been Agent if things had been different.'

'That what you want to be, Paul, a site agent?'

'I guess.'

The two labourers were getting to the end of the wall head again but it was the last phase of finishing that would take the longest. The steel float made the final surface that had to be right and correct and absolutely level because this surface would be forever.

'Feel the heat in the concrete, Tammas,' JB said. 'Lammerton's put in too much cement and it's going off too quick. We'll need to finish and get it covered. Don't want the frost to get in.'

'We'll do that.'

They got to their feet and dropped the wooden floats into the buckets and got back on their knees and went at the wall head again with the steel floats. Now the noise they made was *swoosh* and *swoosh* as they made circular motions across the concrete surface, leaving it smooth and dead level between the two sides of the shutter. Tammas led from right to left making the first smooth surface and JB followed making the finish.

'You going for a pint in Inverness, JB?'

'Need it after this, Tammas.'

'I wanted to ask you,' Paul said. 'Your name is George King. I saw it on the wages list.'

'That is correcto.'

'So, how come you're called JB?'

'Trots called me that when he found out. It stuck. It's okay. It's part of my afterlife. I accept. Tell him what it stands for, Tammas.'

'You sure?'

'Go ahead.'

'It stands for Jail Bird,' said Tammas.

The two men had their heads down and their faces could not be seen.

'Jail,' JB repeated. 'Bird.'

Into the silence of the waves and the birds Paul said that he was sorry.

'Tell him what I did, Tammas.'

Swoosh.

'Sure?'

'The more often it's out the sooner it's over. The punishment I mean.'

Swoosh.

'He was an accountant. He dipped the till.'

'In a manner of speaking. Not so literally. I did it once and did it again and got into the habit. I learned to spread my bets. Moving money around from client to client I stayed ahead of the game for a couple years. That's it, Paul. It's dead simple. Listen, Paul, I'm on my knees here. I'm confessing again. I can't do enough confessing.'

Once again into the silence of the waves and the birds Paul said that he was sorry.

'But he's rising again,' Tammas said, 'and when he does that wife and kids is going to come back. That's what you want, isn't it?'

'Don't stop floating, Tammas. Don't slow down. Keep smoothing this thing over. Don't let it go off on us.'

'And he's going to get out of that rented flat and into his own place.'

'That slum,' JB said.

'When some kind of opportunity comes up he's going to take it with both hands.'

'The punishment doesn't finish when you come out,' JB said over his shoulder. 'It goes on in the names people call you and in the way they don't trust you any more.'

'I trust you, JB,' Tammas said. 'You're going to get on again and I'm going to come with you. You'll take me with you, won't you?'

'I will.'

'You'll be rich again and I'll drive your car and make your coffee or whatever you want.'

'That's right, Tammas. We'll live the life of Reilly or whoever it is. Not the life of Kelly. Ho ho. Or will we? Don't even think it.'

Swoosh.

'Yet I never saw myself as rich. No sir, not even as well off.'

The floats swept across the wall head. The shoulders worked from side to side but it was easier now.

'They teach you about this stuff in the college? Meaning concrete.'

'They teach the chemistry of it and the differences in the mixes and all that.'

'You'll need that qualification to be an agent I guess?'

'Some people make it without.'

'Not many. Most have a degree, don't they? What you need is first to get that qualification and then get yourself to University and get that degree. That's what you need to be like Mac and Swannie. Yes?'

'I guess.'

'You'll find your way. You've still got time.'

Swoosh.

Tammas came to the end of the wall head and stood up and dropped his steel float into the bucket.

'I think about this stuff sometimes,' JB said. 'Concrete I mean. It's a kind of miracle that it should flow the way it does, then go off and harden and be unchangeable short of the breaker. When we make these walls we make something that goes into geological time. When we bury it it's in the ground for ever.'

He made one last swipe along the wall head and rose to his feet. He dropped the steel float into its bucket and together, all three of them, they hauled the tarpaulin over the shutter to hold in the heat and to protect the top surface against a change in the weather and made their way back to the compound, to Paul's car and the long road home, eventually the pub.

14

The first flower of spring

Outside the window of the Resident Engineer's new and well appointed hut, across the road in the verge, there bloomed a solitary harebell, the first of spring. Its blue head bowed by the wind, it shuddered in the slipstream of the site traffic and the traffic from the village of Struie as they passed. Allan Crawford placed his hands on the two sides of the window and leaned towards the glass to stare at the tiny perfect bell and the slender shepherd's crook stem from which it depended.

Harry was at the Struie Pumping Station excavation just a few metres to his left, looking down on Trots and Jinkie. Just out of sight he could enter the hut at any time. The grizzled oldster made him feel like a rookie without hope, a pale shadow unfit to shine the boots of the great Sir Graham Russell, the Almighty GR. At this moment Harry was the last man he wanted to appear.

An hour earlier he had been putting the finishing touches to his monthly report when Trevor arrived with the latest valuation and dropped it on his desk. As usual he had turned to the last page first. His short experience had taught him the bullet list of variations would always hold some surprise. This month it was staggering. Every penny of cost for the tunnel had been included on top of the excavation figures. He flicked forward into the text and read the Contractor's case for his claim and saw that his earlier work in making up the document, his office work, had been at fault.

Putting the sheaf of papers down he noted his hand begin to tremble as Mac's hand had trembled in the days before he was banished from the site, soon to depart the company and recently, if rumour was correct, the country. Reading from the screen of his laptop he amended the facts and figures he would send through to Vernon Street and that Vernon would pass to GR.

He extracted from Harry's notes and, where appropriate, quoted from the Contractor's letters. Adding a few comments of his own he realised he had nothing much to add unless it was an apology. Responsibility would rest with him and very likely he would soon follow Mac down the road.

He scrolled back the report to headline with the essential figures and the essential fact. The Contract would be complete well ahead of programme but it was going to cost a lot more than the Client had budgeted for. The final valuation was going to go through the roof. The great wheels of circumstance and human error was about to run over the first flower of his career. He returned to his desk and attached the report to an email, crossed his fingers and pressed the send/receive. It was 11.00am.

At 2.00pm he received a reply from Vernon. Brace yourself, it said, the Thunder God cometh.

15

Merciless with the lash

'Our whole focus is on the tanks now.'

Harry listened to Trevor, a man fully ten years younger than his own son, who might have been his grandson but for West Africa. In the confidence of his youth he had gone there to line his pockets as he could not do at home, and no ambition to change the world but in the hinterland a young engineer entered his life.

They met in a portakabin much like Allan's at Struie, Graham Russell's blue eyes piercing his own across a desk covered in charts and sketches and sheaves of calculations, his plans for stabilising the sliding face of a deforested mountain. After, that is, the big excavators had cut the worst areas into shelves and the injecting plant had been trucked through the jungle. Mister Russell had refused all bribes and driven the works along the received wisdom of the only Bible either of them recognised, the Contract, and when the job was done had earned the right to be recognised simply by his initials, GR.

His beautiful wife, Diane, had been a second heart beating beside GR's own, another mind that detailed and organised what his own had no space to entertain. All those they met, the tribal leaders, the government officials and all of their women, fell into love or respect or both and she held them in the palm of her hand. Harry knew the liar that time makes of memory, but she was an impossible goddess in his own, and he was still more than half in love.

'Allan tells me he's coming,' Harry said.

'I said our whole focus is on the tanks now. We have to get

them closed and lined before the Plant Contractor arrives. They're contracted to take three weeks and we have to be ready.'

'You're nowhere near ready.'

'James has already asked them to delay for a week. No can do. He's asked them to start at the near tank. Again it's no can do. They say they'll be falling over themselves. They say a contract is a contract.'

'Swannie won't like being told what a contract is.'

'What it means is that we have to get the gas pedal down.

'GR says haste is the enemy of quality.'

'Whatever checks and tests you want you'll get, but we have to get on, Harry. Merciless with the lash, as you never tire of saying.'

'You think Alan Lammerton is up to it?'

'James has already shot a rocket up poor Mr Lammerton.'

'JB would do the job better. You could promote him?'

'Too soon, James thinks. You were saying something else?'

Harry took his camera from the pocket of his duffel coat and tugged the skip of his safety helmet down against a smir of rain.

'I said Sir Graham will be visiting soon. I got it from Allan who got it from on high. The valuation has shot through the roof thanks to the tunnel. I think GR and your Mister James Swann will be having a little confrontation and I wouldn't want to be in Swannie's boots. Now I have to inspect Derek's steel work ahead of the next pour. I'll take some pictures while I'm at it.'

With two further pours required to close the circle of Tank Two the grip squad were working into every night. Trots and Jinkie had already moved the lights and were filling the generator with diesel when Harry arrived with his camera. As the sun dropped behind the hills Jinkie turned the starter handle and the machine coughed and shuddered and the lights flickered on, off and on again. Willie Quinn stood on the wall head.

'Oh wow,' he said. 'That's bright. Reminds me of when Apollo Eleven took off.'

Only Cammy took the bait. 'You were at Cape Kennedy?'

'They asked me to stand by in case the scaffolding bolts needed an extra turn.'

'Shoosh,' said Jimmy Gillies below, impatient, tossing up a spacer to fit between the shutters. 'Get these in and we'll tighten this lot. Jinkie!'

'Yo!'

'Go tell Paul we'll want a level in half an hour – no, say twenty minutes.'

'Ho!'

'Cammy, hold this nut steady with the spanner while I turn the bolt.'

'Okay,' said Cammy whose thoughts, as ever, roamed elsewhere.

'Trots!'

Trots looked over the top of the generator. 'What?'

'Bring the props across.'

Trots dropped into the tank and wandered slowly to the far side. He took one of the heavy props on his shoulder, carried it across the concrete base and dropped it at Jimmy's feet.

'Not there,' said Jimmy. 'There.'

Trots dragged the prop to the other end of the formwork.

'And the rest,' said Jimmy. 'There's another seven.'

'Out in the open air like this,' said Willie, inhaling noisily, 'it's good for your health. The sea breeze! The ozone! The sting of the lash across your back! Why, it's better than a wank with a velvet glove.'

He pointed at the horizon with his hammer. 'Look at this vast expanse of water and how the light flickers on the waves. Why, it's finer than the view from the top of the Sydney Opera House when I drove in the last nail. This is the best job I've ever been on, I reckon.'

Trots grumbled from the tank floor.

'And you know they pay us to be here.' Willie shook his head and dropped to his knees to push a spacer between the two shutters. 'They must be mad.'

Derek's steel tying was a full shutter length ahead of the pour, closing the circle. Harry checked each bar and each bar's centre spacing from the drawing. He noted they would have to be brushed free of rust before the shutters were moved and, looking over his shoulder, peered between the shutters that were going up now. Yes, those bars had been brushed. He looked down at his feet and noted that the concrete surface that would take the new wall had still to be scabbled and made rough.

He made some notes in his book and took out his camera and made sure the date and time were switched on for the site records. He stood back and snapped the steelwork, snapped the props being nailed in place and the formwork as it was tightened. For his personal collection he turned date and time off and snapped the men as they worked.

'What's your best job, Trots?' Willie asked.

'The first after the People take control,' Trots said. 'It's the profit motive that takes the cream out of the job. If the government did it all there'd be no profit motive which is to say no profit margin which is to say it would cost less. There'd be no heat to finish and no sackings. You should think more.'

'And no work done at all,' Jimmy Gillies interrupted.

Trots glowered at him. 'Anybody here know if they'll be on the job after tomorrow? No! We shouldn't have to burst our guts this way. Everyone should have what they need without this, this,' Trots struggled for the right word, 'this indignity.'

Harry snapped Jimmy as the corners of his mouth turned down.

'What's the best job you've been on, Harry?' Willie asked. 'Was it that big pyramid job in Egypt?'

'If he'd been on that,' said Jimmy, 'your feet wouldn't have touched the ground.'

Harry placed his hand on the vertical mat of steel bars and

took some of the weight off his sore back. Best job I was ever on? That's easy, he thought.

It was West Africa where the tropical moon was huge and bright red when it touched the ocean, unforgettable. The sun with strands of cloud stretched across its face. He remembered a young engineer standing against corruption and serving the people, yes Trots' People although illiterate and their skin the colour of washed coal, by making Holy Writ of the contract, an unswerving devotion to the detailed and signed agreement as the only acceptable definition of truth and what is right and, ultimately, goodness. He remembered GR bringing a few young blacks on by pointing at the drawings and pointing at the land and watching them get the ideas in place. He remembered their women carrying machinery in baskets on their heads, rough overland journeys in a bouncing Land Rover, gin and tonic nights in the forest and the sadness of parting.

'No particular job,' he said. 'They're all the same. It gets to be your life.'

They agreed that Harry would do his final inspection first thing in the morning, 7:30am. This meant the grip squad and Paul must be out earlier still to turn on the generator and make any final adjustments. Healey's men could make their usual start and the pour could begin around 9:00am.

Harry felt himself relax. His working day was done. Or at least, the day of beck and call was over although he still had his own work. He pocketed the camera and his notes and drove back to his caravan at the Struie caravan site.

The season being early he had the place to himself but for a few permanent units that stood empty. The contract covered the cost of the owner putting electricity on and making the toilet block available. He entered the site in darkness with the rain falling more heavily. He locked the van for the night and climbed inside, the caravan tilting as he entered. There was very little space, just a bunk, a microwave, a kettle, a table, a built-in wardrobe, a small television, no decoration. On a shelf by the bed were the three books that travelled with him everywhere, The Ragged-Trousered Philanthropists, Children of the Dead End, The Complete Poems and Songs of Robert Burns, all three broken backed and dog-eared.

Home, he thought, putting his mobile phone on charge and taking off his donkey jacket. The jacket was dry enough to go in the wardrobe. No need for the site's drying room tonight. Not a great place, he thought, but warm and dry and his own and better than his real home. Three more years at most and he would retire. They would have to come to terms with that, he and Alice.

Could they face it? Could they face each other in the mornings?

He took off his boiler suit and shirt, put on a pair of cords and a cotton shirt. He rubbed at the bristle on his chin remembering that he hadn't shaved this morning, usual reason.

The phone pinged as he opened a tin of soup. A text had arrived from his son. He should call when he could.

He heated the soup in the microwave and ate it watching the News. He dumped a tin of stew into the same bowl and heated it as well and, when he was finished eating, rinsed the bowl and put it away and put the kettle on. The secret of his housekeeping was to stay on top of it, one bowl, one spoon, one fork, one cup, all clean and in their places all the time. The kettle boiled he made tea.

From beneath the bunk he took his laptop that the company had supplied and connected it to a small printer he kept filled with photographic paper. He connected the camera and downloaded the day's pictures, separating those he wanted for the official site record and those he wanted for his own. One by one he printed them out and then put the laptop away again. He had no other use for it. His notes he wrote out by hand. He did not do emails or internet. The one great thing the laptop did for him was make his pictures.

From a shelf above the bunk he took down two albums. The first was titled in his own block capitals, 'Ness and Struie – Progress'. This was the official record of the contract. The second was titled, 'Ness and Struie – History'. This was for himself and it focussed on the men and their methods, and the machines they used. He had albums like it for every job he had worked on since his apprenticeship ended. Jobs he had served as a working builder, as a trade foreman, a general foreman, as a clerk of works. There were albums from Highland Scotland, the Central Belt, all over England and Wales, and West Africa.

Painstakingly, almost lovingly, he fixed the pictures of the troops in place and titled them. When his working life was done it would be a record not only of achievement but of changing faces and working methods and machinery. Most of all though, it would be people, some repeating the same old patterns of grievance and greed, some unrepeatable, inimitable, unique personalities and unforgettable. Some were sloppy useless tossers like John Kelly, others were craftsmen, Harry's highest accolade for the working man. A few were thinkers.

The phone rang. Harry picked it up and lay back on his bunk.

'Dad?'

'Peter.'

'You're in the caravan?'

'Yes.'

'I can see you there, leaning on the table, reading one of your books.'

'No, I'm lying on the bed waiting for whatever is coming next. Is it the usual?'

'You could be kinder, Dad.'

'I'd say I'm kind enough. How are the kids?'

'Okay, as far as I can tell. Karen still uses them against me. She pages me at awkward times, demands I call when she knows I've something on. She arranges visits so they're difficult. She's a bitch, Dad. She's just a bitch.'

'Don't call her names. I've told you before, you'll get used to it and blurt one of them out when it can do you damage. Don't mess up now. Eventually the divorce will come through and it will settle.'

His son had not called for advice.

'I've told you I'm parting with no more money.'

'I'm in need, Dad. Rent.'

'Horse still running? Okay. Okay. What does your mother say?'

'That I should call you. She says I'm your son too.'

And her husband, Harry reflected. She's not stupid. She knows I'll be home for good soon. She knows we'll have to settle. She's testing her power. Everything she does is clandestine. Everything has another purpose. She's never understood how she doesn't measure up, couldn't.

A wee, home-bound Glasgow lassie she had come into his life when he needed stability. Five years after the goodbyes at Kano Airport his head had still been in a West African forest. He had needed to bring his feet back down onto solid ground and she had appeared and was just what he thought he needed. Except that, now, on his own in Struie Caravan Park, he understood what he really needed back then was a return flight to Lagos and then on.

Although the Russells were home by then as well.

'How much this time?'

Peter told him.

'It's a month's rent, Dad. Buy me that time and I'll find a job.'

'You won't put it on a horse?'

'No.'

'Or any part of it?'

'Definitely not.'

'Straight and narrow?'

'Straight and narrow.'

'Peter, is there anyone else in your life?'

'There was a long silence.

'Peter?'

'Yes, there is.'

'Does Karen know?'

'Maybe she guesses.'

'When the dust settles, can you move in with her?'

'We're not sure yet. The dust has to settle first.'

'Okay, I understand. Meantime it's a secret. Does your mother know?'

Of course Alice knew. Why did he ask? She was in control, or seeking control, of everything in her small world.

As long as other people are in your life freedom is a myth. There was no end to it this side of the grave. Responsibility. Sympathy. Money. Peter thought his Dad wouldn't approve of divorce. He didn't realise Harry's lifestyle was a form of separation for those who want it that way. He and Alice couldn't have formally divorced any more than their parents could. The mistake was in marrying in the first place, but it wasn't a mistake that was all that unusual. Or to understand what and who had been right for him long after the opportunity was gone. He and Alice were locked in an unsatisfactory relationship that wasn't *that* bad.

Situation normal, Harry thought, for half the world.

Peter and Karen could divorce though. Different times prevailed and Harry was glad of it. There was every chance their boys would never marry. They could learn their trade and be lone wolves prowling the world. Make babies wherever they went, and leave them because moving on was the working man's lot.

A gust of wind rattled hail like pebbles against the caravan wall.

Harry drew a curtain back and looked out. There was no light above, cloud cover was a solid black mass. The trees that had been planted by the toilet block were bending in the wind. There was no sign of any let up and he was still unwashed. He put on an anorak and shrugged the hood over his head, tucked his toilet bag under his arm and, when he was out of the caravan, ran for it.

The door to the toilet block battered shut behind him. Inside he stripped and showered and towelled off quickly against the cold and turned to the mirror. He rubbed his hand round and across his chin and squeezed shaving gel onto his fingers and smeared it across his cheeks, working it round and round until it turned into a meagre foam.

He held his hand under the running tap until the gel was gone. When the running water was unbearably hot he scalded his razor and ran it across his cheek, feeling the bristles cut easily and leaving a clean line of pink across the blue white of the foam. He looked at his body in the mirror, its grey hair and distended belly. The skin on his upper arms was slack and loose where once, not so long ago, the muscle mass inside had stretched it tight. Finishing the shave he washed his face, rinsed the razor and put it away.

As he buttoned his shirt he looked at his face. Steady, solitary drinking through the years had turned his nose into a bulb. It looked like you could grow a tulip out of it.

Oh, he could joke with himself, but you have to.

His forehead was seamed and his cheeks were jowly and under his left eye was a flat patch that hung limp where the tiny muscles had given up. He put his hand to it tenderly, as though it gave him pain, which in a sense it did. It was mere chance, though, that had put it in just that spot.

Okay, he had made mistakes but he could live with the results. He didn't like what he had become, but he could live with himself. He could live with himself in his own space. The question was could he share? This late in the day could he share with Alice?

The rain was heavier now. He put on his anorak and ran through it, big drops spattering on his hood, almost slipping on the wet grass but catching himself, hurting his back to remain upright.

Back in the caravan he turned on the television, reached into the cupboard over the sink and produced the bottle of whisky Ikey had bought for him in Brora. Long experience had taught him just how much of this stuff he could take and be all right in the morning. Tonight he would take a drop more. He would have to be up earlier than usual for the wall pour but would trust his stamina.

Watching the News he reflected that his options were reduced to what was real in the here and now. The dream realities had run out of time, those seductive might-have-beens from the otherworld. He could no longer live there. Soon there would be him and Alice and Peter's life of disasters and sponging. Alice couldn't see past the man who, for her, would always be a boy. As long as the three of them were alive Harry's money would pass out of his system through Alice to Peter. He knew this as he knew rain would always be wet.

Poor Alice couldn't compare with what might have been, but then she wasn't *poor* Alice. In Peter's dependency and his own she had all she wanted. It was poor Harry. His hand strayed once again to the limp area below his eye that, yes, chance had put in just that spot although it seemed like so much more.

His mind wandered and, when it wandered, went always to the same place. Whisky drinking in big gulps he reached for his books and his hand inevitably went to his Complete Burns. Beside 'Epistle to a Young Man' he found his copy of the letter he had sent. His mistake had been to obviously put those 'might-have-beens' between the lines. Too obviously, now that he read it again. He should have let his memories lie. Absence had only made her more beautiful in his illusion, more dynamic, more sensitive, wiser and still more perfect. He put his own letter back and turned to, what else but, 'Ae Fond Kiss' and the reply he had tucked away where Alice's hand would never wander.

She was Diana Worthington now, and she lived in Surrey. It had taken him weeks to track her down after he decided to write. Could there be, after all this time, a future? He didn't phrase the question in so many words but it was there and she hadn't missed it.

Still no children, she had written back. Two marriages but no children, it must have been meant. It was too late now, of course. In that sense she was free. The second marriage was comfortable. Not like the first with its adventures, but what could in any way compare to the way things had been back then?

Nothing, Harry mouthed silently on his bunk. Nothing could be like the days of youth and accomplishment and love. He eased his body across his bunk until it was resting against the cold wall. No, but life could always have its own joys and comforts, especially if they arrived at the beginning of another phase.

Alice could never at any time compare with this woman and at every turn in their life together, unspoken by Harry, un-named, was the comparison. What would *she* have done? How would *she* have handled this? And Peter could never compare with the children they would have had, he and Diana. Every inadequacy, every failure, every muffed attempt at something worthwhile was compared to the perfect lives of the perfect children who had never been.

Again he read the letter through. The surface message was as expected; the catching up after so many years, the provision of bland, banal information, but her letter was as carefully composed as his. He had been prepared for 'between-the-lines' messages such as 'might-have-been' and 'too-late' and 'the children' but reading over and over, here and, again, there, was the same unmistakable 'never-was'.

It never was, although he had believed so completely. It never was, for all that his cunning mind had slotted remem-bered words and glances into place. But finally, absolutely, truthfully, the love that had nurtured him through the years had never been. He put her letter again beside Robert Burns' great lyric and lay down and sang it quietly under his breath.

'. . . never loved and never parted, we had ne'er been broken hearted.'

So, it had all been illusion, and the reality was in the distance he had built between himself and his own family, his real family. That is, his family in the world of reality. How might it have been different if he had been without that great yearning? Now he realised that he had to separate the illusion from the memory and somehow hold on.

His hand wandered to the loose flesh below his eye where Diana Russell had kissed him that afternoon at Kano Airport. It felt like a sting even then, leaving the skin for dead. It was something to hang onto though, a real memory, although memory was a lash and it was always merciless.

16

It's the principal tool of my trade although I seldom use it

Pitch black and the hotel's heating full on it felt like waking in the bowels of the earth. GR checked his watch: 3:00am. The pouches of soft flesh below his eyes felt swollen and heavy, his finger joints thick with coming arthritis. He ran his fingertips across his face and down, through the dry, old man's body hair that had grown stiffer as it grew the more grey. Sleep was ended for an hour, maybe two. To lie awake was to go over so many things and all of them repetitiously.

He remembered in his office, at his desk, how the same fingertips ran down the spines of the Lochdon Contract Documents, now due for tender. Emma, his secretary, had placed them on his desk before opening his office door to leave. The same fingers had turned to the pipeline section and the road crossings and the items that covered excavation down through the road surface, the layers of bitumen and roadstone, their excavation, careful removal and costly replacement. The Ness and Struie document was open beside it but in the same section there were no such items, omissions which had survived all three proof readings.

This was why James Swann had chosen to tunnel under the A9. The decision had nothing to do with traffic control or safety, nor the ducts. Stone-faced he had played his card and won and now would claim all the additional costs of tunnelling below the A9. His claim would take the final valuation of the contract far beyond the low priced items the ineffective, now dismissed, Strath Construction management team had priced.

Forty years of experience in contract and claim told him James
Swann had already won and he, yes, GR, had lost.

Well I know you, Mr James Swann, he thought in the small-
hours darkness of his hotel room. You've kept your secret close
all this time and, yes, you are a strong one and clever.

Emma had returned from her long weekend in France
seemingly distracted, more morose even than usual. Things
had perhaps not gone well. It was no great deduction that she
was pining, or manipulating, or angling for a man, husband or
live-in lover, or partner, or whatever such agreements were
called these days. However modern woman looked on such
matters it was a contract the same as all else, possibly written
down and signed, perhaps merely spoken in private, maybe
silent and unenforceable, but a contract nonetheless.

Now thirty she would want this, and children. Likely the
man was married and she was active in the breach of another
contract, which would explain the foreign trips. It wasn't for
him to judge beyond their employer employee relationship.
Besides, he felt himself past such breaches now.

In the small hours he counted off the secretaries he had
employed over the years. Two of them he had affairs with. The
first, with Gail, had destroyed his marriage to Diane but he had
made her his second wife and had his children with her. The
second with (in the early hours he struggled to recall her name)
Theresa, had been turbulence nothing more. Gail had let it run
its course because she too was a strong one. They worked out
their accommodations and silently, discreetly agreed to go
their own ways in such matters and to mostly fulfil the contract
of their marriage. Somewhere between the letter and the spirit
they kept it in place. They adhered or at least observed. People
with such common interests as children, inheritance, home
and lifestyle, people with their intelligence worked things
through. Nothing fundamental ever would or could be destroyed and while each of them recognised their common ends
this would remain the salient fact.

He swung his legs out of bed and tugged his robe from the

door peg, pulling it on as he crossed the sweltering room to look on Brora's empty Main Street. None of the houses had lights on. By God it was dark out there, cold winter with a smir of rain that thickened around the streetlights. Not good, not good, but he had known worse all over the world. He sat at the window table and opened his laptop and thought about the message he would send to his junior partner, Vernon Street, Vernon who was above all responsible for the omission of the road surface items. These things happen.

Mistakes happen and someone has to pay. That's why we have contracts.

Should he send it now? He thought not. An email of such importance timed at 3:15am would look unconsidered although his mind was diamond hard as ever. On screen he flicked through Allan Crawford's weekly reports. The boy was naïve but time would answer that. He could use him on the Lochdon contract and the contract following. He would do.

He thought about the other thing. James Swann was 42 years of age, twenty years younger than he was himself and coming to his peak. His cold far-sightedness had given him the prize. It could do so again in future.

Trevor stood at the corner filing cabinet watching Swannie at the window, looking past him as the sun separated itself from the North Sea horizon. Outside in the compound Derek the steelfixer and his boy were tidying the remaining reinforcement steel while Healey's men emerged from their hut stamping their wellies to the ground and pulling on gloves as the sun's low, slanting light scattered sparkle across frozen mud that soon would melt. Soon the contract would be substantially complete and he would have to lay them off and, having laid them off, might have difficulty getting the best of this team back together again.

'When are you meeting Sir Graham?'

'11:00am.'

Swannie never showed emotion but it was impatience, a saw

toothed aggravation with delay and lack of commitment. Commitment, he said over and over, that's the name of the game. You had to care. You had to care the way he did. Trevor looked in wonder at the man's indifference to personal comfort and rest. There was something there he hadn't managed to put his finger on, something beyond work programmes and progress and cash flow.

'Think he'll resist the claim?'

Silence.

'I've been over the figures a hundred times,' Trevor continued. 'So long as the principle is accepted, that we had no instruction to go down through the road, and no obligation to discuss the contractual point, then the costs of the tunnel can all be drawn into the valuation. That puts 24% onto the contract price and, bingo, we have a profit element that beats the low tender price Strath Construction won the job with.'

Swannie didn't turn from the window, his steady eye on the men moving across frozen mud and broken stone. Trevor felt almost as if he was addressing an authority higher than flesh and blood, or perhaps lower.

'There are two more jobs along the line and no doubt more to come after them. 24% is a whopping addition and it's likely to mean the Engineer, I mean Sir Graham Russell *personally*, going cap in hand to the Client for funds. Believe me he won't like it. If he digs in his heels there is a danger of arbitration and, believe me again, we don't want that. The arbiters go through the records with a sieve and will note that we've had a serious industrial accident that cost John Kelly three fingers and a broken hip, a near thing with traffic control at the tunnel which went as far as the police, and official complaints about muddy run-off from the hill filling the A9 road drains. That's the environmentalists, the Roads Department and the public all with their noses out of joint. We'd win, but would we work here again?'

Swannie's eyes hadn't come off the men on their way to the new settlement tanks. The plant contractor's van pulled in to the compound and his men tumbled out.

'Our record doesn't look too good and telling them we were changing the structure of our team for the better all the while won't cut any ice. If he plays hard ball you might have to revisit those figures and trim 5%, maybe more. If we want to price for Lochdon and after we might have to take the hit.'

'Every possible cost cut is made,' Trevor said. 'We couldn't be better placed to win Lochdon.'

Swannie wasn't listening. 'Those missing road items are an embarrassment to him. The tunnel puts him on the spot but he doesn't want arbitration either.'

Alan Lammerton came into the hut to look at the tank plans, to check a size, and while the new GF was present they said nothing of higher matters, neither the money in bare figures, still less the principles. Trevor stood beside him at the spread open drawing and made the sketch required by the joiners. Swannie stood in brooding silence until he was gone.

'Don't tinker with the valuation. The Contract is on our side for once.' He gestured out of the window at the compound, the stored materials and the men at their work. 'Adhere to it's every letter, Trevor. We'll risk the next job and screw him anyway.'

Harry looked down through the opening to the new Struie Pumping Station, hands clasped behind his back. Why did he feel this undercurrent of excitement, he wondered, at the coming of Sir Graham? Easily answered, he thought, it's because the job in West Africa had been the best job of his life.

Since parting at Kano Airport their lives had crossed several times and always they had recognised each other first through their shared experiences and trust. Their places within the industry were such they never met off site but the GR energy throbbed through his working life and it was a sort of love mixed with envy he felt, although he would not, could not, name it as such. For the last fifteen years he had worked for the Partnership.

Downside the plant contractor was fitting out the new

Pumping Station. JB and Tammas were labouring to them, carrying hooks and chains from their lorry to the derrick by the chamber opening. Acute to the demands of health and safety Harry's eye searched out kick boards, counterweights, hard hats, second cables set against the breaking of the first. All were in place and the area was fenced and tidied as well as could be expected. For two days he had gone over the site with GR's fabled fine-toothed comb and all was well, but how typical to be embarrassed this close to completion.

Beyond the burdened Tammas GR's car appeared around the fence and drew up, and when the Man emerged the throb became a surge because this was a power far beyond Harry, that controlled him but was for all that benevolent. Controlled him yes, although Harry could direct the power, as in choosing when to circumvent the letter of the contract and when not, the aggregate of his experience and wisdom instructing him so, GR trusting him so.

'Harry!'

'Sir Graham!'

'No formalities, Harry. Not from you.'

'Okay. GR.'

They shook hands.

'Thanks for going to Newtonmore at short notice.'

'Pity I couldn't have been in two places at once.'

'The foreman's accident? You would have caught all those safety misdemeanours. So would the RE if he had been more experienced.'

No, thought Harry.

'Still, he recorded it all very fully after the event and that's what's important.'

No, again. He was hiding in the hut right through and got it all from Paul and Conn. What else would he do being weak and directionless?

GR opened the boot of his car, and changed into wellies. He put on his hard hat.

'Allan not coming out?'

'He thought you'd go directly inside. He doesn't know you.'

They stepped across to the new Pumping Station reducing the troops to silence. Harry watched GR's eyes flick from this place to that observing the quality of finishings, the adequacy of the fence, the ladder down into the dark and the torchlight where the sub-contractor was working below. The ladder was tied and safe.

'Wait here', GR said and first of all shouted then climbed down.

JB and Tammas looked at each other.

'No escape from detail', Harry told them. 'That's what Sir Graham says. Good suit and all.'

'Another Swannie then', said JB.

'Better.'

Rising out of the Chamber there came voices, laughter. GR had his common touch still. He would have the men on his side but, even so, nothing would go past him unnoticed. Topside again, GR nodded in the direction of the RE's hut.

'How's he doing?'

'He leaves me to get on.'

'Will he make it?' This GR asked below his breath.

'He wouldn't have gone down into that Chamber. He didn't go into the cofferdam, didn't so much as look at the tunnel.'

'He writes good, clear reports.'

'He only sees the past. Present and future don't figure.'

'Let's walk down the road a bit.'

Side by side they looked all the while at the line of pipe JB and Tammas had laid and then, at the foot of the hill, the surface of the wayleave as it doglegged up to the plateau and the culvert the grip squad had fashioned. Here and there were runnels where the rain had turned to streams and carried away the thin topsoil even though JB had done a better job of directing it than could have been reasonably expected. GR frowned.

'That can never be what it was.'

'I'd say it's as good as it can be given the weather the troops worked through.'

'If you say so I'll accept that – except the Contractor chose to proceed when he might have waited and that, very firmly, is their responsibility under the contract. The Ness side looks worse.'

'Different squad, but also steeper ground.'

'Roads aren't pleased. Neither is the Environmental Agency.'

Harry didn't like this tack that might turn back on him.

'The troops didn't get the silt traps in before the damage was done. I was away.'

Harry heard the whine in his own voice and hated it. Neither GR nor Swannie nor he believed in excuses.

'Okay,' GR said. 'So no job is perfect and the conditions they had to work in were atrocious and the slopes would challenge a team of mountaineers. It could be worse. The Black Isle job was so lousy they're still putting the pipelines right. There have been big changes since the takeover. If anything I'm surprised they took so long. Are these changes kicking in to the good? Is it better? What's the word from the front line, Harry? If James Swann gets Lochdon will quality be better or worse?'

'Everything is better. He's shed the easy-lifers and brought in good grip men. Healey's chancers are mostly found out and gone. He has better men on the job now, thinkers.'

'No replacement for the Agent yet?'

'Trevor will be Agent on his next job wherever that is.'

'What really happened at the cofferdam?'

'Swannie pressured Mac and cut his resources at the same time. That same pressure cost John Kelly his fingers.'

'But that's done and Mac is gone and now he's free to remake Trevor in his own image. There's a new GF?'

'Lammerton's okay. He can do the job.'

'So they could tackle the next two Contracts in the series? I'm not asking for nothing.'

'They're getting better. I'll say no more than that.'

GR took out his mobile phone, punched a memory button and put it to his ear.

'Direct line', he told Harry, 'to the Client's CEO.'

Harry looked away.

'Denis? Graham. Listen, the idea I floated yesterday looks more likely today. Did you fly it past your Chair? Did he receive it well?'

Not wanting to hear this kind of thing Harry drifted over to JB and the plant Contractor's men and Trots and Jinkie.

In the RE's hut GR commandeered the only desk and looked around while Allan filled the kettle. Site plan to the wall, colouring it as the job progressed, dating successful pipeline tests and completed concrete pours, all was regular and ordered, reflecting the mind of a cautious man. Allan was shaping up whatever Harry thought. More detailed drawings were laid out on the plan chest also coloured and dated. GR laid the Contract Documents on the desk.

The Preamble, and Job Description, the Bills of Quantities and the Specification, these were the Russell Partnership documents.

The Standard Specification the job spec varied from, the Conditions of Contract, these were Institution publications.

Together they were the Bible he lived by, that the whole industry lived by although even the likes of Pat Healey had hardly so much as heard of them.

Respectfully he picked up the Conditions, its dark cover creased and folded and marked here and there by muddy fingers and the underside of coffee mugs, and fondled it lovingly. Here was his Bible's Gospel, its essential centre on which all else turned.

Allan put his coffee down on the desk beside him.

'Will you be going into the Conditions today? Challenging principles?'

'Shouldn't think so. I just like to have the book close. It's a sort of talisman to me.'

'Why do we still use the 5th Edition? It's years behind.'

'It's because I know where I am with it. Allan, there is no

creature on God's earth so innately conservative as a civil engineer and when something works we hold on to it against all notions of progress. We have things to build and we get on with the tools we can be sure of. No change for change's sake. It has to work. I love this book and I expect you to love it also. It's the principal tool of my trade although I seldom use it, Gospel, law and moral compass. Was that a car?'

Allan said yes.

'That will be James Swann.'

The Contracts Manager entered and his eyes met GR's. He advanced to the desk and put down his brief case and GR stood up and they shook hands.

Allan brought two seats across along with two more coffees.

James Swann seated looked at the documents spread across Allan's desk.

'I had hoped this would be simple,' he said.

'When it comes down to it the contract *is* simple, James. For you and me it's no more than our promise to do our best and take our shilling and move on. Don't you agree?'

'Sure, but we're here to discuss less abstract matters, meaning the Final Valuation.'

'That includes your claim for additional costs at the A9 road crossing, a variation that amounted to a whole lot of money.'

'There's nothing unusual in varying the contract.'

Allan sat on the desk's third chair and put down a writing pad.

'Yes, do take notes', said GR. 'But don't start yet.'

Allan put his pen on the pad and waited. GR put his hand on the Standard Specification.

'We vary from the Standard Spec here and there of course and that is why we have the job spec.'

'And you allow us to suggest further variations as we go, such as discarding the brick chamber and using large diameter concrete rings. That made a considerable saving that we've put against the additional expense of the tunnel we had to build.'

'Had to build? There was no "had to" about it.'

GR's eyes were suddenly ablaze with judgement, holding the moment, delaying James Swann's reply by force of will. When his defence was eventually articulated it sounded almost like an admission.

'This Ness and Struie Contract didn't give either express instruction to go down through the road surface or any mechanisms of description, specification or measurement.'

'We made a mistake when we omitted those items; yes.'

'And we had no duty to bring them to your attention.'

GR nodded to himself, a weary gesture of resignation and hurt.

'Technically your case was won before you walked in.' GR turned to Allan. 'I take it you've agreed all matters of fact with Trevor, quantities, time spent on additional works?'

'Yes.'

GR looked back at James Swann. 'Let's tie up the final amounts,' he said. 'After that I'd like us to take a walk over the hill, just the two of us. We'll get a different view from up there and develop an appetite for lunch while we're at it.'

In less than an hour they agreed the Contract Valuation was heading for 24% over tender price and responsibility rested with the Engineer, that is the Russell Partnership. Without it ever being said, all three present knew GR would have to go to the Client like Oliver Twist with his bowl pleading for more.

He seemed unperturbed.

The two men in their expensive suits and coats laboured up and along the wayleave fence where the pipelaying gang in their wet rags had laboured previously, the same mud dragging at their feet and the same cold air cutting into their lungs.

GR was a fit man in his sixties. Nonetheless James could have climbed away from him on this slope being fitter still and only in his forties. He would have done if GR hadn't disarmed him with his ready acceptance of responsibility and costs. Instead there were the beginnings of some other relationship and the impression of something noble in the older man. For

Sir Graham Russell he felt a range of emotions that somehow embarrassed him but that also warmed and attracted him.

GR stopped three-quarters of the way up and together they looked along the strath and down to Allan's hut and the village and the mist softened hills beyond, their outline lost to the clouds and distant rain. Without comment each noted work continuing on the Struie Pumping Station and how the pipeline excavation beside the road was so straight and well finished. When grass took its proper hold it would be all but invisible. Not so the pipeline on the hill. Here heavy rain had done its damage, taking the thin and broken topsoil down to the road as run-off, across the road and into the river.

'It's not good enough,' James volunteered. 'I'll return the labour force in the spring if you'll pay for the new topsoil. We must leave it better than this.'

'You might not be in the area. There's no guarantee you'll win Lochdon.'

'We'll come back anyway. The other side is worse, being steeper. We'll do that as well under the same agreement.'

'These are good attitudes, James. They speak more of partnership than contract.'

James silently noted their reaching out one to the other, their tacit agreements, as GR began to climb again. On the plateau they caught their breath and strode out along the line of the culvert. No water erosion here, the land was level and even although soft where Conn had completed his reinstatements. Grass seed and time would do the rest.

'Good driver', said GR. 'But how is your GF?'

'He'll be off for at least a year. At his age, I don't expect him back.'

They reached the west side of the hill and looked down the scarred slope. Huge patches of topsoil were missing. Far below them the new Works neared completion. The Plant subcontractor worked in the two completed tanks fixing scum boards and scrapers and in the Control House commissioning control panels and telemetry. Healey's men laboured to them and beyond, at the shore, worked on the last pipeline that would carry the final, clean effluent from the Tanks on the ultimate leg of its journey to the sea. Man and machine had beaten a path between Works and shoreline through the long spiky grass that would soon spring up again and be as it had through time immeasurable.

'The outfall will be last,' said James, 'although I would expect you to agree substantial completion before commissioning, when the tests are done on concrete structures and new plant. With the outfall complete we can turn on the pumps and hand over to the Authority four months early.'

GR didn't answer. Instead he breathed deep and gestured widely to indicate the Works, the oil rigs, the villages, the towns and cities to the south and across the sea.

'All this,' he said, 'is most usually likened to a machine.'

James took a step to one side to listen more carefully. GR's moral intensity was so controlled it seemed a great heat was being focussed on his mind, the intense heat of a welding flame. He felt his internal defences, tempered and hardened by two decades of contractual exactitude, softening against his will.

GR continued.

'But to me it's more like an organism, a single giant creature that has a life and that will eventually die but, until then, must work to lengthen the duration of its survival and the quality of its living. This means it must continually renew itself and that's where we come in, we builders. This is how we are part of the great corpus. We're its white corpuscles and a wound has appeared in our little part, James. It's bleeding. You'll understand I mean this matter of the tunnel. It was caused by human error and that error rests with me. You know I haven't tried to hide or disguise that, far less shift the burden and blame to you. Just the same, it would have been more easily met and dealt with if there had been openness on your side. You should have pointed out our omission when you saw it and not planned a coup.'

James focussed his gaze on the oil rigs.

'You adhered to the letter of the contract, James, but you pressed down on the spirit. You should have trusted me.'

James felt the ground move beneath his feet.

'There's only you and me here.'

'It was a risk I couldn't allow myself,' said James. 'I didn't know what kind of man you are. The job was priced so keenly there was no way we could break so much as even. This way there was a chance.'

'Think I don't understand? Or that I don't respect your risk-taking? What's your projected profit margin now?'

'4%.'

'Take away that margin and your figure will be a match for the tender price plus stated contingencies plus the invisible contingencies we have stored away in the Report on Tenders.'

'You have more tucked away than I thought.'

'Don't feel cheated. It puts closure at least in sight.'

'Perhaps we could compromise a bit more.'

'We already have the beginnings of an understanding, James.'

'That began with your preliminary remarks in Allan's hut.'

'I would say earlier, with an understanding Client. Perhaps we can go beyond compromise. James, you know we're working to the 5th Edition. It's an unforgiving document that doesn't allow for civilised compromise and it's taken us almost to arbitration. Neither of us wants that. All the Health and Safety failures come out, all the complaints, all the omissions. It's desperately, usually embarrassingly, revealing.'

'I know.'

'The 7th Edition allows for new relationships between the likes of us.'

'Partnering?'

'Yes. Do you know the form of words it uses? I have them memorised. ". . . the parties to the Contract are provided with a co-operative form of contract that should prevent delays or give rise to additional costs . . ." Hear that, James? It means the parties form a team and work together in harmony. It's all about predictive thought and it's the future calling to us. No more conflict. No more claims. A study in America showed that 80% of our time is spent in conflict. At a stroke it will be freed.'

James couldn't see his way through this. He felt confused while GR came across as timeless, a rock solid presence in contract and law.

'A living organism has to adapt in its ways if it is to survive.'

'I can learn.'

'Allan is a clean slate. So, I think, is your Trevor. They could pioneer this method for us. These are interesting ideas, James.'

'I'd like more detail.'

'Detail is exactly what can't be provided. That has to be worked out in the course of a co-operative project, especially with regard to cost. My proposal to you is as follows. You give us a price for the road items we have in the Lochdon Contract and we apply them retrospectively to Ness and Struie. Can do?'

'Of course, but it will cost me what I can't afford. We can't do this job for nothing.'

'Then we take the Ness and Struie prices and increase them by a small percentage for inflation and, frankly, in a non-competitive environment, more realism, and apply them forward into the Lochdon document. This will take care of that 4% and a little more beside although your return will be projected into the future. When the fourth and final Contract is ready, provided the work on Lochdon has gone well, even more so if the rate of improvement between the Black Isle job and here is continued, we award the fourth Contract to you on the same negotiated basis. All you have to do is persuade your Board to proceed to the 7th Edition retrospectively.'

'And the Client?'

'The Client will agree.'

'This is the new way?'

'When the Conditions change everything changes with them. That's how foundational they are. It's not just a new way, it's a new morality. The partnering will go far beyond Contractor and Client and Engineer to include the public. What's good for them is good for the Client and, through the Client, good for us.'

'You don't have to give other Contractors a chance?'

'That's the Client's responsibility. I only recommend, but this way we give the Contractor continuity of employment. That means experience gained in the field isn't lost from project to project. The Client retains the advantage of the first competitive tender but only has to go through that expensive and time consuming process once. Most of all it takes conflict out of our relations, yours and mine, Contractor and Engineer, and that's a money saver in itself. After the fourth job is complete you, the Contractor, are known well and in pole position for whatever comes next.'

'You're asking us to take the hit on Ness and Struie knowing the loss will come back to us over the next two jobs? You're saying it will not only even out but we'll gain in time? I don't know if I can take that hit.'

'A working job on the ground when we're done, a reasonable price for the Client, a reasonable profit for you, gained experience, a better, more assured future, our common ends are the only salient facts. It becomes a sort of marriage. Allan and Trevor will face the unexpected as it appears, as it always does, working out the financial implications as they go.'

'And you, GR? What do you get?'

'No more surprises. In the short term we're saved the embarrassment of asking for more. Longer term? Having learned and honed the new skills we can take them elsewhere. Experience gained we can go anywhere within the reach of our new Bible.'

James Swann looked north in the direction of Lochdon, just out of sight, and beyond. He looked south and eastwards to the great organism that required perpetual renewal as it grew. Finally he looked outwards to the oil rigs that pumped its heart's blood.

'And you can begin right away, James. You can move your staff and your men on to the new job now with all the benefits of a smooth and easy transition and no downtime or forced layoffs. What do you say?'

James felt the weight not of only of his life's experience weighing against this but also the morality of their old Bible. In his head he cast around for anything fundamental that might be destroyed. GR nodded down at the new Works and along the coast.

'All it really means is that the final word on methods and material sources will be with the Engineer, in this case me, as it already is on strategy and procurement. It's more a matter of trust than of money.'

James Swann believed he could perhaps trust.

'In moral terms, think of it as the New Testament growing from the Old. Completing it rather than replacing it.'

'An assured profit on our expenditure?'

'Just agree and all this can be yours.'

The two men looked into each other's eyes and grasped each other's hands and arms and for a moment embraced. There was no one there to see it, unless the sheep are counted, but opponents as they had been under the old contract they now looked more like a single creature joined at hand and arm, and in their minds' purpose as one under those Conditions that were the principal tool of their trade, seldom used but ultimate with the force of law and morality and, when brought into play, absolute in their dictum.

17

Extract from the Final Valuation Report

The Ness and Struie Drainage Project may be considered substantially complete when the Ness and Struie Pumping Stations are commissioned, even before the Treatment Plant comes into operation. Permanent plant, such as that within the settlement tanks, will be in place and functional by the end of the month. At time of writing only the sea outfall remains to be completed of the critical path works.

All pipelines have passed their prescribed tests and all concrete samples have similarly achieved both their seven and twenty-eight day strengths. Water retaining structures (high culvert, collection chamber, pumping stations and settlement tanks) have also been proven. In the course of construction one serious but non-fatal industrial accident occurred. The Health and Safety Executive has now completed its investigation and it is possible that a prosecution will follow against personnel. The Contractor has been cleared of responsibility.

★ ★ ★

Unusually wet weather for much of the contract duration has made surface finishing on the slopes between the two villages impossible and the Contractor will return in the spring to make good. The Client will recall that in the Partnership's Feasibility Report the Engineer did suggest such a likelihood but a single Works, with concomitant operational savings, was deemed the more economic solution by the Authority over an anticipated forty year working life. Some additional costs will be generated but these may be legitimately ascribed (see below) to the forthcoming Lochdon Project and contracts beyond.

* * *

The Contractor has undergone substantial organisational and operational changes between completion of the Black Isle (Beauly Firth) Project and the present time. Nonetheless, a substantial time saving (half of the allotted duration) has been achieved. This, it should be noted, in the early part of the year when the productive working day is shortest and in this winter's particularly inclement conditions. Meteorological references indicate the wettest January of the past fifteen years and some of the lowest temperatures.

The Engineer has been impressed by the Contractor's progress not only with regard to the speedy completion of the Works but also in his internal reorganisations. Experience gained, working relationships developed with the Environmental Agency, the Roads Department, the Engineer's staff and with the client body itself, are deemed invaluable to the successful completion of the two remaining projects. After discussions with senior personnel within the client body it has been agreed that the Lochdon Project will be constructed under a partnering arrangement as prescribed in the 7th Edition of the Conditions of Contract. It is recommended that Ness and Struie rates be applied with an upward revision of 6%.

* * *

In the interests of fairness it is also recommended that the Ness and Struie Contract be included in the new partnering arrangement and the revised rates applied retrospectively. This will allow for additional costs generated by the Contractor's spring revisit and one or two other minor matters. All these developments will conform to the recommendations of the Latham Review and the procurement initiatives propounded by the Egan Report.

With these acceptances in place the Contractor may effect a virtually seamless transition to Lochdon with financial savings passed on to the Client as well as the speediest possible addressing of local difficulties as required by the Environmental Agency. A start within the present calendar month will deflect the possibility of a punitive fine to the Client being applied by the Environmental Agency.

18

It's the Clearances all over again

Last to go would be the towering batching plant with its mounds of aggregate and sand and bags of cement. An industrial relic it overlooked the men's hut like a strange Gothic watchtower. Ikey saw it as having religious significance, the great mixer and maker, an alchemical device that turned loose materials into unyielding concrete. Standing by the plant contractor's van he observed its outline against the blue sky and then lowered his gaze to the wooden cludge that would be the last structure to be moved up the road.

Willie Quinn was also outlined against the sky. Balanced on the men's hut, last to descend, he kicked at the roofing felt where it had come loose at the crest.

'What's it like?' Cammy shouted up.

'It's a hundred years old, bullet riddled and torn. This must be the hut Custer hid in when the Apaches were closing in.'

'Sioux!' Ikey shouted up. 'They were Lakota Sioux, Mr Quinn, and it was the other way round. Custer attacked them.'

Willie pointed at him with his hammer.

'Did you read that in a book? You're spending too much time in that cludge.'

'Lakota,' Ikey repeated.

'I wouldn't argue with Willie,' Jimmy Gillies said, exiting the hut.

'I was a farrier in the 7th back then,' Willie said. 'They busted me after the massacre, said the whole thing turned on a loose horseshoe, but they were covering up for Reno. He was one of them in ways I could never be.'

'Is it usable,' Jimmy asked, impatient, 'the felt?'

'Nope, it's had it,' Willie said. 'No wonder the hut lets in.'

Willie crouched on his hunkers and took the claw of his hammer to the roof nails, drawing and releasing them and letting them slide down and fall to the ground, pulling the felt away from the crest like a blanket, dropping it also to the ground.

Stores had been the first hut down. Too far gone to be repaired and reused Cammy had broken it up and started a fire with the rotted roof joists. He dragged the first sheet of felt over and threw it on to blacken and curl and take light. As it shrivelled he pushed the edges into the fire's heart with his boot.

'More costs for Swannie,' he said. 'He won't like it.'

'And he'd avoid replacing it if he could,' Willie said. 'We're doing the Lochdon troops a favour.'

'Whoever they are,' Cammy said.

Squatting precariously at the end of the roof Willie leaned over and prised at the nails that kept the remaining felt in place. 'Who is staying and who is going, that is the question.'

'Everybody's staying,' Jimmy said. 'Lochdon is a bigger job, more pipelines, three Pumping Stations, four Tanks. I'm seeing Swannie about rates when the light goes. We'll get the work if we're not too greedy. Start maybe next week.'

'The sooner the better,' Willie said, 'because there's no money in this.'

'Perzackly!'

A flat lorry bounced in off the A9 with Derek the Steelfixer at the wheel. By now the joiners had the mess hut, the last hut, down and stacked. It remained to get the panels of all three huts onto the back of the lorry, tied safely down and carried up the road to Lochdon. Two journeys Jimmy reckoned.

Willie shielded his eyes with his hand and made a great play of peering under the lorry.

'Where's Trots, Derek? Shouldn't he be driving this thing?'
'He says it's not his job and won't be until he's paid the rate.'
'So it's yours?'

'There's no money in Lochdon till this is done. The best thing I can do is move the job along and take whatever rate Swannie will pay. Give me a hand with these panels.'

Willie and Cammy each took a corner of the first wall panel and powerful Derek took the other side by himself. When Jimmy moved across to help he shook his head. The three men threw the panels one by one on the back of the lorry.

Where the huts had stood the ground was marked with the rectangle of their floor shapes. The compound fence hung from its posts and the gate swung on its hinges. Where Stores had been was littered with oil drums and loose bolts and spilled gravel. It was a place where life had once been but was no more.

Jimmy came over and stood beside Ikey.

'The place is like a battlefield,' he said.

'The Little Big Horn,' said Willie.

'No,' Ikey said, 'the Clearances. It's like the Highland Clearances all over again.'

'Did you know it was Jimmy burned out Strathnaver?' Willie said. 'He's changed since then. The love of a good woman saved him.'

Cammy's fire crackled and sparked and grew as he scoured the area for odd pieces of scrap timber and threw them on.

'Good women,' Willie sighed. 'Whatever happened to them?'

Panels secured on the back of the lorry Derek fired the engine and drove out, heading back north to Lochdon. Jimmy climbed into his car and followed leaving Willie and Cammy to tend the fire, to make sure everything that could burn was consumed. Later in the day, maybe tomorrow, Conn would dig a hole and doze in the waste and bury it.

Ikey superstitiously tapped the wooden side of his pride and joy, the cludge, as if it contained the spirit of the work, the

Great Manitou of Civil Engineering, as some said all cludgies did, and took a walk to the Settlement Tanks where Conn's jib stood tall above Tank Two.

The double chain hung taut with the load of an aluminium scum trap that he swung in slow instalments closer to the tank wall. Below him on the concrete base the Plant Contractor's foreman opened and clenched his fist slowly and slower still as the dead weight drew closer to the wall. Abruptly he raised both arms and brought the movement to a halt.

Conn locked the jib, opened his cabin door and spat out the remains of his roll-up.

'Yo ho, Ikey.'

With the scum trap hovering gravity neutral by the wall two fitters moved in to sit by either side. They pushed and eased it into exact position and shoved the holding bolts through and into the pockets that had been boxed out before the pour. As they tightened with their spanners the weight of the trap was transferred and the chains became slack.

'You moving up the road to Lochdon?' Conn asked.

'Mr Lammerton has yet to decide, sir.'

'Or if he's decided he hasn't said. That's how these people work.'

'Nil carborundum, Mr Conn.'

'Bullseye, wee man, I hope they take you along. You deserve it.'

'Thinking of movement, Mr Conn.'

'That's Conn, just Conn.'

Ikey struggled against saying to Conn what he wanted to say to Willie but eventually it came out.

'Did you know there were Highlanders at the Little Big Horn?'

Conn eyed him warily.

'I didn't. Which side?'

'With the Long Knives.'

'Joined up? Joined the Long Knives, the White Eyes, Roundeyes, Yellow Legs, Red Coats? Playing the pipes as

the arrows came thudding in? Gathering in a circle at the end
and singing their Gaelic psalms?'

'Yes sir.'

'We were the same in Kerry with the Roundheads, on the
wrong side as ever. In the end they always win. Did you know?'

'I did, sir, and for better or worse we join them. They would
have been cleared from up by. Strathnaver, sir, or the likes.'

Ikey stood talking to Conn and the plant operatives as the light
of day began its departure and Conn switched on the crane's
one headlight, watched while the troops leaned dangerously
over the Tank to tighten the bolts, as they levelled the spill-over
rim to 'near enough'.

Feeling the call of nature he wandered back to where the
compound had been. Inside the cludge he hung up his jacket,
took The Brothers Karamazov from his pocket and sat to ease
himself through the last bowel movement of the Ness and
Struie Drainage Project with the last sustained read.

The boys had killed their father. Well, he understood,
although the reading of C G Jung and the living of his life
had taught him all he needed to know about the slaying of the
father and its futility.

When he came out the sun was gone. All was dark and there
was barely a star in the sky. Willie and Cammy had been joined
by Derek the Steelfixer, returned for the cludge when they had
broken it down. The three were silhouetted against the fire that
overtopped them by twice their own height and might have
been made for the burning of a witch or some other unre-
deemed soul bound for hell.

In the darkness the temperature dropped and a sparkling
frost formed on the ground and on the site's detritus and there
hardened. Ikey joined the three others by the fire and felt its
heat and its call to the primitive and wondered about guilt,
revenge, justice and what they were. Damned little, he
thought, against the great round of history's repetitions and
humanity perpetually breaking up and moving on.

19

All those tiny men working in the distance

Jimmy Gillies straightened from the gabion basket he was filling with stones on the beach. Out at sea, close to the limit of his vision, one of the rigs was flaring off gas. The sea was iron grey, more or less calm, although small waves threw themselves onto the shingle to hush and draw themselves back into the water. His eye followed the arc of the sea's edge southwards to the rocky escarpment of the County of Ross and to Cammy who had wandered off, who was picking stones off the beach and throwing them into the sea.

As dictated by the state of the tide over the next two days they would put down another two baskets below where the shingle broke into sand, presently under water, and fill them with carefully but pointlessly graded stones. A single pipe length per day would do, in fact would be all they had time for. When this first gabion was filled, in another half hour, they would tie on the top mat and extend the outfall on top of it by another length of pipe. They would fix the shuttering and place the concrete before the tide turned and came back in. A can-do operation he had told Trevor, with the right labourers, meaning JB and Tammas, but Lammerton had learned their worth and taken them up the coast.

Jimmy's eye travelled back to where the outfall pipe came out of the long spiky marram grass that waved in the breeze and onto the shore, to the two leather aprons that were draped over it, Willie Quinn's and his own. When the pipe had been laid the marram had been in dieback but now, with spring at last on the way, it had shot up and the line of the pipe was lost to the eye except for Paul's centre line peg. The grass was shoulder high and thick and the land between shore and Works now reminded him of the veldt he had travelled in his early years, when he was still single. Here was a salty veldt.

By the end of the week at the latest, the outfall would be complete and they would follow the troops north to the next site, but it was more time away from home and he missed the wife. He also missed his daughter but she was going anyway, as was only right, as was time. She was a woman now, no longer an apprentice, and her boy friends had turned into men friends. He was better away and letting them get on with it. A cool breeze across his cheek returned him to the present.

Almost lost among the marram Paul stood behind his theodolite. The line for the gabion could be less than perfectly accurate because eventually the whole arrangement would be sandblown, pebble covered and more or less invisible. Only the concrete surround to the pipe would be seen and soon it would be coated with moss and stuck with weed and seashell and no one would care about line and level beyond the troops who put it in, but that was the standard Jimmy set, that he would always set. Placement was to be as accurate as Paul's theodolite could make it provided duration didn't go into funnytime. So, he looked at Paul who had the telescope turned upwards from the gabion and out to sea and the nearest of the rigs.

Willie shoogled the stones in the mattress with his two hands and also straightened.

'Look at this shore,' he said. 'From the sand to the marram it's all stones exactly like the ones we're putting in the basket. Why are we running them a hundred miles from the quarry? Why aren't we just picking them up and sorting them and shoving them in the basket?'

'Because the designer never thought of doing it the easy way and the Engineer won't admit a mistake,' Paul called down.

'Hst! Take a look at Cammy.'

Cammy was standing at the waves' limit, watching them roll to his boots and then stepping back.

'He's a dreamer,' Willie said, 'but you know that. How long has he been with us?'

'Two years,' said Jimmy. 'He's getting tired, maybe pining for something. You and I have been working together long enough to read each other's minds.'

'He'll leave us soon.'

'Think so?'

'We need to be three. Two won't do. Would you want him?' Willie jerked his thumb at Paul.

'Nope. He's to stick in at College and make something of himself. He told me he'd do his best and I won't give him a way out.'

Willie swept off his woolly hat and ran his fingers abruptly through his hair and jammed it back on.

'Why the funny look?'

'You deal in facts, Jimmy. All the time I've known you you've worked in facts, measurements and plywood and concrete and money. Don't go trading on that hope stuff this late in the day. Ten years from now he's going to have a saw in his hand, or a shovel.'

'No. He'll make it.'

Willie waved his hands in the air. 'Paul, back from dreamland! Where's Trots and Jinkie?'

Paul pulled away from the eyepiece and looked back at where the compound used to be.

'On their way with the last load. The lorry's going out the gate so that's that.'

The dumper crested the marram and bounced on to the shingle and skidded to a halt, Trots' head bouncing on his shoulders, Jinkie in his Celtic jersey jumping down behind, smiling and happy to be free of the bosses for three whole days. Graded stones spilled over the edge of the skip.

In the way he sometimes did when they had to wait, or when the work was least intense, Cammy wandered on his own. The shoreline, a narrow strand, was a few metres of shingle that changed to grit and then to sand where the tide went back and forth, the spiky marram grass that hid them from the new Works and made it a world apart. Here all things changed, dry became wet and wet became dry and nature graded rock from coarse to fine more evenly than the quarry could possibly manage. Here Life first crawled from the sea, cast its shell and continued inland.

He could imagine, or try to imagine, how it was when the world was settling, inanimate and senseless and, that done, try to accept that these same elements had somehow assembled without outside aid to take both form and life, developing first consciousness and then self-consciousness, inventiveness and creativity. All this was scarcely more credible than the breath of God, but nonetheless fact.

Bypassing thought as it should his heart sent an arrowshot prayer upwards to the stars. Not repentance this time, for the wavering Christian's diminishing faith that now questioned everything, nor pleading, nor explaining, nor gratitude, nor seeking, this time only acknowledgement of the way things are and of how they fit. Not even thanks, it was appreciation, but now his mind was back in play and Mind ruined everything.

Like the tiny crabs and the bubble-weed he was in an in-between condition, between fact and faith, and the knowledge afforded him a comfort he could not quite explain. No point speaking to Willie or even Jimmy about such things, they lived in the most practical of worlds. Work was their religion and joinery their nation. Their ideology was written in the space between value and independence. That meant though, there could be no discussion of the spiritual.

He looked to his feet. The pebbles which from the outfall pipe had looked so uniform in size and colour in fact were wildly varied. He took in the multi-forms and multi-colours through his eyes, the salt smell through his nose, the cold breeze through his skin and knew beyond all doubt that he was part of it, not merely among it. How could he explain to

Jimmy, whose only watchword was survival, that he would be content to join this inanimate world now? He could turn to stone now but knowing the day would come he was content to wait. He had abandoned the search for purpose.

One pebble called up to be selected and he did so, raising it between thumb and forefinger and tossing it into his palm, hefting its weight there, moving his thumb against its one flat face and feeling its roughness. The light caught its many embedded specks of quartz and made them sparkle and he focussed on it, the whole pebble, all its facets and colours and mass, trying to understand if it had purpose and, if so, was it of less importance than he because he was sentient.

From the corner of his eye he saw Trots and Jinkie arrive with the final dumper of stone for the gabion mattress. Trots had manoeuvred the dumper against the gabion's edge and tipped the stones in. As Cammy watched he reversed the dumper and drove it back into the marram and stopped and climbed down. Willie and Jinkie fumbled at the stones to make their top surface even and started tying on the top mat. Soon they would be ready for the pipe.

The iron grey surface of the sea lay before him with all its depths. Leaning back on his rear foot he stretched still further behind with his arm, twisting at the waist until he could reach no further. Shifting his weight onto the front foot, uncoiling from the waist, swinging his arm forward as quickly as he could, he spun the stone low and flat across the water, watching until it made contact and skipped across the surface and sank. The nearest oil rig lay beyond and when his eyes refocused he could see tiny men on its work platform, far away in the distance and lost in the carrying of tools and loads and the turning of valves. All of them were wrestling with the inanimate, all of them on the side of change whether they knew it or not. The real art, he reflected, the truly fine art, was in a becoming that still eluded him.

Suddenly Paul was at his side. 'The batcher's broken down again.'

'That means we have to call in concrete from Alness as well as get the pipe in and the shutters up and the stuff poured and vibrated. There's not time.'

'Jimmy says you've to come back now.'

Cammy turned again to sea and shore knowing that to go now was to never see them in quite the same way again. His hand strayed to his apron and the hammer that hung by his side, along with his saw the only tools he possessed to effect change in this or any other world; those and a bag of nails.

'Okay,' he said. 'Let's go.'

They joined the others at the gabion to make six. Jimmy Gillies spoke. 'Better call Trevor,' he said. 'He'll see further than us. Meanwhile the mattress is ready so we can get the next pipe in. Trots!'

'Yo!'

'You and Jinkie bring it down from the compound. Don't forget the sealing ring and lubricant.'

Trots jumped back into the driver's seat and revved out a cough of smoky exhaust that blew across Jimmy's overalls. He pushed the gear-stick forward and bounced back onto the marram grass. Jinkie followed on foot.

'He's a clown,' Jimmy said. 'Haste when he's behind a wheel, slow as a donkey with a shovel in his hand. Every idea in the world about working but bone idle when it comes to doing. Paul!'

'Yo!'

'Phone now.'

Paul pressed the memory buttons that put him through to Trevor on the new site at Lochdon.

'Trev! Paul here. Batcher's broken down.'

'Don't say that.'

'Jimmy wants you to bring in a load from Alness.'

'A load is six cubic metres. You can't need all that. Wait you, I'll do the sum.'

Paul could hear Trevor's fingers tapping on the calculator.

'Pipe's 15cm diameter, 15cm concrete around that. Point four five by point four five.'

Jimmy couldn't hear as Paul could. 'When will it arrive?'

'He's doing a sum.'

'Times six metres less the area of the pipe also times six. Paul, that's just over a cube. We're not paying for six and the journey, which is what we'd have to do to bring it up from Alness. Get Trots and Jinkie to mix it by hand.'

'He says we've to mix it by hand.'

Jimmy took the phone from Paul.

'Jimmy here. The tide's going to beat us.'

Words passed back from Trevor. When the call ended Jimmy looked at the phone as if it was responsible for some great stupidity before he returned it to Paul.

'Willie!'

'Yo!'

'Get the shutters oiled. Cammy!'

'Yo!'

'Cut the dwangs, 45cm perzackly and twelve of. Paul!'

'Yo!'

'You and me'll get the pipe in while Trots and Jinkie are breaking their backs up there.'

'Trots? Some hope.'

'Look at that.'

Breaking out of the marram grass again Trots had a length of ductile iron pipe balanced across the skip of the dumper, the pipe sticking out two metres to either side and Jinkie running alongside steadying it with his hand. On the shingle the dumper bounced away from Jinkie and the pipe rolled off.

'As well Harry's not here,' Jimmy said. 'Take the pipe over to the mattress. Where's the gubbins?'

Trots reached into the skip for the jointing ring and tin of lubricant and showed them.

'Put it all over there by the mattress.'

Trots frowned but did the job, carrying the pipe at opposite ends from Jinkie. 'We'll fit it too,' he said. 'That's our job.'

'Not this time. You two get back up there and mix us a cube of concrete. There's none coming from Alness this day.'

'Mix by hand?'

'Quick time too, we're fighting the tide.'

'Who says we've to break our backs for nothing? If the bosses want, they can pay.'

'Trevor says no.'

'We work for Pat Healey.'

'So, ho ho. Want a job up the road? Think Healey wants to stay in with Trevor? That's to say Swannie? There's no money in this. There'll be money up the road.'

Angry Trots clenched and unclenched his fists.

'We can do it, Trots,' Jinkie said. 'Couple of hours back and forward.'

'Or we can stick together against the bosses. We can get the price we're due for busting our backs.'

'Stand arguing,' Jimmy said, 'and the tide beats us and everything goes back a day. Worse than that, since we're right on the ebb just now work time gets less every day. Two pipelines down we're that much further into the water with the tide taking that much less time to turn. We have to do this today.'

'That's it,' Trots said. 'That is the case. That's what you put to them. They're not daft. They'll give in first time. Trevor's organising the new compound, working out impossible pro-grammes to kill the workers, ordering materials. He hasn't got time to argue. C'mon, Jimmy, we're in this together. Get him on the phone.'

'I told you, Paul and I will get the pipe in. You start mixing now, I mean right now, and we'll finish this today.'

Jinkie, that small man, took hold of Trots' sleeve just above the closing and unclosing fist.

'He means it, Trots.'

Trots jerked his arm away. His eyes found Jimmy's eyes and remained deep inside them as he spoke.

'Need is the capitalist game but we can play it as well as they can. They don't think twice about exploiting the workers. They do it all the time.'

'There's a job to do and no time to argue.'

'You know they do!'

Slowly and carefully Jimmy took his hands from the pockets of his overalls.

Willie began to whistle loudly.

Cammy stopped sawing and stretched his back.

'There's another job coming up the road,' Jinkie said. 'Don't lose it for us.'

'Round these parts we remember the Clearances. We remember the dogs as much as the shepherds, the shepherds as much as the masters.'

'Think I'm a dog, Trots?'

'Jimmy!'

'What is it, Willie?'

'Forgot your name for a minute, I was just making sure.'

Jinkie took hold of Trots' sleeve. 'C'mon, Trots.'

The rasping sound of Cammy's saw carried in the breeze.

'Okay,' said Trots, 'we'll do it. The Workers know how to wait. We've been doing it for a long time.'

He climbed back onto the dumper and gunned the engine, turning it in its narrow circle and bumping back uphill into the marram with Jinkie running along beside.

His instrument set plumb above the centre line Paul swivelled the powerful telescope onto the nearest rig, centring the vertical cross hair on the tower above the platform. Swivelling it down again he found he could pick out lifting gear, windows, hand rails, crates stacked one above the other.

A door opened and a figure came out into the weather, pulling its collar up around its neck before running to a standing valve and taking its wheel in its hands and turning it anxiously, shoulders working, sturdy legs transferring all the forces both static and kinetic down into the platform. At sea level silent waves broke against the rig's three massive round legs

'See that, Paul?'

Willie Quinn had finished oiling the shutters and tucked bucket and brush upright among the marram grass.

'See what?'

'Three legs are more stable than two. That's what we should have, three legs. We wouldn't fall over as much. Not then.'

'No?'

'Proof positive there's no God. He'd have given us three legs so us joiners could stand up better in the wind that way and slaters wouldn't get blown off roofs. Fishermen could stand up in their boats.'

'We'd walk different though,' Paul said. 'We'd spin along like those waltzer things you get at the Fair.'

Willie considered sagely. 'We'd need ball bearings in our neck to keep the head steady while the body went round and round. Great things the ball bearings are. What do you think, Cammy?'

Cammy shook his head.

'We'd do a better job than God. Three legs instead of two.'

Cammy was thoughtful of this blasphemy. 'God gave us four legs,' he said at last. 'It was men that got up on two. That's when it all went wrong.'

'Paul, I need a rough line for the pipe,' said Jimmy at the mattress.

'You'll miss the banter,' Willie told Cammy, 'if you go.'

'Three legs,' said Jimmy, 'and three arms to go with them; one to steady the wood, another to work it and the third to scratch your arse, which is what you guys do most of the time. Paul, give me that line.'

Paul turned his instrument to sight the mark he had made on the wall of the closest Settlement Tank and locked it into position. On top of the wall the fitters were fixing the scraper rails on the walls. By tonight the job would be done and they would be away. Swivelling the telescope on its axis he focussed down on the mattress and guided Jimmy's pencil onto the centreline.

'Spoteroonie!'

Jimmy made a mark. 'Near enough then.'

'No. Spoteroonie.'

'Boy's getting confident,' Willie said. 'He knows his worth.'

'Shoosh, Willie,' Jimmy said. 'He's worth nothing without that qualification he's promised me he's going to get.'

Paul turning a stone with his boot frowned.

'What's your qualifications, Jimmy?'

'Possession of the tools is all.'

'So what's your worth?'

'A hammer and a few nails.'

'You were the highest paid man on the site until the plant fitters arrived.'

'A hammer and a few nails is all any joiner's worth.'

Jimmy took his hammer out of his belt and spun it on his finger like a six-gun and pointed it at Paul. 'Paper is worth more. Get that and you can do what you like.'

'You listen to him, Paul,' said Willie. 'He knows what he's talking about. A lifetime on the tools and what's he got to show for it? Beautiful wife, big house, a nearly new car and a daughter at Uni, is all. Some hammer. Some nails.'

'And a sore back,' Jimmy said, still pointing, 'arthritis coming on from endless soakings, the state pension and nothing with my name on it bar the label on my overalls.'

He put the hammer back in his belt.

'Now Paul, help me fit this pipe. Willie, help Cammy finish off the dwangs.'

Between them, Jimmy and Paul, they lifted the pipe onto two blocks of wood on the mattress, its socket end looking up at the spigot of the pipe that had been laid from the settlement tanks. Jimmy took a clean rag from the bucket and lifted the pipe ends and wiped them carefully.

'The tiniest piece of grit can spoil the joint.'

'No matter,' Paul said. 'This open end won't be tested.'

Jimmy looked at him out of the corner of his eye and it was a complete answer.

The pipe ends absolutely clean he took the rubber sealant ring from the bucket and coated it with lubricant and pushed it carefully into the socket. 'That's a fit,' he said and replaced the pipe on the mattress. 'Now, give me a piece of that timber for a cushion, and the pinch bar.'

Cammy passed him a piece of sawn wood and he and Willie stationed themselves at what would be the pipe joint. Jimmy went to the low end and placed the wood between the spigot and the pinch bar that he jammed into the mattress and placed his boot behind.

'Ready?'

'Yo!'

Jimmy pressed the pinch bar forward onto the wood, the wood onto the spigot and so eased the pipe forward into its mate. 'Now Paul. Line again.'

Paul returned to his position behind the theodolite and guided Jimmy left and right until the new pipe end was in line with no margin for error either side.

'Spoteroonie!'

'Do you mean it this time?'

'I mean it *again.*'

'That's good. Now just stay there. Willie and Cammy, bring the shutters over. This won't take long.'

The six shutters were two metres long and a half metre deep, marine ply lubricated with linseed oil and fixed to a wooden frame simply with nails. Willie and Cammie placed them in pairs to either side of the pipe, spaced them at the bottom with the two-by-two dwangs Cammy had cut to size and at the top nailed them to the correct 45cm width. They took their line off the pipe and when they were done Paul again checked it. Jimmy nailed on the stop end and the box was ready for concrete.

'These days they say the first men were blacks,' said Willie. 'Roaming up to the north out of Kenya.' He shook his head. 'Not true. They were white like us. It's been proved.'

Jimmy looked at him for a long moment. 'Where do these

things come from? No, don't tell me. Paul! How's the concrete doing because we're ready and the tide's on the turn.'

Paul's mobile phone rang. Trevor had a question.

'The shutter's ready,' Paul told him. 'If we get the concrete now we'll finish, yes.'

'Ask him,' Jimmy asked, 'if the fitter is coming out to fix the batcher. We won't manage with hand batching tomorrow with less time. We'll need the machine.'

Paul repeated this and waited again.

'Trots and Jinkie are working away at the mix now,' he said.

He listened again and switched off.

'The fitter's on his way. Trevor says to call him when we're about finished.'

'Do that,' said Jimmy. 'Listen, that's the dumper on the way back.'

The dumper broke out of the marram grass and bounced onto the shingle spilling concrete. Jinkie ran out behind.

'Here's the Lone Ranger and Tonto,' Willie said. 'Remember that on the telly, Cammy?'

'Before my time, Willie.'

'You won't remember who played Tonto then.'

'Nope.'

'Jay Silversleeves. He got the name when he was a joiner on the Hydro dams. With his colouring he couldn't take the cold. His nose ran like a waterfall and he used to wipe it on his sleeve, over and over on his sleeve. He changed the name a bit when he got to Hollywood. Good joiner he was, started the same day as me on that big pyramid job in Egypt. He was on the wrong side at Little Big Horn though. We never spoke again.'

Trots manoeuvred the dumper so he could tip the concrete into the shutter. 'Ready, Willie?'

'Not without vibrators. You haven't brought them down yet.'

'Nothing works here,' Jimmy said. 'Look, pour half the concrete in.'

Trots pushed the tipping lever forward and the skip rose on its hinges. Jinkie pushed the back of his shovel into the flow, directing it into the shutter, allowing very little spillage.

'Easiepeasie,' he said. 'Lemon squeezie.'

'Now move over here and drop the other half.'

Trots reversed and moved the dumper sideways and tipped in the rest.

'Now drive up and bring the vibrator unit down. It's the wee electric one.'

Trots and Jinkie roared up towards the compound.

The concrete was mounded above the top of the shutter. 'Will we shovel out the extra while we're waiting?' Willie asked. 'It's their job. They might not like it.'

'No. Wait until it's vibrated down, there might not be enough. They might have to mix some more. Look at the tide, though. We're getting beat.'

The tide was lapping the base of the shutter.

'Paul! See what they're up to.'

Paul climbed up off the shore and stood by his theodolite, looking uphill towards the compound.

'They're on their way. No dumper though. They're carrying the vibrator between them.'

Jimmy took his hammer out of his belt and spun it. 'They've left the dumper behind. The vibrator weighs about as much as a mini car and they've left the dumper behind.'

Willie stroked his chin. 'We're going to have to get them put down,' he said. 'Cammy, do they deserve to live? As a moral philosopher you know about these things.'

'What's "deserve"? What's that?' Cammy asked.

'There's more in that question than in any possible answer.'

Trots and Jinkie reached the edge of the marram and rested the vibrator on the shingle.

'The dumper's broke now,' Jinkie shouted. 'The fitter's on the batcher and he'll fix the dumper when he's finished that.'

Willie looked at sweating Trots. 'Working hard?'

Trots and Jinkie again picked up the machine by its two

handles and carried it to the shutter where Trots grasped the starter cord and pulled. It whined into action first time and the half-inch poker jiggled on the stones of the beach, rattling like a beggar's cup. He picked it up and tossed it into the mound of concrete and the mound slumped down in the shutter.

Paul shouted over the noise. 'Willie, what were you saying about the first men? They were black. Everyone knows that. From Kenya.'

Willie pushed at the concrete with a shovel, forcing it in mounds against the vibrator, watching the tiny air bubbles come out and the cream form on top.

'Look at that,' he said, 'lovely stuff. Trots, you can mix concrete all right. This would even make Harry happy and he is a famously grouchy person. The first men, black? Not so. All the new thinking says white, like us.'

'That's racist,' said Trots, scowling. 'You're a racist.'

'Just a thought. Can a thought be racist?'

'Yes, it can.'

Trots lifted the poker out and put it in again, moving along the shuttering's six metre length and as he went Willie looked at Cammy. 'We are apes,' he said. Right?'

'So some say.'

'No tails.'

'True.'

'But unlike all other apes we are hairless. Also unlike all other apes we have noses that stick out from our faces.

Jimmy ran his fingers along his own. 'Some more so than others.'

'Don't worry about that,' said Willie. 'In more advanced specimens, such as James here, it signifies a great astuteness and the correct understanding of the bounds of truthfulness, very useful qualities when dealing with the likes of Swannie. How's the measure doing anyway?'

'There's nothing in this beach work. The sooner we're up the road the better.'

'So listen, it's several millennia ago and the Ice Age is

blowing down from the north and here is a tribe of our still not quite human ancestors, *Homo Hairiarsus*, covered in brown fur with their noses flat as toad in the hole.'

'I've got the picture,' said Paul.

The vibrating poker shrieked and dulled as Trots pulled it in and out of the concrete. 'This is all racist nonsense,' he said.

'I'll be a Fascist then, Trots?' asked Willie.

'Sure sounds like it.'

'Well, never mind that. So they come across this hot spring and one of them jumps in and, hey, this is good, I mean really warm and comfortable. There aren't too many of these apes so they all get in and just sit around in the warmth for years while the temperature drops all around and the other ape tribes get hairier in order to cope, as do the mammoths and sabre toothed tigers and all the rest that manage to survive at all. The temperature continues to drop and their shoulders and heads get very cold indeed so they lie a little bit lower in the water and then a bit lower still until eventually only their noses are poking up and only the apes with long noses survive. They pass this characteristic on to their successors and, eventually, here we are.'

'Hoho,' said Trots.

'I tell you true.' Willie raised a hand and swore on his joiner's apron.

'The males had to get out of the water every so often and go find food for the females and the young. That's why men today are hairier than women. When the ice eventually receded and they came out of the water for good and walked off through the long grass their skin was white. Like ours.'

'Racist,' Trots muttered, but Jinkie was staring into space with his mouth open.

'That makes sense,' he said. 'It explains why white men are superior to blacks. The blacks lost their fur later, and their noses are flat.'

No one contradicted Jinkie who would need to believe he was superior to someone somewhere. Willie slapped him on the shoulder. 'Ever meet a black man, Jinkie?'

We'll have the fitter standing by the batcher just in case. He's the best insurance we can have.'

'We'll be quicker by then. Jimmy will have it down to a fine art. This was just the first.'

'We're sending JB and Tammas down for the next two days. That should help. Now you can wrap up, early start tomorrow.'

'Four labourers? They'll fall over each other.'

'Never mind that.'

Trevor hung up.

Paul put the phone back into his pocket and looked at Jimmy.

'JB and Tammas will be here tomorrow as well.'

Jimmy and Willie and Trots looked at each other and something unspoken passed between them.

'We'll tidy up now,' said Jimmy. 'We have to carry all this gear back up to the compound.'

Paul went back to his instrument and out of their way, turning its telescope on to the nearest rig and focusing on the platform. A group of men were working at something, he couldn't tell what, but they were intent on their business and all their attention was on this unreadable activity. Two were speaking animatedly together and pointing. Others were laying out what looked like a rope but might have been a chain or a hose. They were thinking and talking and working together on their man-made world and he took the impression somehow that they were working against the possibility of some future catastrophe.

He turned the wheel at the side of the instrument to bring them as close as he could and refocused.

Yes, they seemed to know what they were doing and what they couldn't be sure of they worked out as they went. Now other men appeared, walking past them in pairs, in threes, ignoring them it seemed, all in the service and protection of the great machine that stood on its three sturdy legs in waiting for the power of the sea to turn against it.

'Can I see?'

Cammy put his tools down among the marram grass and stepped into Paul's footprints behind the instrument. He turned the focusing wheel to suit his own eyes and, that done, his hands went down to rest on his thighs and take his body's weight against the crouch, against back pain, and as he watched with visible admiration all those tiny men working in the distance his forehead creased and a thoughtful smile formed on his pressed together lips.

Paul's mobile phone rang again. This time it was Pat Healey calling from Glasgow.

'Trevor said it was okay to call. I need to speak to Trots.'

Paul held out the phone to Trots on the shore. Trots took it and put it to his ear and listened and turned it off and handed it back. Jinkie stared at him with his mouth open, waiting for the inevitable.

'We're paid off. This lot don't want us any more. Healey says he'll call when something new comes up.'

Jinkie walked into the long grass with his hands to his head and Trots swayed where he stood before sitting down on the beach pebbles.

Paul couldn't look at them. Instead he looked at the Grip Squad, Jimmy, Willie and Cammy, one by one. None of them could look at the labourers either. They couldn't even look at each other. Jimmy and Willie kept on gathering together their tools and Cammy kept peering through the telescope until Trots and Jinkie had recovered. In this way Paul learned that, although tomorrow their cares would be about income and provision, today the searing truth they had to contend with was expendability and insult. Jimmy spoke.

'You guys heading back to the compound? We'll take you to Inverness. You won't need the company bus then.'

Trots nodded slowly.

'That's good of you.'

'Next time it might be us.'

It wouldn't though. Paul knew it.

Deep down all of them knew it

Trots folded the vibrator's air hose and gripped the generator handle and hefted it but no, the beast was too heavy. It would take them both to carry it.

'She won't like this,' he said. 'She won't like it.'

'There'll be another day, Trots. We're never out the game for long.'

Each took his handle and together they put their backs into it, leaning outwards and away from each other, as their ancestors had done when between them they took the weight of an animal they had killed, to carry it back to the compound.

Paul unscrewed the theodolite from its legs and clamped it in its case. The tripod stand he also broke down, unscrewing the butterfly bolts and pushing the extensions inside and tightening them again. With the gathered legs on his shoulder and the heavy case in his hand he nodded to the joiners standing with their hammers hanging from their belts like long knives and their saws and pinch bars over their shoulders like spears, providers and protectors for their women and their children no matter the colour of their skin.

Now the labourers entered the long grass and Jimmy Gillies and Willie Quinn and Cameron Stobo also entered it and all moved through it and eventually were lost in it and none of them left anything to mark their existence in this place at all, at this time, but the scrapings they made on the ground in the course of their passing. Burdened by the weight of his tools, the tripod legs and instrument, by his book and the pencil he wrote with, he followed.

20

What can't be cured

These are the best of months, April and May, the daylight
hours stretching but the ground still hard in the morning, with
a skin of frost that melts away in the time it takes Malky to mix
the first batch of mortar. It never gets really hot like in the
summer so the shirt doesn't come off but I prefer that. The sky
is a clear, bright blue and the sea matches it in its own way. I
am looking out towards the oil rigs from just below the A9,
looking down on the shore and the new Works and behind me
is the hill and over the hill is the village of Struie and behind
that the big mountain ranges that reach all the way across
country to the Atlantic shore.

Today we're working on the new Collection Chamber. It's
as deep as the pumping station we did on the Black Isle job but
Swannie had his way on this one and they used those big
manhole rings backed with mass concrete, no bricks. This will
have taken them a fraction of the time I would, but there will
not be the same qualities of appearance and care for that
whoever-he-will-be that will one day enter it for some un-
known reason and look at the walls and make his judgements.
No one will want to sign the walls on this but that isn't going to
weigh much on the Swannie scales of importance.

There is only Harry and me left that give much of a toss
about these things. Good guy, Harry. We're getting to talk that
bit more now. He comes down from the new job in Lochdon
and, let's face it, there isn't much to do beyond poking the
rubber end of his pencil into Malky's mortar mix and discuss-
ing that big pyramid job in Egypt. Those were the days.

The roof slab of the chamber is below ground level and all Joe Public will see is a cast iron bitumen coated entry cover embedded in the grass. The cover will sit on a brick shaft and it's the shafts to all the site's chambers we are building now. It's not too demanding except on the small of the back and half the time I do it on my knees, the other half sitting on a fish box. This is how it is now. From time to time Malky leaves off mixing to make a roll-up. He also has a fish box and from time to time he sits on it and dips his nose in his comic. Meanwhile I sit here and place brick on brick, mortaring them and placing them and knocking them flush one with another. No problem, but no rhythm either.

For this bitty kind of work Malky does the mixing with a shovel on a board. No machine required for these small amounts. The day stretches out and there is no wind and no rain and the sun is shining. I tell myself I am happy and if I can say so, why, it is so. It's all in the mind.

This work is easy but there isn't much money in it and I could use some more of that stuff now that I've lost the other squad. When we finished at the factory Big Tam got the idea he could do as well on his own. There's another building going up but I'm not bidding for the work this time. He can have it. Between the troops and the client, too much hassle. The accountant, that crook. The tax man. For years I've put enough away to cover the government bill but this time, first time, I had to dip in and it won't be there when the Big Man comes along wanting his cut. If there's a problem with this work it's that it gives too much time to think.

All the big chambers were built with rings when it's bricks shown in the drawings and priced for. That's money into Healey's pocket and out of mine. Along the line it's money into Swannie's pocket, or the guys above him, ultimately the Authority's and then, yes, the People's. That's the justification for turning out crap. It's good for us. Ho!

On this new job further north, Harry tells me, they are adopting the rings from the start and that is reducing the price.

So that's Harry's nose out of joint because he strives for quality but like the rest of us he accepts these things. What can't be cured must be endured.

So, I sit here on my fish box beside the A9 and the traffic rushes past and I don't suppose that Malky and I get so much as a glance. The fish box sits on the concrete roof of the chamber and there is an opening in the slab just big enough for a man in breathing apparatus to get through. Round this opening we build the shaft. Below the slab there are the concrete rings and, in the base, concrete benching shaped in channels to take the flow of sewage. Round the whole thing, but buried and out of sight are the cofferdam piles and, somewhere down there, John Kelly's fingers. Out and under the road is the pipeline tunnel, now infilled. Working Man did this. Past goes the traffic and no one gives a toss so long as it doesn't block up somewhere and overflow and make a bad smell and a mess. This is what you have to understand: no one cares.

Except, for some reason, I care. I care that these bricks go one on top of the other and that the bond is correct, even in a wee box of walls no more than 45cm high. So, why? Why keep checking the diagonals on *this*? The bricks have to be sound. They've not to slip or crumble and when that guy goes down the hole some time in the future, whatever he thinks about the rings and the benching he's to think; hey, good brickwork to the shaft. Later we'll manhandle the cast iron cover into place and after that shovel the arisings around it and smooth them off.

Yep, we're doing our own labouring now. Malky says he should do all that himself but I won't allow it. What would Sandra think if I called her from the hospital about his ruptured disc? She'd have my balls for dangly earrings.

I smiled just now and Malky looked at me. Better not say what I smiled at. The places your head goes.

The system is now what is known as live. That is to say the pumps over at Struie are working and the diversion has been made from Ness. Looking down into the Chamber through the slab opening I can see the flow coming in from under the A9 and the flow from Ness joining it and turning left and the two together running out towards the Works. The access ladder is in place, as are various pieces of safety ironwork but, for all that, I can't go into the chambers, any of them, because of the danger of gases. Of course I am liable to drop things, bricks, mortar, into the chambers when I work. Coming on the job this far along I can't go in and tidy up. They should have let me get this done before they turned it all on. These are the results of haste but nobody cares. It's money first, money last and money all down the line.

Down below us the Authority's troops are getting the new place in order, the instruments building, their own mess building. Of course they are putting their own building in order first and looking at the Works second. No surprise in that. Three of them, they have their new van, their clean overalls and their ordered, limited days. They have rules and hierarchies and jealousies and their own jobs to do and they don't like us much, Malky and I. We're beneath them. Also, we are a threat. We could do their jobs better and quicker and cheaper. Everyone knows this. Their easy jobs have cost them their edge. They keep their jobs for reasons other than how well they do them. That's the politicians for you. They look after their own.

I pick up a brick and sit straight up on my fish box to ease my back. The clean blade of the trowel enters Malky's pile of mortar and I like the dry *shushing* sound it makes, like the wife, way back, when she'd hush me in the night and me not knowing I'd made a sound. I don't dream the way I did now I've put the wackybacky aside. I miss the deep relaxation but not the Technicolor cartoon nightmares. It got beyond the bearable when the beheadings and castrations started popping up and I woke thinking it was me. No more. The trouble is the vodka tide goes up. There's a balance to be struck between the substances and whatever the need is but try telling that to a quack.

The idea of affecting a bond on these shafts is a joke to many builders. The strength required of the shafts when they are off the road like these is not so great. Harry doesn't agree. He says a vehicle could come off the road at any time and pass across it and, anyway, English Bond is what it shows on the drawing, right there at the side in the notes, and that's what the Client is paying for. Okay, the Client's wallet, but I'm still kind of stuck on that guy from the future finding the ladder with his foot and lowering himself and his breathing apparatus down into the chamber and his eyes running across the bricks just naturally as he descends. He's a skilled man too, must be. He would notice if it was crap. Success is that he notices nothing. He is to be supported in his assumption that the job is sound. Maybe not even born yet, he is my brother.

Mortar is a mixture of sand, cement and water and, because we have to dot about the site to the different chambers, we carry the sand and cement in the van. The shafts being small don't take such great quantities. Malky gets the water locally. At Struie he knocks doors and what, you might wonder, do douce middle-class incomers from the English Home Counties make of the man from Govan via the BarL and his single syllable grunts. Do they understand a word or just respond to the empty bucket? At Ness he goes into the hotel where, of course, they know us, but here we take it from the burn. Harry wouldn't like that but it saves Malky from carrying it up from the Works and the culture clash with the easy-lifers.

The mortar is what holds the bricks together, along with the bond, and gravity. As far as I can see all that holds the workers together is money. Maybe there are invisible bonds. Malky and I are good pals but I'd shag Sandra if she'd let me. Naturally she won't, so Malky and I get closer. We need each other. Come to think of it he's all I've got now the teacher is out of it. It was only ever worker's playtime anyway, and I didn't wander in the Land of Illusion for long. She got what she wanted, which was plenty of dick, then let it slip to her man. Going on six months without his hole he had the idea something might be up anyway, because it sure wasn't him. Ho!

Office workers, teachers, doctors, social workers, all the serried ranks of the respectable, all hypocrites and liars, they're all useless showers and no different from Malky and me when the chips are down. He skelped her a few times and she thought she'd made her big mistake in telling him. She came away with the usual 'we have to talk' number. If only we'd talked before it would never have happened, she told him. What this boils down to is that the whole thing, her getting off with me, six months of lies and double life, was really his fault. She wasn't responsible. How many times have I heard this one? He believed her. I would have straightened him out if he'd given me a chance. Instead he came straight at me with his mitts and that was only going to have one result. I guess he'd rather take a kicking than face the truth. The truth being that he doesn't even have the dignity of being responsible. How do I know for sure about the things I couldn't see? She told me in bed when she came round afterwards for that 'one last time' they always do.

So now I've been without for three weeks. I'm missing it but not worried. What I have noted through the years is that for some guys there is always a woman. Even when things are straight there are other women looking on from the sidelines and they are biding their time. You can never tell who they are but you can be sure they will appear at a time of their own choosing. This is how it is now for me.

It's not Sandra though, and there's part of me sad but maybe that's just a case of what you can't have is what you want. The other sides to this are, firstly, I could not do without Malky, not now, and secondly, he is one of only two guys I would admit could take me apart and fill me in if they wanted, the other being Derek the Steelfixer.

This one is Donna, wife of Dave who owns the pub I sometimes drink in. No longer that young although younger than I, she has large, well-shaped breasts and a broad arse such as my always-fit, too skinny teacher did not. She was angular and hard and uncomfortable to lie on. Donna will be otherwise. She will be like a double divan and if she gets on top she will be like one of those four poster beds with the roof thing that comes down and smothers you while you sleep. I can't wait. Sometimes I order one of those high-shelf single malts all true vodka drinkers hate just for the pleasure of watching her stretch.

When you come out of a relationship, which I should be expert in by now, you give out all kinds of availability signs without ever knowing it and the interested pick them up. The interested have sensitive receivers. They are ever alert, as is Donna who has the reputation of being hot. She replies with looks that are different and a hand that lingers and she leaves open seams in conversation that will sound innocent to the unaware. Whether Dave is unaware, or just used to it and comfortable enough within their accommodation, time will tell, but it is written in the stars that I will shag that woman.

Harry's receivers are also sensitive, but only to matters of quality in the work and to the strange politics that go on slightly above his head and far above mine. Swannie continues to hold a special place in his bile duct but Harry knows the beast is here to stay, or at least until he battles his way upwards onto the Board and, no doubt, back to England. The first parts of the Great Swannie Mission, says Harry, are now in place.

All the Strath Construction guys are gone. Alex Matheson went with the merger. Mac got more and more sidelined and eventually couldn't take it any more. He's in Saudi now. John Kelly won't be back from losing three fingers and a broken hip, not at his age. John was a slob in his work. He deserved what he got. Harry also tells me that Health and Safety have pinned responsibility on Kelly and Mac. That's how it should be, agent and foreman, the men on site, but it takes no account of the pressure Swannie put on them. It takes no account of his intent to rid himself of them and put his own guys in their place. It takes no account of their natural resistance and their striving to survive.

All the staff joiners are gone. They went on the grip and couldn't cut it. I would have told them, don't give up on security, not if it's in your nature to live within systems. Everyone hears the call of the wild. Not everyone can live this way though, and those of us who do can't manage for ever.

So now Swannie has Trevor as Agent on the new job, Trevor that came north with him and is young and single and energetic and will be working for half of Mac's money. Trevor will eventually be remade in Swannie's image. Decent bloke still, he won't be for long. Paul comes along after him and with Paul Harry is in two minds. Deeply committed in the main discipline of getting it right first time he can't be arsed with the College. He's going to fail, says Harry. That will be correct, but Swannie will use him to the limit first. My guess is he will end up on the tools like me, and that makes sense for what are all too obvious reasons to me and to his mother. I should care?

Lammerton has taken the place of Kelly, of course. Healey's men from the Black Isle job are gone because Harry made enough of a fuss about the quality of their work, sure but, more to the point, applied the letter of the spec to the crap they turned out. This cost Swannie money in the lifting and relaying and endless testing of pipes. The new Healey's men are half way decent on the job but they will pass also because the turnover of men is relentless. The industry eats them and it has a wide and gaping mouth and a bottomless gut.

What does the watch say? 11:45am. Too much thinking doesn't do. The work has slowed and Malky has been giving me the occasional questioning look. Everything good needs rhythm. Lift the brick and heft it, reach into the mortar with the trowel, spread it on the brick, edge and arse, knock it into place. This won't take long. Then we can get the cover on and concreted. That will be about 1:00pm and we'll go to the Ness

Hotel and maybe we'll see Ikey hanging about there. Trevor didn't keep him on for Lochdon so, now the Works are built, he's back to cleaning glasses and doing what he can. They won't have him in the bar for much longer, he tells me. The tourists will be back soon, taking big breaths of the newly fresh ozone, and they don't like to see handicap. It would break your heart. Ikey played his part. He's damaged? Okay, he's damaged. He arrived that way. The rest of us achieve it.

Already I am thinking of those big Whitbreads and perhaps, when it's getting on for back-to-work time, a wee voddy. I am eating less just now. I've noticed that. There has been a loss of weight. Hopefully this is not a sign of some underlying horror more than the usual. Right now, life has spiralled down to building, Malky, and drink. I'll pull out. It goes with the round of the work. As soon as we get back onto a decent housing job I'll be okay. The fine bricks and the colour mixes, the demand for real skill, I'll respond. I always do.

Meantime though, it's just continuation. Spread the mortar and lay the bricks; labour. Oh yes, I'll pick up a shovel if I have to. I'll earn. I'm worth my bread. So is Malky. So is Ikey. So is Paul. So are all those other names I went through earlier. We are worth our bread even if the rest of the world drives past without looking and likes to pretend we don't exist. So is Swannie who refines the whole thing down to its sharpest economic edge, the edge that cuts us to the quick.

We are the hard-handed ones but we are not necessarily the foul-mouthed. We are the less educated but we are not the stupid. We are the temporary and the used. If we are wise we learn not to feel. In the full depth of winter Derek's first move in the morning is to grasp a frost bound reinforcement bar in his two hands and hold it tight.

This is the way we must be. We must confront the resolute and the inanimate and turn it into the structures and systems that encourage, allow and contain that thing I have heard called civilisation. Not that I know what civilisation really is. Whatever it is though, that thing that is not for us. Without this deep numbness we could not go on and nothing would be built. We are the slabs you walk on and the water you drink. This is the working life; toil, exposure, frustration and injury are all built in and, as far as I can see, can't be built out, nothing can.